DUMPING HILARY?

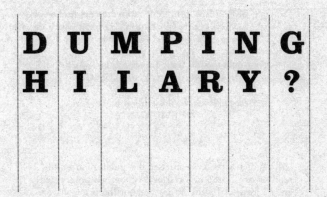

DUMPING HILARY?

PAUL REIZIN

review

First published in trade paperback in 2001 by
HEADLINE BOOK PUBLISHING

First published in this edition in 2002 by
REVIEW

10 9 8 7 6 5 4 3 2 1

ISBN 0 7472 6670 0

Typeset in Perpetua by
Palimpsest Book Production Limited, Polmont, Stirlingshire

Printed and bound in Great Britain by
Mackays of Chatham plc, Chatham, Kent

Headline Book Publishing
A division of Hodder Headline
338 Euston Road
London NW1 3BH

www.headline.co.uk
www.hodderheadline.com

For Ruth

Thanks to Imogen Parker for the encouragement;
Clare Alexander for the surgical interventions;
and Martin Kelner for the musical advice.

PROLOGUE

In his youth, the Conservative politician Michael Heseltine famously wrote a list of things to do on the back of an envelope.

1. **Make a million by age thirty**
2. **Enter Parliament by forty**
3. **Be in the Cabinet by fifty**
4. **Be prime minister by sixty**

My own list is longer. I wrote it last night on the inside of a cigarette packet somewhere between the second and third Martini.

1. Tidy flat
2. Dump Hilary
3. *Get* Yasmin
4. Buy groovier specs
5. Get a proper haircut
6. See doctor about pain under arm
7. Buy filing cabinet – sort papers
8. Get a proper car – or fix Peugeot
9. Get a proper flat
10. Finish books (esp *Crime and P*)
11. Have dinner party – invite C&M; Steve & ??
12. Rationalise wardrobe – take unwanted clothes to Oxfam
13. Do same with books
14. Be nicer to parents – or visit more often
15. Finish with psychotherapist; find tennis coach instead
16. Stop obsessing about Olivia
17. Tell Maria to clean fridge
18. Think of really good – untraceable – revenge on Clive
19. Cancel *Sunday Times*
20. Give up smoking

Although Heseltine gave himself the best part of a lifetime to tick all the items off his list, he notably failed to accomplish his final ambition. With me it will be different. I shall begin today and the target date for completion will be . . . soon. I am easily old enough to have a proper car, flat, girlfriend, back-hand . . . you know, *lifestyle*.

I have just come back from making a phone call to the newsagents. Things are looking up already.

Cancel *Sunday Times* ☑

1

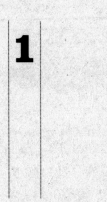

[illegible] There [illegible] morning smell of toast.

I was [illegible] lying under the duvet, pretending to be asleep [illegible] nothing not to have a hangover, crawling to [illegible] my eyes and began the twenty-four hours I [illegible] about to spend in the unrelenting company of a woman who should really be my sister. That's how I've come to think of Hilary, as an annoyed younger sister, though we [illegible]

ONE

1

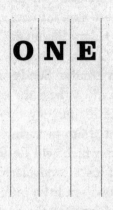

'There's no *Sunday Times*,' says Hilary the following morning, returning to the bedroom with the *Observer*. There is an all-pervading smell of toast.

I am hiding under the duvet, pretending to be asleep, pretending not to have a hangover, unwilling to open my eyes and begin the twenty-four hours I'm about to spend in the unrelenting company of a woman who should really be my sister. That's how I've come to think of Hilary, as an annoying younger sister, though one who I have sex with. As I am an only child, this does not count as an incestuous thought.

'It's that dopey paperboy,' she says sliding back into bed. Pause. Two, three. Wait for it. 'You should make sure they knock it off the bill.' A *crunch* as perfect white teeth sink into her breakfast; a gulp; and now, I hear Hilary Bloom raise the broadsheet sails of Britain's Oldest Newspaper into the uneasy calm of a North London Sunday morning.

Silence. I fancy I can hear the carriage-return of her big blue eyeballs pinging their way down the columns of print. I am picturing the small frown of concentration which will be forming between her eyebrows. If it's a particularly complex tale – tax havens, Kosovo – a little pink piece of tongue might just be poking into the daylight. And now I do something unforgivable. I fart. If there were windows down here, believe me they'd be rattling.

'Mi – chael!!' My name elongated to express mock irritation followed by a half-hearted kick under the covers. But I know that deep down she's secretly amused, even pleased that I feel comfortable enough, *familiar* enough with her to express my coarse masculine side in her presence. Yes, don't talk to me about comfortable and familiar. When it comes to familiarity, Hilary Bloom is not your favourite old armchair, she's the whole bloody furniture department.

Hilary is loyal to the point of blindness (which is annoying), caring to the point of soppiness (very annoying), and almost always unnaturally cheerful (maddening). Oddly, she is not stupid. She reads more difficult books than me (how many people do *you* know who got through *A Brief History of Time*?) and she can make herself understood in French, German, Italian and Spanish. My tired old boast is that my girlfriend can speak five languages . . . and can't say No in any of them. We've been going out, on and off, for years. It feels like she's always been there, which as a matter of fact she has, because we knew each other as children. If she wasn't so . . . well, 'happily shaggable' is the phrase that comes to mind, I'm sure it would have ended long before now. What she sees in me, you'll have to ask her.

In the mysterious way of The Hangover – now lucidity, now shash – I find I have segued into a dozy little meditation about smell. I remember once hearing in a psychology lecture that smell is our oldest sense. It arrives in consciousness unmediated by thought. With sight and sound it's different; that loud bang appears in your head as 'thunder' or 'bomb'; the blur streaking across the park pops up in your consciousness as 'dog' or 'squirrel'. But with a sudden unexpected smell, you merely think, 'What the fuck is that?'

And those words – what the fuck *is* that? – are now suddenly very much in my mind as I become aware of a bad smell, a really bad smell; and hang on . . . it's getting *worse*. It's a powerfully terrible smell, a truly *evil* one, much nastier than my own production; it wouldn't be overstating the case to call it a *stench. A whiff of the charnel house*. In seconds I twig. It's *her*. She's dropped a retaliatory SBD – Silent But Deadly – and if this was a foxhole, the Nazis would be tumbling out with their hands in the air.

I hit the surface fast. 'Oh Christ, that's disgusting.' Hilary is staring straight ahead at the newspaper, trying to keep a straight face. She is wearing one of my shirts and there are toast crumbs round her mouth.

'How's your head?' she asks, eyes never leaving the page. 'Nurofen?' She picks up the pill bottle beside the bed and rattles it louder than strictly necessary.

Who was it who told me that the late Kingsley Amis's favourite cure for a hangover was sex? I guess in my time I've tried them all. The hair of the dog (risky). The bloody great fry-up (can go either way). The bracing walk to 'blow away the cobwebs' (life-threatening). Sex is a funny one, however. There is definitely something about sex and hangovers that go together. Evolutionarily speaking, they're both a bit 'old brain', higher mental function in the case of the hangover having been damped down nicely by a skinful the night before. And there's something about the *fury* of sex that speaks to the guilt and stupidity of a hangover. Or is it simply that when you're feeling like death, an orgasm is, as the French say, *le petit mort*.

And now I remember who told me. She'd read it in a magazine. Snatching away the paper and hurling it over the side, I roll on top of her.

'Good morning, Miss Bloom.'

Hilary gazes up at me with that slightly dumb look that smart women know men like. Her hair is all messed up and she's spilling out of my red striped shirt in the nicest possible way. In my mind's eye, someone has rolled a tape of slow-motion vodka flowing into a tall glass. A sexy smile is spreading across her features. A fingernail does High Barnet to Morden down my spine. Suddenly her tongue is in my mouth. The *Observer*'s profile of Greg Dyke was evidently not that unputdown-able. And the last thought I have that can be expressed in words is, oddly enough, another *aperçu* of Kingsley Amis: he was delighted when he finally lost his sex drive, he said, because for years he felt like he'd been chained to a mad dog.

Afterwards she asks me, 'What are you thinking?'

'Woof,' I reply enigmatically.

2

Hilary is having a post-coital moment. Something funny has happened to her face. Her mouth has gone a little slack and she's staring dreamily at the smoke from her cigarette, curling into a shaft of sunlight that slices through my bedroom at this particular hour. (Cool jazz piano music accompanies the film version of this scene. In the book, it's just the traffic on Haverstock Hill, I'm afraid.)

Hilary is one of those smokers who aren't really smokers. She has two a day – after eating, after sex – and not the slightest desire for any more. Even the fags she does smoke she doesn't smoke *properly*. It looks to me like she's *toying* with smoking; she barely inhales, and stubs out long before a twenty-a-day girl would. Oddly, even though a packet lasts her more than a week, I'd still say she was addicted to her two a day. Tragically, her brand of choice is Lambert and Butler, possibly the naffest cigarette you can buy. She claims *she likes the taste*, though the truth is, in common with all smokers, she'd smoke *anything* if that was all that was available.

I'm lying beside her, watching the smoke coiling and uncoiling. After my triumph with the *Sunday Times* – yes I *do* like myself more for not buying it – I'm wondering what I can tick off my list today. After last night's booze-fest (bar; party; club; Steve's), tidying the flat is clearly out of the question, as is all the practical stuff about books, wardrobes, filing cabinets, specs and haircuts. Even being nicer to the parents seems unlikely. With a sound very like the sigh of a contented woman, Hilary sends another plume of smoke into the cloud gathering over the bed.

Actually, I've never been much of a one for the post-coital cigarette. Don't know why, because I'm inclined to smoke at most other tobacco opportunities, including post-prandial, pre-prandial and inter-prandial, though I do draw the line at chopsticks in one hand, Silk Cut in the other. First of the day is usually post-breakfast. Next in the car to work. Another on arrival at work. Several during the morning. One after lunch. More during the afternoon. Loads more if I'm writing or in the edit suite. One with the first drink in the bar. Then a steady stream through the evening. If I end up having more fags than drinks, I wake the next morning feeling unwell. If I have more drinks than fags, I wake feeling very unwell. It was a recent occasion in the latter category that prompted me to add 'Give up smoking' to my list of Things to Achieve.

Hilary had gone to her reading group, so I decided to catch up with 'the lads', two school friends now so tightly shackled in wedlock, you can see the chain marks on their wrists. By midnight we were in a Chinese restaurant, and it was there that I did one of the stupidest things that I've ever done. I asked for directions to the gents toilets from a man who turned out to be my own reflection in a full-length mirror.

Pretty stupid, you've got to admit. And it gave Peter and Mouse a big laugh. But hey, I was drunk. As a matter of fact I was as pissed as a rattlesnake. Do you think I would do something that dumb if I were sober? The next morning I had a hangover. No, that doesn't do it justice. In the vivid Australian phrase it was 'an overhang you could photograph.' And this was very nearly the moment that I finally, finally, *finally* decided I have to give up smoking.

Not drinking, you'll note. Smoking.

Because it wasn't the drink that made me feel this rotten. OK, perhaps the night's fuel-load of vodka, red wine and sake might have had something to do with it. But at least we'd had *fun*. As in, got pissed, had a laugh. Young people being loud and happy in bars and restaurants. What young people are supposed to do. Alcohol fuels that stuff. (And don't get me started on romance. Who in the world ever snogged anyone without a decent measure of C_2H_5OH somewhere in the equation?) The odd hangover seems a fair price to pay. In the words of Winston Churchill, 'I have taken more out of alcohol than alcohol has taken out of me.'

No, there's another reason why I woke up paralysed, afraid to move or even *think* of moving; a more insidious cause of the thick, nauseous feeling in my head and lungs. And it lay, I saw clearly, in the *empty* packet marked 'Silk Cut'. That harmless, almost *innocently* white box was why I felt so lousy. Actually lousier than lousy. There was the immediate lousiness caused by a neckful of tar and nicotine; and then the longer-term lousiness you develop after ten years as a serious smoker, almost a philosophical lousiness, a condition you could describe as *morbid dread*. The feeling that you know this is doing you terrible harm, inextricably intertwined with the feeling that you can never stop.

I dragged myself out of bed and into the sitting room. What pleasure, I asked myself, had I taken from those twenty Silk Cut that could make up for these Two Types of Lousiness? What wondrous, secret joy had those cigarettes delivered that could outweigh the huge health risks I knew I was taking? In the absence of any answers, can you guess what I did next?

I lit a cigarette.

And here is the moment. Slumped in a busted orange armchair in an off-white towelling bathrobe (stolen from hotel), fag in mouth, dreadfully hungover, I strike a match. It flares, and casts a phosphorescent little bomblet on to the robe, which ignites and spreads a low carpet of flame alarmingly across my chest.

OK it was a cheap bathrobe. OK it wasn't strictly, technically, in the legal sense, mine. I do a frantic bongo drum solo on my rib cage to extinguish the blaze. The smell of burnt artificial fibres hangs in the air, mingling unpleasantly with scorched chest hair. Even through the fog of the morning after, I recognise this as one sordid scene. I resist the urge to weep. This is my nicotine rock bottom. And the precise moment when I finally, finally, *finally* decide that I have to give up smoking. The end of the affair.

3

Maybe it's because I used to work in newspapers but, to me, a Sunday newspaper sort of Sunday morning with only *one* Sunday newspaper isn't much of a Sunday morning. We've been lolling around in the sitting room for an hour, swapping the *Observer*'s Business section for the Sport, the Review for the News. But it's not the same. I realise I'm actually missing the *Sunday Times*, its spiteful little articles, its entire frivolous supplements, the sheer *waste* of it all. Still, that's the thing about change; it's painful. If you do what you've always done, you'll get what you've always got. (Christ, that could have been the shrink talking; which reminds me, I've got to cancel her as well.)

I haven't lit up yet today but, to be honest, this doesn't seem like the best day to try and give up smoking. If I tell Hilary that I'm quitting, she'll be so incredibly, sickeningly . . . *supportive*, that I don't think I'll be able to stand it. She'll trot out all that bollocks about how you should alter your habits and avoid smoky situations – how exactly? Leave your job? Change all your friends? Move in with Buddhists? – she'll think up strategies for Taking My Mind Off It, start a jar for collecting money that You Would Have Spent On Cigarettes, cut up little sticks of carrot to nibble Every Time You Feel Like a Fag. Oh, do me a favour. She'll probably even give up her two pathetic L&Bs in solidarity.

I pick up a biro and scribble my options in a big white space in the middle of a Volkswagen ad.

1. **Decide to give up; tell Hilary (surely more than flesh and b. can stand).**
2. **Decide to give up; *don't* tell Hilary.**

3. **Carry on smoking. Try not to think about fatal illnesses.**
4. **Take up cigars instead. Or pipe. (Don't be ridiculous).**
5. **Decide *not* to decide, just stop and see what happens.**

Number five's my man, I decide, circling the digit. An interesting philosophical position, doing something without *deciding* to do it. But there is a pleasing symmetry to the idea; after all I *became* a smoker without deciding to become one. So to avoid the possibility of trying to give up and *failing* – and the inevitable cycle of disappointment, depression and heavier tobacco use – I shall make the conscious decision *not* to make the decision to give up. Instead, I just won't smoke. There'll be no great declarations. No decisions. No Supreme Acts of Will. I won't be 'Trying To Give Up Smoking' in great big inverted commas, I just won't be smoking. Well, not just now anyway. With a bit of luck, I might eventually forget about cigarettes altogether.

Total bollocks or what? Only one way to find out.

4

Most of my friends are fond of Hilary, and I know they'll be disappointed when we break up, i.e.

when I dump her. Some like Mouse and Claudia will be incredulous. We're round at their big old house in Crouch End for Sunday lunch and right now, while the girls are policing the twins in the back garden, Mouse and I are in the kitchen, draining the last of the Chardonnay. He's just lit a Marlboro and my desire to do the same is so great I can barely follow the conversation. No-one has noticed that I haven't been puffing away like a train as per.

'When are you going to make a decent woman of her?' he asks annoyingly, the phrase adding roughly fifteen years to his own. 'Bloody good girl is Hilary. Best *you've* had.'

Mouse has met all my girlfriends. Weirdly, I've known him since I was a boy. His real name is Eric Humphrey but the childhood nickname, on account of his sticky-out ears and squeaky voice, has stuck. Even Claudia sometimes calls him Mouse. He takes a long, lingering drag on the Marly. There is something dreadfully disturbing about my old schoolfriend's *facility* with tobacco. The *practice* in the movements, the vaguely corrupt thing his mouth does as he inhales, the seasoned way he blows the smoke at the ceiling. I'm going to ponce one off him. No, I'm not.

Mouse was never the brightest button in the box, but he was always one of the straightest. A classic Decent Bloke. It's very clear that he hasn't enjoyed a single one of the four cigarettes he's smoked since we finished lunch.

'Why do you still do it?' I ask as casually as I can.

'Can't help it mate,' he replies. 'I'm hooked.' And he laughs. That infectious, knee-slapping laugh of his that defies you not to laugh along too.

Well, that's Mouse. Fags, Claudia, twins, whatever life throws at him, he accepts his lot and doesn't gripe about it. He brings the cigarette to his lips again and narrows his eyes as if *this is going to hurt*. The end of the Marlboro glows red. My head is empty of all thoughts but one: *Offer me a cigarette. Just one. Now. Go on. Don't make me ask. Give me a fucking cigarette, fuck you!* Mouse blows his smoke off at an angle, but I catch some, snorting it up silently, 'passively' re-consuming the fumes. That smell. The distinctive Marlboro smell. A smell with an *edge* on it, a side to it, a note that somehow echoes the hot little kick you get in the back of your throat from each dragful of smoke. Marlboro smokers wince *before* they inhale. For them, truly, love hurts.

GIVE ME A FUCKING CIGARETTE YOU FUCKER!!!

You know those thoughts you can have which are both good and bad at the same time? Well, now I have one: Olivia smoked Marlboro. This is a good thought because, while I'm thinking about Olivia, I'm not actually craving a cigarette. I'm picturing her on my long yellow sofa, the way she looked after a bath: wet-combed blonde hair, wearing nothing but a big white towel and a pair of glasses. We'd be watching TV. Well, she would be. I'd be watching her. The way she'd fire up a Marlboro without taking her eyes off the screen, absorbed and unselfconscious. The way she'd throw her arm over the arm of the sofa, tilt her head back, shake her hair out and blast a stream of smoke straight at Trevor McDonald. The way she'd lean forward, just far enough and no further, to reach the ashtray to tip-tap a little ash away. The way she'd let me slowly remove her glasses – *but my God, you're beautiful*; our favourite joke – and how there was something exquisitely pornographic about snogging this beautiful young woman with tobacco on her fresh, pink breath. (That line about kissing a smoker being like kissing an ashtray has never put me off. I mean, ashtrays are *dirty*, right?)

I loved the way that on those evenings – how many were there altogether? Twenty? Thirty? – my world resolved itself to four elements: the cigarette, the glasses, the towel and Olivia. I loved the way that, if she was in the mood, one by one they could be discarded to leave only the last.

The *bad* thing about this thought is that, according to my list, I'm not supposed to be having it at all, never mind the full-blown Olivia fantasy. On the positive side however, it's nearly 4 p.m. and this is the first time she has entered my head today. Something of a record.

Out of the window, Hilary is playing chase with Mouse's twins. They shriek with delight as she repeatedly just fails to catch them. If it had worked, would Olivia have slipped into this scene as easily?

Mentally, I digitally superimpose her into the garden, lying on her side in a cornflower-blue summer dress, that spooky half-smile – am I laughing *with* you or *at* you? – the full meaning of her expression masked by the sunlight dancing off her specs. I suppose I'm a sucker for a mysterious woman and Olivia was your classic Sherlock Holmes three-pipe problem. What lay beyond that calm, creamy exterior? Surely not calm, creamy *interior*. For three feverish months, I tried to find out, and maybe never even got close. When she left, naturally Hilary had me back within twenty-four hours.

A peal of laughter from the garden. Hilary rolling in the grass with the twins climbing on top of her. Hilary. Great, galumphing, big-hearted happy old Hilary. Born to please. One of the world's nice people. Children love her, animals love her, even I love her – but in a pathetic way, the way you love a faithful Labrador. Or a close relative. You know way too much about their foibles and you're sort of stuck with them.

'Getting broody?' Mouse has been watching me gazing at the women and children. 'You should have a couple of kids. They'll give you something to think about apart from yourself.' He does his over-the-top Mouse laugh again and I want to slap him.

'Actually, Mouse, I was just thinking about how to get rid of Hilary. You don't know anyone who might want her, do you?'

He pauses mid-drag. 'You're not serious.' I give

him my sad, dead face. 'You *are* serious. Jesus, Michael, for someone who's supposed to be smart, you can be pretty fucking stupid at times. I mean . . . *why*?'

How am I going to explain it to him? How Hilary can't be faulted on affection, devotion, loyalty, on sheer bloody *being-there-for-you*. How you can't argue that she's not intelligent enough. Or boring (she's certainly no more boring than most people after a few years). How I can't even claim not to *fancy* her any more, when the truth is that she's so ridiculously fuckable that one minute she can be sitting there, tap-tapping away at her laptop, and the next we're down on the white rug, banging away like a pair of Bonobos. Once we even finished before the screen-saver came on. Christ, I've been known to wake up to find we've started doing it *in my sleep*. Whatever it is, it's not a sex thing.

I sometimes wonder if it's the fact that she never, *ever* argues with me. Yes, she might ever-so-discreetly, passive-aggressively *disagree* ('Are you sure about that, Michael?'), she might sweetly proffer an alternative point of view ('There *is* always the new Woody Allen at The Screen on the Hill'), but so hypothetically, so tentatively, that there's never any danger of her having her way. And there's something so insidiously *wheedling* about the rising note at the end of her sentences? You know, how she makes everything a question? That always seems to be asking for *permission*? To even bloody *be there*?

Don't get me wrong. I hate arguments. I can't

bear those women who are never happier than when they're chucking plates and calling you a wanker. And I certainly don't want to come home and go twelve rounds with some Jemima Paxman about European farm subsidies. Just every now and then, a bit of a *challenge* might be nice.

But even this is not the whole story. I guess it boils down to my feeling – more than a feeling, my *belief* – that She Is The Wrong Woman For Me. That I can't be happy with her. Not properly.

'I dunno, I think I lost all respect for Hilary when she said she'd show me hers if I'd show her mine.' Mouse splutters on his Chardonnay.

It really happened. In a park in North Finchley. Edward Heath was prime minister. We'd been putting bangers in Airfix models and blowing them up – a very gratifying explosion, as they come apart along the glue lines.

When we'd finished doing that we hid in the bushes for a while, and then, neither of us having any brothers or sisters, Hilary outlined her proposal. Shamefully, after she kept her side of the bargain, I reneged. In recent years, I feel I have more than made up for it.

They come tumbling back into the kitchen, the twins dressed in loud primary colours like cartoon characters, followed by Claudia and Hilary. Hilary is saying: 'We're going to Michael's parents? It's always a bit of a nightmare for him, because he hasn't told them he smokes?'

She stands there smiling, panting from mucking

around with the kids, hair beginning to stick to her forehead and, looking up at this unforgivably happy, healthy creature, I have a sole powerful, *physical* urge. It is *visceral*. (I feel it in my viscera.) It is a great yawing pull of desire for one single, silly cigarette.

In the moments that I've been stewing about Olivia and reflecting on Hilary, I've forgotten all about tobacco. Perhaps it's true, perhaps men *can* only think about one thing at a time.

Mouse feeds himself another Marlboro. *Give me a fucking fag you cunt!!!!*

5

The car ride from my flat in Belsize Park to Finchley only takes about twenty minutes. But, for me, the trip between these two North London suburbs is a journey into the past, a few miles down the Finchley Road back to my childhood. Belsize Park has a kind of genteel yuppie buzz to it – there's an arthouse cinema, a few modern bars and restaurants, Oddbins, a hardcore delicatessen. The place I grew up in, Finchley, has *never* buzzed. To call it dull or suburban – and it is spectacularly both – is missing the point about Finchley. As a child I had the powerful feeling that nothing was supposed to happen there, or ever *could* happen. The place seemed to have a sense of pride in its own blandness. Olivia put her finger on it, the first and only time I ever took her there. As we drove in silence along Ballards Lane, the main street, one afternoon, she suddenly remarked it was like being in the Midlands.

'Hilary, would you like another cup of tea? Or I could make you a sandwich? I know, some fruit. Would you like strawberries? I have nice strawberries. Or melon. Some water-melon. Would you like some water-melon?'

My mother has always been absurdly anxious to feed me, as well as any visitors to our house, usually to the point of physical discomfort, though always stopping short of actual asphyxiation. My father is staring hard at Hilary, lasciviously, I'd say, for a man in his seventies. His eyes flicker into her cleavage. I become aware he's about to launch into a story. This is how my father communicates. He doesn't have conversations. He makes speeches. A lot of people with hearing difficulties are like that. They'd rather talk.

'Monica,' he begins. This is a genuine mistake. These days I think she reminds him of someone he knew called Monica, maybe a girlfriend.

'Hilary, Dad.'

'What? Oh yes. I'm sorry. *Hilary*.' He taps the side of his head with two stubby fingers. *Old age. What can I tell you?*

'Hilary,' he resumes, 'do you know the story about the old Italian? Luigi. He's sitting on the balcony of his villa in Umbria. The sun's going down in the valley, he's got a glass of grappa, and he's talking to one of his sons.'

Hilary beams, nodding furious encouragement, tilting even more bosom in his direction.

'You see those vines?' My father has assumed a ludicrous Italian accent. 'I plant them when first we come to this valley more than forty years ago. With my bare hands, I, Luigi, plant them, and now this valley is full of vines. But do they call me Luigi the Vine-Grower?

'You see those houses? I build those houses. Fine, beautiful houses with the best Umbrian stone and marble. Yes, I, Luigi, build those houses, but do they call me Luigi the House-Builder?'

My mother sets a teacup down noisily. My father shoots her a glance: don't you *dare* ruin the ending.

'You see those roads? When I first come here fifty years ago, there are no roads. Just dirt tracks. I, Luigi, build those roads. But do they call me Luigi the Road-Builder?'

My father takes a deep breath. Looks to the heavens. Spreads his fingers in exasperation.

'I fuck . . . *one* pig . . .'

I've heard it before and it still makes me smile. My father does bitter old Luigi very well. My mother is amused but isn't sure about the F-word in front of 'young people'. But it takes Hilary a full minute to stop laughing. She's actually wiping away tears with a Kleenex. My father is hugely gratified by the response and I can see he's got another funny story in the bomb bay ready to go the minute the hilarity dies down.

My father loves Hilary. When we moved to this

house when I was nine and she was eight, she was the rumbustious little girl next door who was somehow better at being the Daughter He Never Had than I was at being the Son He Actually Did Have. In the two passions he tried to pass on to me – football and chess – Hilary was demonstrably superior. In the park, I'd sulk, but she'd chase round him like a *boy*, harrying for possession, leaping for headers, doing diving saves between the two jumpers for goalposts. And when they moved to the mental plane of the chessboard, her keen, young face would grow tight with concentration as she threw herself into the unequal struggle. Even though he never let her win, she never minded. When it happened to me I was furious.

I did eventually inherit one of his passions – for cigarettes. And at the thought, I feel another lurch of desire, a clamour in the gut – or is it in the head? – that's craving, demanding, *insisting* on a cigarette. Only one. But right now. OK then, soon. I'll buy some on the way home in the Shell garage by the North Circular. No, I won't. Yes, I will. *No, I won't.*

As Hilary is telling my mother and father about what we did last night – a nicely sanitised, low-alcohol, zero-tar version – I slip away upstairs. Good old Hilary. Keeping the old folks happy. Such a nice girl, I think in my mother's voice, you could do a lot worse. I know, Mother, I reply silently, I fully intend to.

My old bedroom is not exactly a shrine to my

childhood, *kept exactly as he left it*. It's been cleared of the worst excesses – what *did* happen to my Salvador Dali poster? – and now it's used as a spare room for guests. My old books are still there though and, ritualistically, I scan the spines. *A Study in Scarlet. A Book of Things a Boy Can Do. The Care and Maintenance of the Budgerigar. A-Level Physics. The Lord of the Rings. The Godfather. The Royal Road to Card Magic. The Avengers Fun Annual*. Through the floor, I hear Hilary downstairs still gamely entertaining the troops. Out of the window I look out on what used to be the Blooms' back garden. They moved years ago. Today, it's all neat lawn, patio and white plastic furniture. Then, it was a wilderness. Then, it was our playground.

We were never Doctors and Nurses; we were Restaurateurs. I am the chef, she the waitress; and we are *busy*. I mean this is one hot fast-food outlet. Through the window of the garden shed, we do a roaring trade in dishes chiefly featuring earth, stones and weeds; we yell orders through to each other, mimicking the controlled hysteria we've witnessed at the Tally Ho Corner Wimpy Bar.

'More greens!' I cry. 'I need 'em now!'

'Coming up!' she responds, tearing up great hunks of undergrowth. 'Where's that mixed grill for table five?'

'Chips! Get me chips! Mixed grill, table five. Ready!'

'Coming right up!'

(For two well-fed middle-class kids from

Finchley, this was much more exciting than Doctors and Nurses. Hospitals were for sick people. In restaurants you could *eat*.)

When we tire of the catering trade, we become The Avengers. Emma Peel and I – though hopelessly outnumbered – are beating the shit out of our imaginary attackers.

'Need some help, Mrs Peel?' I inquire laconically, despatching a villain with my tightly furled umbrella.

'It's OK, Steed, I can manage,' she replies, karate-kicking two felons insensible.

And then, lying in the long grass, there follows a scene of our own invention. From the pockets of his short trousers, John Steed produces a packet of sweet cigarettes, ten lengths of white candy each tipped with a blob of red. I offer one to Mrs Peel and have one myself. Well, we deserve a cigarette, when you consider all the crime we've put a stop to. We loll there in the sunshine, puffing on the sugary simulacra (their cloying powdery aftertaste), striking attitudes, doing things with our fingers and lips that are much, much too *knowing*. We suck. We exhale. We tap, tap on the barrel of the sweet cigarettes, disturbing the imaginary ash. We even do that one – cigarette between index and middle finger – where you flick *up* at the filter with your thumb. All the mannerisms of smoking are in place without a real cigarette ever having passed our lips.

Well, almost.

At nine years old, if I am John Steed, I am also David Nixon, bald maestro of the rabbit and the top hat. I own a conjuring set; I can do annoying things with coins, cards, ropes and rings. And when we put on a show for our mums and dads, Hilary Bloom is my glamorous assistant.

Does she perhaps steal a little too much of the magician's limelight as she prances about in her bathing costume, pointing dramatically and mugging shamelessly when The Egg Has Completely Disappeared . . . or Your Handkerchief No Longer Has a Hole In It? Yes, I feel she may be overplaying her role.

But I hold no bitterness. She only ever wants the best for our show. And she knows the First Law of Magic, which I have read to her from the instruction manual: always leave your audience wanting more.

There is a trick we do with a cigarette. A real one. One of Mrs Bloom's stubby little Embassys. I sit Hilary on a chair and she suddenly becomes very serious, as if she is concentrating hard. I take the borrowed cigarette and hold the end that you light by the thumb and fingertips of one hand. I put the filter against her ear. Slowly, with much gasping and wincing on the part of my young assistant, I appear to push it all the way in. (Of course it slides safely behind my palm.)

Behold, I have shoved a perfectly good Embassy into the Bloom girl's ear. How can this be? Is she hurt? Will she need hours of corrective surgery?

Before the audience has time to consider these questions, I place my fingertips to my lips and – can you believe this, ladies and gentlemen? – I pull the same cigarette out of my mouth.

Ta daaa!!! Hilary is grinning like a lantern, pointing and prancing like this is the neatest trick since Harry Houdini escaped underwater from a shackled sack. With a flourish, she reunites the cigarette with her mother. There is applause. If we had music, there'd be a fanfare. Parents are wondering how much more of this there is. And I have the taste, the distinctive fruity taste of un-smoked tobacco on my lips.

Maybe we *will* stop at that Shell garage on the way back home. No, fuck it, we *won't*.

6

We've done that Sunday night thing. When you've read all the papers, and done all the visiting, and it's crap on the telly, *and I still haven't smoked a cigarette today*, we've gone to the cinema.

Personally, I don't find Hugh Grant all that amusing. But Hilary laughed quite a lot and I suppose the film does just manage a weak grasp, like a sick person's, on what's left of your attention this late in the weekend.

So now we're in Café Flo on Haverstock Hill having a bite and Hilary is acting rather strangely. She's gone a bit serious, for her, and asks me if I think there's anything *special* about today. Can't say I do. Feels like another Sunday in North London to me.

'Hitler's birthday?' I venture.

'No, Michael,' she says, 'something special about *us*?'

Oh Christ. What?

She reaches into her handbag and hands me a small, flattish box, wrapped in gold paper with a ribbon round it.

Shit shit shit. *What am I missing here?*

'Michael.' Her eyes have widened as she looks deep into mine. I resist the urge to laugh stupidly. 'We've been together exactly two thousand days. You know . . . *together* together. I bought you a two-thousand-day anniversary present. Sorry. I couldn't help it. I love you.'

Oh Hilary. You sweet dumb mutt.

It is a Ronson silver cigarette lighter.

7

In bed, Hilary is reading a book called *Cod*. It is apparently a social history of the fish of that name and she says it's as gripping as a novel. I tell her that, personally, I doubt whether anyone would bother to write a novel about a cod, which makes her laugh and kiss my ear, and then return to the North Atlantic. Lately I have failed to complete three books in a row (*Birdsong, Ralph's Party* and *The*

Tesseract – I mean, *what the fuck was that all about?*) so I am re-reading *Scoop*, which I know I adore. The desire for a cigarette is a constant dull . . . emptiness. A little like hunger. A headache without the head. I've got through the whole of Sunday without a fag. How will I do tomorrow?

At the thought of work, a dim but distinct pain pings on like a lightbulb somewhere under my arm. Is that a lymph node on the blink? *The British Medical Association Complete Family Health Encyclopaedia* (the world's scariest book) which I've been consulting in Waterstones has been inconclusive on the subject. First indications of heart disorder? Possible lymphoma? Whole body *riddled with disease*?

Hilary closes her book and throws herself on her side, jamming her warm bum against my hip. I reach over and squeeze her thigh. I guess good magician's assistants aren't all that easy to come by. 'Goodnight, Michael. Have you set the alarm?'

My little pain turns up the volume a notch and bites a bit deeper into the armpit. The palms of my hands are dampish.

There's a saying in our business that people use when something goes wrong, or maybe doesn't come out quite as well as expected. *Hey*, they say, *it's only television*. They might even add, *nobody died*. By which they mean, *it doesn't matter, it's not important, who cares?* But the truth is they're only saying it to make themselves feel better. When they say 'it's only television', then you know they really believe it *does* matter, it's *very* important and they care *deeply*. It was the last thing that little fucker Clive said to me on Friday evening. 'It's only television.' You don't *have* to be an arsehole to say 'it's only television', though somehow I suspect it helps. Surely Yasmin would never say anything as *empty* as 'it's only television'. I try to imagine those words coming from her lips in that deep, raspy voice. But in my mind's ear I find she's saying an altogether different phrase. Something older, much darker and totally unexpected. *Yasmin* . . .

By the time I finish the cigarette, Hilary is already snoring.

I have just written a Post-It Note for the cleaning lady.

Tell Maria to clean fridge ☑

Yes, some men merely daydream. Others *act*.

TWO

1

'She said *what?*' In my peripheral vision, I see the Bearded Lady leaning forward in her chair. So *now* she's interested. Well, this will give her something to think about. 'In this . . . reverie of yours, Yasmin said *what?*'

The Bearded Lady is my shrink. I started going to see her about a year ago when the thing with Olivia broke up and Hilary and I got back together again. Of course, it was Hilary's suggestion. To Go And Talk To Someone. I wasn't even particularly against the idea; after all, I was once a psychology student. Actually, I rather warmed to the thought of going to an address in North London, lying on a couch, and telling a grey-bearded Freudian everything that came into my head. Also, I'd just read that psychotherapy can have the side-effect of improving your tennis. The theory is that it's your personal issues – not lack of talent – that sends the ball long, or into the net. Certainly there's got to be *some* reason why I can never get more than a game or two off Steve when we both *know* that he's crapper than me.

Anyway, the old Freudian turned out to be a woman, but the beard thing sort of stuck. Her real name is Augusta Tuck and that single fact, along with any clues I might pick up from her front garden, hallway and consulting room is all I am supposed to know about her. Naturally I am very curious – is there a *Mr* Tuck? Yes, surely there is, and he must be English because she is so reassuringly Mitteleurope – but I know she will decline to answer any personal questions (*'Why do you ask?'*) so I do not inquire. Her nickname is one of a number of things I haven't told her. Since I fork out £40 a session, I reckon I've got a right to a few secrets.

Mainly I bring her my dreams. And we've got quite tasty, the two of us, at picking them apart like crossword clues. The one about the country lane that splits into three (sex, and which woman to have it with). The one about the leaking radiator (sexual fears about dodgy plumbing). The one about going down the bouncy slide with Hilary (have you ever heard of a better visual pun for the *act* of sex? Bouncy slide. Get it?).

Sometimes when I don't have any dreams of my own, I bring her other people's. Mouse had a good one recently. He dreamt that he got his P60 from the Inland Revenue which showed that he'd earned £88,000. Now, Mouse works for an insurance company and doesn't make anything like this. So why £88,000? (And not £90,000, or £85,000?) Well, eighty-eight is twin eights. *Twin eights*. A play on words voicing Mouse's anxiety about earning enough to pay for what his *twins ate*.

So what have I discovered since I began seeing the Bearded Lady?

1. **That the unconscious is full of cheesy puns. The person who scripts your dreams used to work for the *Daily Mirror*.**
2. **That I'm worried about work, which I already knew. I mean, who isn't?**
3. **That I'm worried about women. Ditto.**
4. **That while I'm lying on the couch, I never once have the urge to light a cigarette. The unconscious is a non-smoker.**

'She said she was late.' *Yasmin*.

'Those were her words? As it were, the words you put in her mouth.'

'I think she said: "Michael, I'm late." Which was

a surprise, as I say, because I was trying to picture her saying something completely different.'

'"It's only television."'

'Yes, "It's only television." It's a sort of terrible cliché.'

'"Michael, I'm late." You take it to mean . . .?'

'I mean, this is a woman I've barely spoken to. I think I asked her if she knew how to rename a file in Microsoft Word. And once I cadged a fag off her. Which I didn't need to because I had a whole new packet in my bag.'

'You are attracted to her . . .'

'She's got those sexy hooded eyelids. And a beaky Roman nose. A long face, like a horse. She's very thin. Like a thin horse. Or maybe a greyhound. Actually she reminds me a little of a witch. Or a nun.'

'This "I'm late" you take to mean . . . ?'

'To mean that she may be pregnant. Expecting a baby.'

'And the father. In this fantasy, the father would be . . . who exactly?'

'Well . . . I suppose that would have to be me.'

Silence. In a distant part of the house, a door slams. *Mr Tuck?* Pause. Two, three. Get me William Hill. Five hundred quid on what the next line's going to be.

'So how did you feel about this?'

'Well, here's the funny thing. You know I think I was really rather *pleased*.'

2

I see the Bearded Lady at nine o'clock Monday morning in West Hampstead. If I'm out of there at 9.50, and I put my foot down on the Westway, I can be at my desk off Shepherd's Bush Green about quarter past ten.

I love the Westway. Only five minutes of motorway in the heart of London, but with the right track on the radio to yell along to, five minutes of Pure Car Epiphany. *Up The Junction* by Squeeze will do it for me. Or Talking Heads' *And She Was*. Especially – though I wouldn't admit this to too many people – *Desperado* by the Eagles. Red Peugeot, outside lane, driver in tortoiseshell glasses doing the tortured vocalist bit? That'll be me.

Today, the best I can find is *I Am The Walrus*, which is acceptable at 70 mph but not, you know, *mood-enhancing*.

Belvedere Television is named after the posh restaurant in Holland Park where the founders celebrated their first commission. (Let's face it, Andy's Kebab House Television doesn't have quite the same ring, does it?) The company started out making docu-soaps. *Car Park*, that was one of ours. We also did *Sweet Factory, Tax Men* and *Pet Cemetery*. We nearly won an award last year for *Tree Fellas* but we were just beaten by *Tooth Fairies*, a six-parter about the gay dental practice in Soho. Since the bottom fell out of the docu-soap market, we've tried to move into leisure (gardening, cooking, DIY) though the truth is that, in common with the rest of the industry, we'll make just about anything if someone can be found to pay the bill.

I've been several things in my time in television – reporter, producer, director – just at the moment I'm Belvedere's Head of Development, which means dreaming up ideas for new TV shows, making them look sexy on paper, then trying to persuade broadcasters to give us the money to produce them. Right now I'm writing a one-page treatment for a job-swap series in which a Bradford policeman goes to work in Rio de Janeiro. It's called *Copper Cabana*. Channel Five, apparently, are very interested. This afternoon, I plan to spend a couple of hours seeing if there's any mileage in a late-night post-ironic quiz idea about Satanism entitled *I Love Lucifer*. I find it usually helps to start with the title and then think up a show to fit it. An earnest woman at BBC2 got quite excited for a while about one such programme, a history of the creation myth called *Would You Adam and Eve It?*

Does it surprise you to hear that I can get through rather a lot of cigarettes in this job?

Monday is always a slow start. Most of the younger people look half asleep, still wrecked from doing their Es at the weekend. Yasmin is different. Even from about twenty feet away, there's an intensity about her, a heat that comes off her that feels a little *nuclear*. This morning she is at her terminal, rattling away at some script, eyes blazing, cigarette drooping from the corner of her wide, *wide* mouth. I'd say she is practically glowing. Through the glass walls of my office, I find her directly in my eyeline every time I look up from the screen. She joined Belvedere as an Assistant Producer on our religion-meets-cookery show, *Holy Delicious* (vicars and rabbis compete in the kitchen; you don't want to know, believe me).

Now she stops typing and tips back in her chair. Two thin ankles, one crossed over the other, pop out from beneath the desk's front 'modesty panel'. She's kicked her shoes off. Thin feet point across the carpet at me. She gazes off into the middle distance, searching for the right word, or a phrase. I do this all the time myself so I know what is going to happen next. She takes a massive drag on her cigarette – Camel, what else? – a really huge, re-fuelling infusion. Just watching, I feel the powerful jolt of nicotine that's about to whack her round the head like a slow-motion sandbag. I begin to count. It will take seven seconds to travel from lips to lungs to brain.

Five . . . six . . . seven.

Yasmin allows a thick creamy soup of smoke to swirl out of her mouth. Rather astonishingly, like ectoplasm, it's hanging above and in front of her face; and now she's blowing a thinner, faster stream of smoke, from deeper down; it's gusting through the soupy cloud, dispersing it. Her eyes have gone very wide and I have the feeling that they meet mine for a fraction of a second. But they lock back on to the screen, her feet vanish, and she falls on the keyboard like a pianist.

I'm afraid I find this irresistibly sexy.

Two minutes later, as I pass behind Yasmin on the way to the water machine, I shoot a glance at her terminal. She's writing an e-mail. And the only phrase that leaps out at me is '. . . must give up smoking'.

I knew it. We're made for each other.

3

Television is all about agonising over the silliest of details. Grown men can spend hours deliberating whether a show should be called *Copper Cabana* or whether it 'works better' as *Cop@Cabana*. Is the shimmering chrome on the new titles of *Holy Delicious* (or should it be *Holy Delicious!*) regrettably *eighties*, or ironically retro? Is the notion of Nicholas Parsons as the host of the devil-worship show *I Love Lucifer* inspired or terrible? Actually, that's an easy one, but these things *matter* to television people. I've heard it said that the secret of good TV is going to more trouble than *anyone would think worthwhile*. The sad truth is that *bad* TV is just as hard to make.

Actually, I'm finding it quite difficult to concentrate on *Copper Cabana*. Every time I stop writing and glance up, there she is. Come to think of it, it's worse than that; it's the specific knowledge that *there she is* that's causing me to glance up. She's wearing one of those clingy Chinese silk dresses, all butterflies and orchids in electric colours. Shiny black hair swings against pale shoulders. Walking past her desk just now, through her perfumed cloud of Camel fumes, I had the tangible urge to bury my face in her neck.

People assume working in television is glamorous. Oh, that must be exciting, they say to me at parties. Do you know lots of famous people? What's Dale Winton *really* like?

Glamour? Let me tell you about TV and glamour.

At an industry dinner – a drunken awards ceremony at the Grosvenor House Hotel or somesuch – I once saw four of the most famous women on television. They had formed a little circle and they were chatting away, quite plausibly actually. You might even have supposed that they liked one another and weren't in fact bitter rivals for work and fame. Each was a household name, the star of her own show, or shows. Each could have done the work of the next. Each was pretty and blonde and 'young'. In fact the sight of them *together* felt impossible, like the transgression of a physical law, an unstable, critical mass of pretty, blonde TV presenters. And yet as you looked from one to the other, all made up and sparkling, these four painted performers could not even *collectively* match the glamour, the allure, the sheer sexual heat that's rising off Yasmin like air rippling over hot tarmac.

Here's where you'll find the glamour in television today. Not in the arrogant vacuity of the stars (yes, us producers *are* envious, but *they* are still arrogant and vacuous). Not in the sexiness of the technology (most of which you can buy in Dixons). It's in young women like Yasmin Swan.

I get up from my chair and begin rearranging the Post-It Notes on my glass wall. They're a bit of a con really, little more than scribbled *aides-mémoire*, quarter-baked ideas like '*Really Sick* – health series where presenter contracts new disease each week.' Or '*Strangers in the Night* – chat show with no host. Guests talk among themselves.' The information on this blizzard of yellow stickies would not fill more than a single sheet of A4. But TV folk like to look creative. A *busy* office wall denotes a mind in ferment with ideas. I redesign the Post-Its into concentric circles, which I think is rather effective, conveying, as it does, a mysterious sense of *plan*. When I take my seat again, I discover Yasmin perfectly framed in the centre.

No, this is ridiculous. I can't sit here *mooning* at the girl. Go and *talk* to her . . .

My hand is actually on the doorknob when the phone rings. It's Hilary.

'Michael, shall I cook supper for us tonight? There were some fabulous aubergines in the market this morning. I could do that ratatouille you like?'

Hilary walks through Berwick Street every day on her way to work. Tragically, she's in TV too, a researcher. Sometimes they call her Associate Producer and other times Assistant Producer (though I've never met anyone who could explain the difference). It's perfectly possible she may not be nasty enough to ever be a *Producer* Producer. Her company makes respectable popular-science documentaries about black holes, earthquakes, epidemics and the like. They've got quietly splendid offices in Soho though, unforgivably, they're called Plasma Productions. If they weren't so corporately level-minded and generally *pleasant* about life, they might sneer long and mightily at the likes of Belvedere TV and all its tacky works.

I don't know where she got the idea that I like ratatouille. Who does? Do you know *anybody*? 'Yeah, fine. I'll bring a bottle. What's happening in Plasma-world?'

'Hugo's in the States pitching *Secrets of the Lobsters* to the Americans. You know, how apparently they're a lot more intelligent than anyone had realised? Julia was telling me she's got this amazing footage of a lobster actually playing a tune? On an underwater keypad?'

'*Lobster Confidential*. Better title surely?'

'Michael, can you believe it? I waited in all morning, and that plumber never showed up. *Again*.'

I can believe it. After we hang up, I scribble on another Post-It and add it to the Great Wheel of Television. 'Show about musical animals. *Pet Sounds?*'

Through my glass wall, across the open-plan

office, Yasmin has become animated. She's laughing, raking her fingers through her hair, throwing her head back, eyes sparkling, mouth wide open. There's a lot of soft pink tissue on view. Looming over her, with one buttock resting on the corner of her desk, a picture of blond male insouciance, is my nemesis, Clive Wilson.

He is lighting her cigarette and my heart is full of hate.

4

They say the best revenge is to live well. Or that it's a dish best tasted cold. All very icy, all very cerebral. And my official position in regard to Clive is indeed one of lofty disdain. I've Risen Above It. He won, I lost, next. That sort of thing.

Actually, the reality is this: my most frequent revenge fantasy is so vivid, so hallucinatory, I think even the *thought* of it may be illegal. Here it is: he's twitching on the carpet, almost *bouncing* at the fleshy *slap, slap* of the bullets that spit from my Kalashnikov. I've floored him with a single non-fatal wound to the leg and now, as I work my way up his body – *slap, slap, slap* – he is whimpering and I am reminded of that Japanese poem about the snail.

Oh snail!
Climb Mount Fuji.
But slowly, slowly.

Slowly would definitely be the way to do it.

Fantasy is normal I tell myself as, with a final well-placed meaty *slap*, the roof of his skull comes off and the bloodbath is over. Fantasy is healthy – OK, one more in the eye just to make sure – *slap* – it may even be *necessary*, as long as you can distinguish it from reality. And, in truth, the only thing I am liable to do to Clive – unless I can come up with something really brilliant – is to subtly undermine him on every possible occasion. Subtlety is of the essence, because nearly everyone knows why I have a grievance against him, if *grievance* is the right word for someone who comes to your birthday party – brings a really *nasty* bottle of red wine – and then leaves with your girlfriend. Grounds for war, more like.

Slapslapslapslapslapslapslapslap.

Yes, she did *say* she wouldn't be staying because she had to be up early for a flight the next day. And yes, he *was* only giving her a lift home. But they *were* flirting chronically with each other all evening. By the mantelpiece, on the arm of the sofa, later against the bookshelves, she was doing funny things with her eyes and hips at him; he playing a straight bat, friendly but not *over*-interested; you know the type, the jut-jawed captain of the sodding cricket team. Even Mouse commented on it.

'Here, your bird's being a bit hugger-mugger with that very *handsome* fellow over there isn't she?'

When I stepped out on to the balcony and found them together, there was still a slight disturbance in the air, as if they had only just settled into their positions. They had, I am sure, been kissing.

'Michael,' she'd said a little too enthusiastically. 'Clive's been telling me that you thought up the title for his new show, *Holy Delightful*. That's rather clever.'

'Delicious.' I forced through clenched teeth.

They claimed their relationship didn't start until long after that evening. That they'd never even thought about one another until they'd met again months later, at a charity do. But by the time she'd returned from Los Angeles, where she'd had a chance to do some *serious thinking about us*, in her mind it was finished. It had been very *nice*, you know, *lovely really*, but ultimately she knew she needed something – *someone* – different. What – *who* – she couldn't say. She'd love to stay friends, but she'd understand if I didn't want to see her.

I'll always remember the way they left that night. Midnight. The party still going. Clive clapping me on the shoulder on his way out. 'She's a lovely girl, Michael. You're a lucky bugger. Don't worry, I'll see she gets home all right.' And Olivia just smiling. That slow, mysterious smile. With you or at you? *With* you or *at* you?

Slapslapslapslapslap.

5

As the producer of *Holy Delicious*, Clive has about a hundred reasons a day to talk to Yasmin. I have fewer. On a Post-It Note I survey my options:

1. **Bum another fag off her (and come across as a tiresome scrounger).**
2. **Offer *her* a fag (why?).**
3. **Ask a computer question (something to do with headers and footers?).**
4. **Go to water machine, 'trip' and spill water down her like Hugh Grant in *Notting Hill*.**
5. **Ask what she's doing for lunch.**

I go for a hybrid of options four and five, but by the time I return from the water machine, omitting the 'trip' and spill stage, she has vanished. From my office window, I watch as she leaves the building, Chinese silk dress flaring in the sunlight, right hand on the strap of her shoulder bag, cigarette fluttering from the left, a pair of huge white trainers propelling her off towards Shepherd's Bush Green, smoking like a train all the way. Gratifyingly, she is alone.

So now I am in the pub with Steve, though strictly speaking BarBushKa is no longer a pub but a themed leisure outlet, the theme being young people getting pissed quickly as opposed to old people getting pissed slowly. A frozen vodka cabinet and nightly karaoke are the main innovations; they've also taken up the carpets to reveal the floorboards and ripped out the curtains to let the daylight in. I guess it was hoped that the old lags who used to nurse their pints through the afternoon would be offended by the redesign and migrate to gloomier boozing grounds. Hideously, however, they stayed. Mostly in the same positions. Steve likes it because he reckons they still keep the best draught Guinness in West London.

Steve is currently producing Belvedere's last remaining docu-soap, about a group of crisis counsellors in the Midlands, *Traumarama*. But the two of us have been crossing each other's path for years, since we first worked together on local newspapers. As a result, the present scene, Steve and I in a pub, smoking and drinking, has a reassuring familiarity about it. Women and jobs may come and go but this tableau somehow endures. Steve's about the only person I can talk to about Clive and how much I'd like to bugger him up in some way. We enjoy dreaming up terrible fates for him and, to further this end, as I return to our corner with a second Guinness and another red wine, Steve feeds himself a Silk Cut and lights it in a very characteristic way.

Ping, rasp . . . snap.

This is how I first became aware of him. Fifteen years ago. Sitting at the next desk, stick-thin, built like the spindly cigarettes he then used to hand-roll and fire up in the three unmistakable sound effects that spell, to those who have ears for these things, Zippo lighter.

The metallic ping of the lid flipping open, the rasp of flint sparking flame and then, after the incendiary pause – during which you might even catch a sexy little crackle of paper and tobacco strands – loudest of all, the satisfying, businesslike crescendo of lid snapping back home. Good job Zippo, it seems to be saying. The classic lighter of the US Military with its fat petrol flame holding the promise of plenty more where that came from.

He smokes greedily, eyes half-closing in pleasure. His passion is for Old Holborn. Rolling tobacco in a stiff silver paper packet. And the smoke smells sweet. Aromatic. If it were food, it might be something chocolatey or gamey. Some fascinating duck dish. If it was a drink it could only be brandy. It rises from him in a kind of masculine perfume, the papery cylinder glowing orange between his already yellowing fingers like a fuse. He is twenty-one and I am just a year younger.

I am drawn to him instantly.

We are junior reporters on the *Wrexham Examiner* in North Wales. A traditional weekly whose first three pages are filled with the court reports that are believed to be the main reason most people buy the paper. Shoplifting, assault, drink-driving. The odd indecent exposure. Neither of us is Welsh and we laugh cynically at the way the local population seem to revel in the misfortunes of others.

Steve, all bony shoulders and elbows, is hunched over a typewriter at the desk in front of me, hammering prose from his shorthand note of the words of some prosecuting police inspector. How the defendant was discovered in the driving seat of a car whose front wheels were found resting in the shattered window display of Victoria Wine. How, upon opening the driver's door, the accused fell out on to the pavement and appeared unable to get to his feet. How the officer at the scene noticed his eyes were glazed and his speech was slurred. How the PC formed the impression that he had been drinking.

The pounding stops. There's the barely audible whisper of a Rizla slipping from its packet. Silence. And now, the familiar mechanical . . . *ping* . . . *rasp* . . . (pause) . . . *snap*. Steve tips his chair back and the great cloud rises over his head, like smoke from a distant blaze.

I don't remember how many sets of *ping-rasp-*(pause)-*snap* I heard before I cracked. Maybe not that many. But I do remember how hard it was at first to roll the moist, clingy tobacco. How the trick was to get an even consistency, no lumpy, matted stretches that you can't inhale through. How the *making* of the cigarette was at *that* stage as important as the smoking.

And the smoking? Well, let's say it was like inhaling chocolate vapour. Or soup. It curled and swirled, delivering a hot physical shock as it hit the back of your throat on its way down into your lungs. And the effect was like being hit over the head with a blunt instrument. The dizziness, the nausea. And the roll-up would keep going out. And sometimes the paper stuck to your lip. And if you tried to re-light it when it was very short you could scorch your nose. And when you smoked it really far down, the last drag nearly burnt your fingers. And after each one you couldn't really see why you'd ever particularly want another. So, of course, it *was* love.

I never blamed Steve for getting me started. If it wasn't him, it would have been somebody else. And eventually, of course, we both grew out of roll-ups. But now, in this Shepherd's Bush theme pub all these years later, he's looking at me through the haze of alcohol and tobacco fumes with what looks very like an evil grin on his face.

'A bereavement solution,' he says. 'Get a bench engraved in his local park. "In Memory of Clive Wilson. Rest a while in a place he loved." That'll spook the little fucker.'

6

Always a mistake to have a couple at lunchtime. You arrive back at your desk all red-faced and buoyant, ready for anything. Ten minutes later you realise you are completely useless. So, if you work in television, this is the time to watch tapes or make phone calls. I call Steve who works one floor up.

'That Argentine Merlot has gone straight to my head.'

'You should stick to Guinness. I can't feel a thing above the neck. Ideal state for viewing three hours of Redditch burns-victim.'

'Have you noticed that woman who sits near my office? She's new-ish. Works on *Holy Delicious*.'

'The one who Clive's shagging?'

My stomach descends six floors.

'Only kidding. Yes, I have, as a matter of fact. Very nice. Do you fancy her?'

'Well, I do actually. Trouble is, though, I'm finding it a bit difficult to make . . . an approach.'

'Send her an e-mail. Something neutral to do with work. If she replies, you send her a witty reply. If she then sends you a witty reply, you know she's intrigued, so you send her a witty reply. You get a whole witty dialogue going and then you ask her out.'

'In person?'

'On e-mail.'

'Bit stupid when I can *see* her from where I'm sitting.'

'That's the beauty of it. It's a parallel form of discourse. There's no embarrassment. If she knocks you back, you needn't mention it. But if she goes for it . . .'

My stomach descends another floor. 'Have you tried it?'

'Read about it in the *Evening Standard*.'

'What if she did as well?'

'Then she'll know the rules of engagement. Fortune favours the bold, Michael.'

An hour later I click on SEND and light the twentieth cigarette of the day. It is four o'clock.

To: Yasmin Swan
From: Michael Roe, Head of Development
Subject: I Love Lucifer

I am playing with an idea about a post-ironic Satanism quiz. Late night. C4, C5, that sort of thing. Can you think of any game clergymen from Holy D who might be induced to take part?

The next forty-five minutes pass in a daze. I channel-hop furiously, settling finally on Eurosport. Ladies tennis. A tournament in the Far East. Jana Novotna versus Anna Kournikova. Every now and again, I shoot her a glance across the office. Still at her post. Typing, phoning, talking, smoking. A day in a life in TV.

Plink. An e-mail. From her.

To: Michael Roe, Head of Development
From: Yasmin Swan
Subject: RE: I Love Lucifer

Sorry, no. Ours are all v. serious.

Promising. I can work with this.

To: Yasmin Swan
From: Michael Roe, Head of Development
Subject: Dodgy Vicars

What, you mean they all believe in God or something? No jokers? No pisstakers?

5.15. Novotna is a set and a break up at 3–2 in the second. *Plink*.

To: Michael Roe
From: Yasmin Swan
Subject: RE: Dodgy Vicars

Sorry, no.

Shit. Bloody bollocking fucking cunting shit.

7

'Michael, I'm late.'

Yasmin is standing in my office doorway. My stomach free-falls into the basement.

I have been concentrating so hard on torturing the *Copper Cabana* proposal into shape – 'the Yorkshire bobby on the Latin beat' – that a couple of hours have slipped by. The office has emptied.

'Sorry, I was miles away. I don't think I quite heard you.'

She smiles. I can feel sweat forming in the divot above my upper lip.

'I said it's late. I think we're the last here. Will you be OK to lock up?'

She's on her way home. Sunglasses ride shotgun in her hair. Orchids, tigers and butterflies are doing something complex and sinewy down her long thin body. Absurdly, she terminates in a cartoon pair of oversized white trainers. Poking out from the top of her bag is a paperback copy of *The Talented Mr Ripley*.

'Sure. No problem.'

She turns to leave.

'I love that book. The Highsmith. Are you enjoying it?'

The horsy face swivels round in my direction. The great hooded eyelids bat once, twice. The palms of my hands are a swamp.

'Well, it's not my normal cup of tea to be honest. But I think it's amazing, the way you find yourself rooting for this total, amoral bastard . . .'

'Actually *willing* him to commit murder.'

'Yes. I was like, go on, *do him! Do him!* Quite scary really.'

'Listen, do you fancy a quick drink? I was hoping to pick your brain about something.'

'Oh?'

A quarter of an hour later we are in Damien Hirst's trendy bar-restaurant, the Pharmacy, sitting side by side directly below a giant packet of Canestan. A beautiful young waitress in a surgical gown brings our drinks. Dry vodka Martini. Two of them. I can't describe my pleasure at hearing Yasmin say in her husky, toasted voice *That sounds like a very good idea* and asking for the same. Dry vodka Martini, the turbo-charged Bentley of the alcohol world. There's no faster, classier way to reach cruising altitude.

She's smoking of course. Camels. I'm on the Silk Cut. And we've been twittering away about all sorts, about naughty Tom Ripley, about *Holy Delicious*. About Belvedere Television and about Montgomery Dodd who owns it. About *I Love Lucifer* (ludicrous, but You Never Know). About working for the BBC (I have; she hasn't), about Television In General, about What We'd Be Doing If We Hadn't Got Into It (journalist; academic). And there is an *excited confidential* tone to our conversation, an intensity about her huge, lidded eyes, something about the way her nostrils flare when a new idea strikes her that is combining with the Stolichnaya in my veins in the most intoxicating way. But this is still two colleagues having a drink after work, I remind myself. Just because I'm pissed and slowly dissolving in the presence of this woman who looks to me like a sexy horse, doesn't mean she necessarily feels the same. Does it?

We chatter on about books we've liked and disliked (she liked *The Information*; couldn't finish *Underworld*), about films, flats, TV shows. Through a second vodka Martini, we find ourselves back on to Belvedere. I give her what I hope is an amusing overview of the politics of the company, including a not very subtle stiletto in the ribs for Clive ('Not very good at *television* really, but that's what makes him such a delightful chap'). In return, she tells me a funny story about a priest they had on the show the other day who turned out to be an unemployed actor. She lives in Queen's Park. She is twenty-eight. Of course she's got a boyfriend. Nick. They're all called Nick, the men in the lives of desirable women.

Do you think it would be wise to have another Martini? I ask her. Her face is flushed and she lights a cigarette. She's smoked a bloody caravanserai of Camel since we've been here and I've matched her fag for fag. I tell her the third Martini is known as the Mona Lisa Martini because, after three, you can't get this stupid smile off your face. She is sweet – or is it drunk? – enough to laugh.

We dive into a pair of Mona Lisas. The waitresses are replacing the ashtrays as fast as we can soil them. And then, because I badly want to touch her – though we are just colleagues having a drink together after work – I do something a bit cheeky. I do the ash trick on her.

'Want to see a good trick,' I ask?

Sure, she smiles. Her eyes widen. Staring straight at me. Almost flirting. Isn't she?

Put your hands out like this, I say, holding mine out, palms downwards, fingers slightly apart, like a pianist; as if I was just about to launch into Rachmaninov's Second.

Gamely she does likewise. And I take her surprisingly cool hands in mine and move them a little closer to me. She doesn't flinch. Holds my gaze.

Clench your fists, I tell her, doing the same. She obliges. Her knuckles go very white. There's a single ring on her right hand. It's a Love Heart set in Perspex. It reads 'Passion'.

I lick the tip of my index finger and dip it gently into the ashtray. A grey blob of ash adheres. A flicker of alarm on Yasmin's face. Don't worry, I reassure her. It won't get too mucky. Keep clenching.

I touch a little smear of ash on to the back of her left hand. The blemish is almost offensive. Like a dog turd in a Ming vase.

I pick up the plastic stick with the olive from my Martini glass and perform some ironic magic passes with it over her two fists. She's laughing. Buying this schtick.

Go like that, I tell her, demonstrating how to pass right fist over left. Now like that. Left over right.

I lean over and blow the ash off the back of her hand, brushing away what remains, my fingers touching hers again.

Unclench that fist and look inside, I tell her.

She looks. Nothing. There's nothing there.

Shit. The trick has failed. I appear genuinely perplexed, Yasmin vaguely disappointed. But hang on. What about the other hand? Look in there . . .

Inside – *inside* – her clenched right fist, daubed on the palm of her young thin hand – *she can't believe this* – is a rude smear of cigarette ash. Her mouth has literally dropped open in amazement. If her eyes go any wider, they'll fall out. She is speechless.

'Quite good, isn't it?' I say modestly, draining my Martini. Actually, I think this trick is quite brilliant in its simplicity. It rarely fails and most people cannot begin to see how it's done. I say *most* people, because right now a light is dawning in Yasmin's face. My God, she's sussed me, even with three Martinis inside her.

'You put the ash on my palm when you pulled my hands towards you.'

I smile at her. Innocently, I hope.

'Michael, that is so fucking . . . sneaky. I love it.'

She cocks her head to one side. Frowns.

'So what's the one after the Mona Lisa called then?'

8

They should call it the Zen Master Martini. Because, after four, you reach the sort of clarity, of transcendence of the everyday that mystics and yogis can take lifetimes to achieve.

The world distilled into a single object, a single thought. A mantra.

Her.

Or if you prefer . . .

She.

We're in that restaurant, Kensington Place. I couldn't tell you much about what I've eaten – it involved squid – but I know we've sunk one bottle of Chilean Merlot and we are halfway through another. She's been rattling on about something for the last ten minutes or so, though I'm afraid I haven't been listening too closely. I've been lost, gazing at her eyes, her hair, her lips, her teeth, her tongue. And that voice, the Camel-cured vibration coming out of her mouth doesn't seem to be words any more, it's *noise*. Changes in air pressure. Abstract sound sculpture. The way it is when you're fascinated by the colour of her gums, not the structure of her sentences.

'You don't really enjoy it, you just *think* you enjoy it because it stops the pain.' She lights another cigarette. 'That's the theory. I just wish I believed it.' Her long neck muscles flex as she sucks down hard. A beat. Another. And now she is wreathed in ectoplasm.

What is she talking about? I am far too pissed to know. But down this fast flowing river of red wine, I have spotted an overhanging branch. I grab for it.

'What's the difference between enjoying something and only *thinking* you're enjoying it? It's the same, isn't it?'

'Well, it is a bit philosophical,' she says. *How come she is so sodding . . . articulate? When I am almost on my knees*. 'But I think there actually is a difference. *Real* enjoyment is the positive addition of pleasure to your life. Like eating ice-cream. Or having sex. *Imaginary* enjoyment is the mere cancellation of pain. Smoking is imaginary enjoyment.'

Oh, smoking. That old thing.

The rest of the evening is a series of jump cuts. Now we are in the middle of an argument, no let's call it a spirited discussion, about the nature of addiction. I am talking drivel. Or I *think* I am talking drivel. Perhaps it amounts to the same thing. I wish she hadn't said that. *Having sex.*

And now we must be paying the bill because our First Direct Visa cards are falling together deliciously on the plate . . .

And now we are outside on the pavement, scouting for taxis . . .

And now – *Michael, it's been a fun evening* – her long pale face looming towards mine, eyes huge, a chaste kiss from those full, promising lips.

And now, alone in a black cab bowling through Camden, the memory of that kiss, repeating like a multiple-edit.

And now, as we sail past The Roundhouse, a horrible, queasy thought. Ratatouille. Hilary. Oh shit.

When I get home, I phone her. I think she was asleep. Honesty is always the best policy in these circumstances in my experience. I'm really sorry, I tell her, I'll make it up to you. I got drunk. With Steve.

That's *OK* Michael, she says wearily. You can buy me dinner tomorrow night. Goodnight.

I sit for a while, smoking a cigarette in an armchair. Listening to the traffic on Haverstock Hill. Replaying fragments from our evening. And then I call Dave Cleaver, another old colleague from the *Wrexham Examiner*. Not a friend like Steve, but a man with more than a passing interest in the wicked world of television. We swap stories for a bit (he tells me a fantastic piece of gossip about two of the female contestants in *Big Brother*. Shit, or was it *Countdown*?).

I swallow a couple of Nurofen, brush my teeth, and stare at the reflection in the bathroom mirror. A man wearing unfashionable glasses with a toothbrush in his hand stares back. I loom right in and peer into his eyeballs. Wasn't there once a little boy who used to do this? Who would narrow his eyes until they were nearly shut, trying, but never quite succeeding, to see what he looked like when he was asleep? Whoever *this* bloke is, he definitely needs a decent haircut.

There's been progress. Definite progress. Despite one twinge around Clive, I've barely thought of her all day.

Stop obsessing about Olivia ☑

That night, Yasmin and I play a game of tennis. Except for a pair of giant white tennis shoes, she is naked. I marvel at the way she athletically steps into each shot, the way she follows through on the forehand, so the racket head ends up over her shoulder. The way her empty left hand is in the game too, fingers splayed, sinews stretched. Running back towards the baseline to reach a lob, she slips, and falls to the ground, grazing the back of her hand. As I lean down to ask if she is all right, I wonder, will she allow me to suck the poison out of her wound?

In your dreams, Michael Roe.

THREE

1

Around the same time on Saturday night that I was in the bar writing my life-plan on the inside of the Silk Cut packet, the man who lives in the flat downstairs, a concert pianist, died during a recital he was giving in Harrogate. They say he was in the middle of his final piece when he collapsed. Of a heart attack or a stroke, no-one knows. Apparently Howard was seventy.

What a great way to go, everyone's been saying. Not from some squalid, degenerative disease; but suddenly, up on stage, in front of his public, doing the thing he loved doing, right up to the end.

I don't know though.

I think it would be incredibly disturbing. Like the time I was at the cinema – *The Usual Suspects* – and the projector broke during a crucial scene towards the end of the movie. It was in the police station, there had been several minutes of nervy dialogue between Chazz Palminteri and Kevin Spacey; we knew the resolution to the mystery was coming soon when . . . *WHUMP!!* Suddenly the screen goes black and the house lights bang on. The shock was positively *rude*. Like being kicked awake in the middle of an exceptionally absorbing dream.

I don't think Howard would have wanted to go like that. From the look of his post in the hall – alternative health catalogues, private medical insurance, copper bracelets – I don't think he was planning to go at all.

So it is with me. I have no wish to leave. I'm guessing that by the time I reach Howard's age, they'll have come up with something. A cure. Or a system of payments one can make instead.

There was an urgency about Howard in the last few months of his life that perhaps spoke of what was to come. At a House Meeting a few months ago, a dozen of us sat round a table to study carpet samples and reach agreement on precisely what shade of oatmeal we wanted for the common parts. As the arguments went back and forth, I noticed Howard wasn't listening. The fingers of his right hand were playing a tune on the tablecloth that no-one could hear but him. Now I wonder if it was the same piece of music that closed his last performance.

I sometimes talk to the Bearded Lady about death.

'How do you feel about it?' she asks. (Such an original question. How does she think of them?)

I'm against it, I tell her.

But you smoke. You drink. You take risks with your health.

Yes. Bit of a weird one that. But look at it this way. If I led a blameless life I would die too. Maybe later. But I would die. And it's dying that I object to.

Today, though, I am talking about living. About Monday night. And Yasmin.

'We seemed to get on so well together. We liked the same books, hated the same films. And she *challenged* me. We actually had an argument. I can't remember much about it. I was a bit drunk to be honest.'

Over my right shoulder, I feel – or I *feel* that I feel – a twitch of disapproval from Augusta Tuck. Just a straightening of her tweed skirt, or a resettling into her armchair. That generation doesn't drink. They don't approve either. (Or am I just projecting my guilt, fuck it?)

'I mean I can't remember the last time Hilary mounted any sustained disagreement with me.'

'You think she is too passive?'

A bolt of irritation flashes through my head. I

don't want to talk about boring old Hilary. I want to get stuck into sexy Yasmin. I sidetrack the Bearded Lady with the dream.

'I don't think there's much mystery to it, do you?' I ask.

'Well how do *you* interpret it?'

'I want her to *fall* for me, don't I? – that's why she falls over. And that thought about wanting to suck the poison from her wound, that's pretty sexual wouldn't you say? Quite apart from the fact that she's not wearing any clothes except a giant pair of . . . oh shit.'

'What?'

'I've just realised what brand they were. The trainers. In the dream.'

'Yes?'

'They were Wilsons.'

2

I see the Bearded Lady Mondays and Thursdays. So, this Thursday morning I'm flogging down the Westway – Al Green, *Tired of Being Alone*; great but not epiphanic – and I'm wondering why my unconscious took the trouble to equip Yasmin with Wilson tennis shoes when her actual brand is Nike. I mean she's only Clive Wilson's assistant producer, not his bloody property.

Today, as I pass through the open-plan office, I see she is not wearing any sports gear at all. She's in tight green jeans and a sleeveless blouse that stops short to reveal a fascinating inch of bare midriff. Her hair's up in some sort of clip and, not for the first time, I think that there's something about her face, at a certain angle, in a certain light, that is almost blokeish.

After the monumental hangover that followed Martini Night and the delightfully conspiratorial exchange of looks we shot one another on Tuesday – *Jesus, did we tie one on, or what?* – I am trying to ease us into a happy routine of chatting several times a day. So this morning, on the way towards my glass-walled cell, I stop off at her desk. She's lighting a cigarette.

'Hey, how's the no smoking going?' I offer.

'No problem. Nothing to it.' She blows a stream of smoke at the ceiling. I notice a book lying open by her keyboard.

'What are you reading? More Ripley?'

Yasmin flashes me a meaningful look and turns the slim volume over to reveal its cover. *The Easy Way to Stop Smoking* by Allen Carr.

'My boyfriend bought it for me. Apparently it's a classic.'

'What's the thrust?'

'Well, as I was telling you the other night . . .'

Whoops. 'Ah yes. The Alzheimer Martini. Can seriously affect the, er . . . Sorry, what were we talking about?'

She laughs. Her bony shoulder-blades bounce up and down and I feel slightly helpless. She continues.

'Giving up smoking is not a sacrifice but a *liberation*. The pleasure you get from smoking a cigarette is like taking off a tight pair of shoes after a hard day at the sales. It's *relief* from the symptoms of addiction, not a positive addition of happiness . . .'

'Like an ice-cream. Or . . . steak and chips.'

'Exactly. Smokers say cigarettes help them to concentrate. Or they really like one after a meal. Actually, the most important reason that smokers smoke is to reduce their withdrawal craving . . .'

Sorry. I'm not listening any more. For the moment I've lost interest in the psychology of nicotine. It's the planes in her face that have caught my imagination. And inappropriately, *absurdly* – after all, it's 10.25 on a weekday morning and she's *got* a lover – I find myself wondering what this face might do during sex. I imagine her clenching her teeth. Eyes blazing. A bit wild, like a horse . . .

No, come on. Concentrate.

'. . . And that's what was so interesting about your trick with the cigarette ash.'

Uh?

'Not many people rumble it the way you did.' *Silver-tongued flatterer*.

'I thought it was perfectly symbolic of the way smokers get hooked.' *Like that perfectly*.

'Really? Just thought it was a harmless little bar-room trick myself. Got loads more where that came from.' *Who did I just remind myself of? Oh Christ. Leslie Phillips*.

'No, seriously. I've been thinking about this a

lot. With cigarettes you start off thinking you're not getting addicted. That you can just take them or leave them. Brush them off like ash on the back of your hand. And then one day when you look inside, you find a dirty great smear. You were . . . *marked* all the time. Even before you thought you had started. Does that make any sense, Michael?'

No. 'Yes. Absolutely. Listen, you don't fancy running this past me again at the Pharmacy this evening do you? Just the one Martini. Maximum two.'

'I'd really love to. But I'm having a bondage session with Clive tonight.'

'Sorry?'

'He's taking the whole *Holy Delicious* team. For a bonding session. It's only beers and pizza, but I guess I should go.'

Bonding session. Maybe I should get the doc to check my ears as well.

3

I'm currently 'developing' three ideas. Which is to say I am trying to think of enough things to say about each of them to fill a single sheet of A4. There's no point wasting more effort than necessary. In television, for every fifty ideas up for discussion, only one will ever get made, and even that will end up quite differently to the original concept. Yes, we loved the idea about traffic wardens, they'll tell you. But can you do it about spaceships? Or badgers. Or with Dale Winton. The cliché is still true: how many television executives does it take to change a lightbulb? Just one, but does it *have* to be a lightbulb?

So right now I'm toying with *Stir Crazy*, a cookery series where a 'personality' chef goes round Britain's jails, using the ingredients he finds in the prison kitchens to create mouth-watering meals for his 'captive audience'. I think it would be nice to find a sympathetic cook who's perhaps spent a little time behind bars himself, though probably not for poisoning. Then there's *Cordon Bleagh!* Another cooking show, where all the recipes look beautiful but are actually disgusting. Things like seafood-stuffed duck; tandoori boiled egg; beetroot ice-cream. (I don't know why this idea appeals to me, it just does.) And there's a third project which at the moment is only a title, *The Sweet Furry Baby Animal Show*. Which I think speaks for itself.

I'm just wondering which file to open on the computer – *Stir*, *Bleagh* or *Furry* – when my door opens. It's Olivia. I haven't heard from her in nine months and the very last place I expected to see her again was here. In the background, in the open-plan office, do I imagine it or is Yasmin staring wide-eyed over the top of her screen at the blonde apparition in my doorway?

'Michael, it's Daddy. He's had a stroke.'

Daddy. I recall a tweedy geography teacher.

Rather deliberately eccentric. Thought he was a 'character'.

'I'm sorry. Is it serious?' *Why is she telling me this? Where's bloody Clive?*

'They don't know yet. It's only just happened.' She drops into the chair on the other side of my desk.

Olivia is one of those women who look better when they're serious. Smiling only seems to undermine their beauty. Right now, grave, and not that far from tears, she's looking as gorgeous as I ever remember her.

'Where is he?'

'In the hospital in Newton Abbott. They're doing tests.'

Daddy. He's coming back to me. A winter evening in my second year at Manchester University. Olivia says her father is passing through the city after attending a conference and wants to take her, and some of her friends, out to dinner. So five of us find ourselves at an Asian restaurant in Rusholme, being subjected to a series of ponderous anecdotes by a raconteur who clearly believes he has an amusing outlook on the world and its curious ways. Ridiculously, even now I can hear him droning – *when one wakes up covered in pine needles, it is reasonable to assume one has been sleeping beneath a pine tree*. A quotation I think. I used it for months afterwards whenever anyone was being pompous and boring.

'He liked you, Michael.'

Liked me? How could he even have *noticed* me? If I spoke to him at all, it was to ask him to pass the takka dahl.

'He said he thought you were touched with a mordant wit.'

The old bastard. He was taking the piss. Afterwards, I remember he lit a pipe. Not some lovely old meerschaum. But one of those metal-stemmed jobbies, a *technical* affair that spoke of clinical efficiency in the pipe-smoking department. No doubt he had a top-of-the-range pipe-cleaning kit to go with it.

'Has Clive met him?' *The c-word.*

'No, but we're supposed to be driving down to Devon this afternoon.'

Ha fucking ha. That could bugger Clive up nicely. A nasty little family crisis to deal with. But as soon as I have this thought, I have the equal and opposite one: that this could actually bring them closer together. If Clive is sensible and calm, a rock in stormy seas and all that malarkey – fuck it.

'Have you got a cigarette?' she asks me.

'I thought you stopped . . .' *When you started going out with Clive.*

'I did. But you know . . .'

'It's really not such a great idea . . .'

She starts to cry. Great fat tears drop out of her eyes. I see one fall on to her sleeve, darkening it. Then another, like the beginning of a summer shower.

'Please, Michael, just give me a cigarette.'

She is halfway through a Silk Cut when Clive walks in.

4

A tad embarrassing for everyone, I suppose. And when they leave, Olivia pale and red-eyed, Clive with a wordless manly nod in my direction, I tip my chair back and consider how many times I have witnessed this scene play itself out before. Me, sitting in a room, Olivia leaving with some bloke. Over the years the rooms change, the actors playing the role of bloke change – I even played him myself for a short season – but somehow the scenario seems timeless. Like Steve and I in a pub, it's me watching as she leaves. With someone else.

I can't remember who introduced her into our little circle at university. One day she just seemed to be there. But I do recall the word that sprang into my head the first time I set eyes on her. 'Creamy.' She was your classic English rose. Perfect clear white skin. Fine blonde hair. All set atop a sturdily girlish frame that included a strikingly ample chest. She was nineteen and I fell for her on the spot.

The longer I got to know her, however, the clearer it became that Olivia had unusual taste in men. Eclectic, you'd call it. She didn't seem to go for one particular 'type'. Rather, her boyfriends were so ridiculously diverse that you began to wonder whether she was simply working her way through the male species until eventually she found something she liked. This was good news, I speculated, because, on that basis, one day she might even get round to me.

Many years later, one night during our short-lived affair, it came to me – the single quality her boyfriends at university had in common. They were all *smokers*. It felt a little like a revelation. Could it be that for her, smoking represented maturity? Not in herself – because, in those days at least, she felt herself to be a shy young thing and therefore a non-smoker – but, in others, was it the sign that said, I have passed into the adult world? I am worthy. And I might even have a chance with you. When I thought about the encounter with her father, the argument was even more persuasive. Perhaps the roots of her attraction to smokers lay in childhood. At an early age, did she absorb the spectacle of Daddy creating clouds of fumes from his ridiculous metal appliance? Eventually, did fatherhood, and by extension maleness, become inextricably intertwined with the fug of tobacco? When I put this theory to Olivia, while we were sharing a cigarette in bed, she laughed out loud and immediately changed the subject.

But think about it. Why else would she have found Brian Barnes irresistibly witty? This short, dough-faced son of a Blackpool bookmaker had little going for him except a comic trick where he could make quite banal statements sound funny simply by speaking more slowly. How often had I heard him reduce a roomful of otherwise intelligent people to fits of hysterical giggling by uttering in his curiously camp Lancashire accent, O o h, y o u d o n' t g e t m a n y o f t h e m t o t h e p o u n d, d o y o u?

This was mildly amusing, particularly when heard in the context of mood-altering drugs. But Olivia thought he was hilarious. Throwing her head back, hair flying, teeth gleaming, she'd laugh so full-heartedly, you could see all the way down her lovely pink throat. Did young, sexy Olivia make this limp lettuce think he was Oscar bloody Wilde just because he was a smoker? Dumpy little Brian Barnes – who was known to read *science fiction* – who smoked John Player Special and was therefore, in Olivia's eyes, a Sophisticated Man of the World.

Brian Barnes was the first male I watched Olivia leave a room with. Brian Barnes who, it turned out, never made a move on her. Who probably took her off to look at his collection of Ursula Le Guin paperbacks, smoke fags and s p e a k s l o w l y f o r c o m i c e f f e c t.

I guess her first proper boyfriend was Ralph. My drugs mentor. Only two years older than me but light years ahead in all the stuff that mattered. He was a hyperactive driven character, eyes bulging behind his John Lennon glasses, intensely alive to the possibilities of being a work-shy student in the big, northern city we found ourselves in. He too was 'studying' psychology and was genuinely fascinated by the issue of consciousness – its problems, paradoxes and interesting reactions to a widespread variety of Class B drugs. He loved music. And how much sweeter it sounded after a pipeful of hash. He wore a fur coat – a *ladies* fur coat – had longish hair and sported a piece of pottery on a leather cord round his neck. He said it never ceased to amaze him, the lengths people would go to, to render themselves unconscious. Sellotaped to his bedroom door was a tiny scrap torn from a newspaper, 'Love conquers all.' Naturally, he'd been to a public school. And he smoked twenty Dunhill a day.

I watched Olivia and Ralph leave many rooms together, usually through a low-lying haze of marijuana smoke. As she didn't smoke 'straights', he taught her – as he taught me – how to smoke dope through a hash pipe. There is a particular evening in a room in Chorlton-cum-Hardy. The three of us are there. I've mastered the art, but I watch enthralled as Ralph offers the stem of the pipe to Olivia's lips and holds a lighted match to the crumbled resin in its bowl. She knows the theory – to breathe in *through* the pipe – but it's hard to convince the body that what it really wants is a chestful of burning vegetable products. Her lips, as they close round the brassy nipple of the dope pipe, reflexively suck.

A coughing fit. At least she hasn't coughed out

through the pipe, scattering precious drugs all over the carpet. She tries again. Another suck. But when she breathes out, a stream of thin white vapour floats out of her mouth. The Pink Floyd on the stereo seems particularly . . . *rich* tonight. She composes herself, shoulders dropping as she lets the air out of her lungs. And this time, as her lips clamp on to the pipe, the flame is tugged into the bowl. The resin glows orange. She holds her breath. She daren't blink. Ralph is nodding encouragement furiously, his goggle eyes red-rimmed behind his specs. Finally, she lets it go, breathing out through her nose, two lovely great plumes of thick white adult smoke. She's done it. They hug. She's part of a Great Tradition.

Later that evening, when they are capable of standing up, I watch them go off to bed.

Ralph and Olivia stayed together all through her third year, so I got used to seeing them leave many times. Ralph thrilled with his gorgeous blonde girlfriend, Olivia happy to be with someone who *knew things*. Ralph may even have taught her to smoke Dunhill eventually. I think she broke his heart when she left him for Stuart.

Stuart was as far removed from both Ralph and Brian Barnes as it is possible for members of the same species to be – save in one respect. He was a smoker. I never quite knew his exact occupation but, put it this way, he was the very last person alive a geography teacher from Newton Abbot would care to see his daughter with. A lithe young man who looked like he could outrun any policeman in the city, Stuart seemed loosely connected with the provision of drugs, or possibly car crime. Degraded front teeth spoke of amphetamine abuse. Or fighting. Or both. To my soft, southern eyes, he was most definitely a 'hard nut'.

And yet there was a gentleness in the way he wooed Olivia. He seemed genuinely awed by her girlish beauty and its Devonian associations of hidden valleys and verdant cow pasture. She, no doubt, was attracted by the romance of her exotic suitor, his charm and gallantry appealingly at odds with the windblown streets, doomed housing estates and shabby pubs of his native city.

He took her off in his Ford Cortina Mark II and she brought back breathy stories of how they'd been to a *shibeen* in Moss Side where black people had been playing dominoes, cracking their tiles down on the table tops like gunfire. Or how he'd taken her to Belle Vue Stadium for the dog racing, and then on to a Turkish restaurant, an upstairs room where people were sitting around smoking opium. Or they'd gone to watch Manchester City and afterwards she and Stuart had gone to a club where he seemed to have been at school with half the players.

I would attempt to conceal my envy and jealousy as Olivia reported each exciting foray into the *demimonde* of a city that was still a mystery to me. I tried to imagine what they talked about. God knows, they had nothing in common. I, given half a chance, could have banged on endlessly, chiefly about psychology of which we were both students. How dazzling I could have been on the topic of Festinger's Cognitive Dissonance Theory. How could she have missed my critique of Irving Maslow and his 'Peak Experiences'? I guess if Stuart hadn't been a smoker, he wouldn't have had a prayer.

By the time she finally allowed me to seduce her, girlish enthusiasm had been replaced with a kind of studied enigmatic charm and I, of course, had become a smoker.

Although I've lost contact with almost all of my university friends, I had always kept in touch with Olivia. Or rather it was she who kept in touch with me. It was she who sent the Christmas cards, made the phone calls, dropped in on her way through London. I think I had rather given up on her. But she, perhaps sensing my frustrated desire, had kept the pan bubbling over the years. Wanting to be wanted. Knowing maybe that one day I would make a perfectly serviceable interim boyfriend.

We'd fallen into a pattern of meeting two or three times a year in the West End. Drinks followed by dinner at Mr Kong on Lisle Street. I'd talk about the world of television. She about educational software which she had somehow ended up in. This time, as the chopsticks brought a trembling scallop up to her lips, I noticed her eyes holding mine rather longer than usual. And, instead of departing in two taxis, that evening we took one. So it was that, for a few months, I became the man that others watched her leave the room with.

But now, with her perfume still lingering in my office, I am thinking about a very beautiful thing that has just happened. In the moments before she left with Clive for the West Country. Clive, looking rattled. Clive who *does not smoke*. Clive pointing at my packet of Silk Cut on the desk saying, *I think I'd better have one of those.*

And I, only too happy to oblige.

5

To: Yasmin Swan
From: Michael Roe
Subject: Bonding

I gather Clive has had to leave suddenly. If tonight's bonding session has been cancelled, how about that drink? I have startling new thoughts about smoking.

I have no such thoughts but, fuck it, I'm sure I can come up with something.

To: Michael Roe
From: Yasmin Swan
Subject: RE: Bonding

Sorry. We're bonding without him. Next week?

That'll do nicely.

To: Steve Panic
From: Michael Roe
Subject: Tennis

How do you fancy a game after work? Then a drink or two. Or if you prefer, just a drink or two.

Four hours later, I am 5–4 up, serving for the set. I think it's Yasmin's positive e-mail, its promise of another vodka-assisted evening together, that has boosted my game to within sight of this historic landmark. Steve *always* wins. And I have to say my old friend is not looking terribly comfortable in defeat. His father was half-Croatian – you pronounce it Panitch – and, without wishing to peddle any crude cultural stereotypes, Steve can get quite worked up over a little matter like winning or losing.

Neither of us are really natural tennis players, but it's the only sport I enjoy where you can compete, vent your aggression and be an individualist. And did I mention the fun? The sheer comedy in the difference between what you *meant* to do, and what actually happens. Half the time I'm using the filthiest language I know, the other half, I'm helpless with laughter. And although most of it, I guess, is pretty poor stuff, occasionally Steve or I will produce a really great shot; like, where did *that* come from? And on these occasions, you have the feeling that you haven't played the shot, *the shot has played you*. The whole hour or two is worth it just for the kick you get from hitting one of those.

Today I'm playing well for me. Remembering to bend the knees, watching the ball. For improved clarity of focus, I'm even trying to spot the *seam* in the ball. I'm in that desirable yet paradoxical state of relaxed concentration. And then it happens. Something seems to impede my triumph. Steve digs in grimly, takes the following two games, I win the next and rather than piss around with a tie-break, we agree to draw the set 6–6. Must talk to the Bearded Lady about this. No, better still, sack her and hire a coach.

'Dreamt up any evil new schemes to bring about the ruination of Fuckface?' Steve asks me, as we settle into our traditional positions. Study for Two Gentlemen in a Bar with Alcohol, Crisps and Tobacco.

'Thought I might try to turn him into a smoker.'

'Yes, nice idea. All those diseases. Not to mention the expense.' And looking at Steve firing up a Silk Cut *ironically*, I remember the precise thought that occurred to me when I realised *I'd* become a smoker. It felt like a profound thought. The moment I graduated from just smoking cigarettes to being A Smoker.

I was in North Wales. Still a reporter on the *Wrexham Examiner* and bumming so many roll-ups off Steve that one day I bought him a replacement packet of Old Holborn. A fortnight later I bought him another. And then, finally, I bought my own. (This is not yet The Moment however.)

And so at work, in the pub, at parties, I'd be rolling, rolling, rolling; taking a perverse pride in the manufacture of these nasty little rollies. Like a cottage industry I was, full of contempt for 'proper' cigarettes which required *nothing of yourself*, no art, no craftsmanship. And of course packets of fags were Big Tobacco, shiny products of capitalism that I would have no truck with. It was a studenty, hippy thing. Ready-made cigarettes represented the 'straight' world. To roll your own was to cling to the counter culture. And of course, to buy cigarettes was to *be* a smoker. Rolling your own was a hobby.

'Why do you bother with those stupid things,' asks Gwilym Griffiths, the *Wrexham Examiner*'s sales manager one night in The Egerton Arms, a gloomy watering hole that stands by the town's central bus station. (It is a toss-up, which is the fastest way out of Wrexham, the D34 or four large whiskies?)

Because I don't want to be like you, I think. I don't want to wear a suit like that. Or a shirt and tie *that match*. Or have my hair cut like that. Or sport the sort of fat, gold wedding ring favoured by butchers. Or a Round Table badge. In short, I never want to be so *corporate*, so grown up. And the twenty B&H are somehow all part of the package.

But, yes I will have one of your Bennies, thanks Gwilym.

There is, it must be said, something *rather impressive* about a fresh Benson and Hedges, the first or second out of the iconic gold packet. Some cigarettes have a cheaper self-image (John Player Special); others have a more exotic, aromatic spin (Marlboro); and some are just plain weaker (Silk Cut). But Benson and Hedges is somehow the gold standard against which all the others are judged.

So one day I buy my first packet of cigarettes. In The Egerton Arms with Steve and Dave Cleaver, who liked to pretend he was a hard-bitten hack – actually he had an English degree from Cambridge – so naturally forty a day was an essential part of the image.

We've been drinking and smoking and laughing. About our editor, a shy morose man with over-large ears. About the sports editor whose ears were, if anything, even larger. About the Clerk to Wrexham's Magistrates who had the largest ears any of us had ever seen. We laughed about the stories we'd written (only that morning I had covered the case of a man charged with indecent exposure after he had been spotted masturbating in a field). It was the cruel laughter of young men who fancied themselves a little, confident they'd soon be moving on to bigger towns, bigger stories and bigger laughs.

I drop coins into the cigarette machine, but which brand to buy? Not Number 6, favoured smoke of builders, plasterers and the unemployed. Not Embassy, with its collectable gift tokens and concomitant suburban associations; or Gold Leaf, whose advert featured a man in leisurewear tampering with a red setter. Surely not Rothmans. Didn't you have to be an airline pilot to smoke Rothmans? It was obvious really. What was the problem? I yank open a drawer and liberate a sexy gold packet of Benson and Hedges.

Peeling off the cellophane like I've been doing it for years, I pull away the little bit of gold foil and there they are, twenty Bennies, packed tight as a drum. I offer them round. Steve lights us up with his Zippo and away we go. More beer; more cynical laughter, now at the expense of the paper's chief photographer whose Nikon used to shake chronically until he'd drained two pints of Wrexham Lager. Or the hilariously quotable councillor who was prone to thundering Churchillian oratory on matters like provision of lamp posts. Or street numbering.

And now I'm buying a pack of Bennies nearly every day. I don't know why they are my brand, they just are. I'm not even a smoker, I tell myself, I just smoke.

And then one night, at a party, I have a little revelation. Three-quarters pissed, standing in a room full of people I barely know. Almost everyone is smoking and I'm talking to a thin young woman called Erica, whose skin is stretched across the bones of her face in such a dramatic way that

I am losing the power of speech. Her huge brown eyes are staring back at me, the full lips of her wide, wide mouth are saying *something*, but I'm buggered if I know what. I reach into my jacket.

'Cigarette?' I ask.

'Thanks.'

I light her up with a miraculously steady hand, pulling that expression that men pull when they offer a naked flame to a woman they fancy. The one that says, *Regard the steadiness of my hand, the firmness of my jaw and the command in my gaze. I know better tricks than this one, believe me.*

Erica aims a plume of smoke at the ceiling, allowing me a lingering view of her wondrously upstretched neck. She seems oddly unmoved by my cigarette-lighting technique and shortly afterwards begins a conversation with a former member of the Welsh Lions who owns a share in a wine bar. But I am not bothered. I watch her from across the room, throwing her head back with laughter at some pre-Cambrian quip, raking slender fingers through her thick chestnut hair. I am unconcerned. There are many more women to offer cigarettes to, now and in the future.

I light up. And somehow this simple act seems to have filled the space that was ready and waiting for it. A temporal and psychological gap in my life at that exact instant. A little moment at a party – but in truth, one of many moments that day – when lighting a cigarette was the natural, the *obvious* thing to do. So cigarettes are the answer.

Cigarettes are the answer.

That is the thought that made me a smoker and that was The Moment I became one.

6

'This is ridiculous. Have you read this twaddle?'

Hilary and I have just eaten. We're having what we call A Quiet Night In. I'm reading a celebrity quiz in a magazine with one eye, watching *Newsnight* with the other. Since the main item is something to do with the Liberal Democrats, I feel that sleep may not be long in coming.

'What twaddle is that?' asks Hilary. She is at the other end of the sofa reading a book called *The Physics of Immortality*, a scientific argument for the existence of God and the resurrection of the dead. One of the reviewers has called it 'a remarkable speculative tour de force'. There are a lot of equations in the back.

'This actor. He's in *The Bill*. They asked him, "What is the most important lesson life has taught you?" And do you know what he said?'

'What?'

'"That life is not a rehearsal."'

'What's wrong with that?'

'Well, it's so bloody . . . *serious*, isn't it? So *dedicated*. And offensive to all us people who thought that life *was* a rehearsal. Who thought it was OK to spend time mucking around, *trying things out*.'

Hilary gives me one of her level looks. Well actually it's her *only* level look, but she gives it to me nonetheless.

'Michael, it's all right. This book says you're coming back anyway. We both are. For all eternity.'

At this thought, I have a horrible sinking feeling. It's not the eternal return I have a problem with. Far from it. It's *we both are*.

Hilary lights her nightly Lambert and Butler. I watch her smoke it, inexpertly. Not even *holding* it quite right. I know she'll stub it out nearly an inch from the filter.

'Why do you bother?' I ask.

'Oh, I enjoy a cigarette after a meal. Sort of rounds it off.'

I think of what we've just eaten. Ratatouille and baked potato. Followed by Ben and Jerry's out of the tub. Yes, I can see how a Lambert and Butler would round that lot off perfectly.

'You're not really enjoying that cigarette. You only *think* you are. You're actually only relieving your withdrawal craving.'

Hilary furrows her brow. Nods towards the ashtray on my arm of the sofa, crammed with Silk Cut butts. Can't bring herself to say, *Speak for yourself smartarse*.

'I've been thinking about this. Smoking is a cancellation of pain. Not a positive addition of pleasure into your life. Like Ben and Jerry's. Or having sex.'

Hilary puts her book down on the carpet and rubs her toes along my thigh.

Uh-oh.

Was that a positive addition of pleasure, I ponder afterwards as we're lying in bed? Or the mere cancellation of a sexual urge. Hilary has snapped her light off and is burrowing down for her eight hours. *The Physics of Immortality* hasn't detained her long this evening. Her breathing becomes slow and deep. Within less than a minute she is impressively asleep, making low rumbling sounds, like a central heating boiler that needs a service, but without the clicking thing from the thermostat. Most of the women I have ever gone to bed with have been able to do this. Switch themselves off like a TV set. Myself, I need to drift away. Words and pictures in my head, getting weird in the moments before oblivion.

Did I enjoy that, or just *imagine* I did? With Olivia, it always felt like positive pleasure. Just the sheer *achievement* after all those years was joyful, like finally winning a Wimbledon championship. Or passing a driving test at the eleventh attempt. It was always *filthy sex* with her. In taxis she used to whisper in my ear, *Michael, let's go home and have lashings of filthy sex*. Somewhere in her head I think she thought it was dirty. Well, as Woody Allen famously remarked, it is if you're doing it properly.

With Yasmin? A positive addition too, I should

think. Steve said today that she looked like a class bird. Top totty, he called her, trying to be funny. Must send her another e-mail. Make a proper date for next week. More Martinis underneath the Canestan tube. Any time, any place, anywhere, it's a wonderful world you can share. Ooh, Miss Jones. Yes, Mr Rigsby. May I call you Ruth? Yes . . . Earnest? Simon? Bernard?

Shit. What *was* his shoe size?

7

Montgomery Dodd, the big cheese at Belvedere is on the phone. I was stupid enough to e-mail him a copy of *Stir Crazy* at close of play yesterday.

'Michael, sorry. Haven't got long. Bumped into Electra Fuchs at a reception last night. Pitched her the *Stir Crazy* idea and she went loopy for it. Loves the poignancy between the horrible daily life of the convicts and the really great grub they *could* be having all the time. Told her I'd get her a detailed treatment by Monday. Can we do that?'

We. Love that we. Sure *we* can.

Electra Fuchs. Five years ago she was the researcher on a pilot I produced about people with shitty jobs called *Why Do They Do That?* Now she's head of her own bloody channel.

'Oh and Michael. She wondered if a better title for the show might be *A Crime Not to Eat It*. Anyhow, would you play with it?'

So I'm rattling away at the PC, smoking like a train because, I don't know about you, but I can't write a word unless there's a fag burning between my typing fingers, ash dropping nicely down the keys. I ignore her suggestion to change the show's name – what sort of a crap title is that, *A Crime Not to Eat It*? – though I do briefly flirt with *Apple Pie and Custody*. It is not my intention to waste one moment of my weekend on this document, so I'm anxious to wrap it up today. In the end, Electra Fuchs will almost certainly tell us, *Yes, loved the treatment, but could we make it about hospitals. And play down the food aspect. Put in more gardening*.

When I look up, Yasmin is leaning against my doorway, arms folded, ankles crossed, one slender hip describing an arc that cannot adequately be expressed in words, an odd smile playing about her long, horsy face.

'Are you in here, Michael? I can't tell through this bank of fog.'

'I always smoke a lot when I'm writing. I find it helps me concentrate, though no doubt you're about to tell me it's an illusion caused by an excess of nicotine.' *Did that come out a bit tartly? Never mind. Shows I'm not drooling and drivelling over her*.

'The Good Book says it's actually your *withdrawal pangs* that are disturbing your ability to concentrate. Smoking a cigarette is a cancellation of that distraction, not an addition of concentration.'

'Cigarette?'

'Yeah, thanks.' She drops into the comfy chair

and I light her up. She's gone Chinese again. The tigers and butterflies are back in action. She drags powerfully on the Silk Cut, throwing her head back for added depth of inhalation.

'I can see that Quit Smoking book has made a big impact on you,' I quip. 'Perhaps I can borrow it some time.'

'I buy the theory *totally*. I just can't stop. Anyhow, I didn't come here to lecture you about cigarettes. I suppose you've seen the papers.'

'No. Too busy. What?'

She tosses me one of the tabloids. On the front page, in huge print, the headline reads:

VICARS IN A TWIST

In a smaller typeface above:

Fake cleric scandal hits TV show

In white letters against a black panel it adds helpfully:

**Jobless actor poses as
Greek Orthodox priest.**

Under a photo of the programme's beaming presenter, a caption says:

Angelica Doubleday: 'Devastated.'

Below the legend, *by David Cleaver*, the first paragraph of the story runs:

> **Furious MPs were demanding an inquiry last night as yet another popular TV show was discovered to have used fake guests.**

'Michael, do you think there's a chance Clive will get into trouble over this?'

8

Get a proper car – or fix Peugeot ☑

I'm so happy, I've bought a new car. A two-year-old Golf. Black and very sexy. I've never had a German car but my twinge of guilt – my father swore he would never drive one – dissolves the moment I close the driver's door – *clunk* not *clang* – and count the eighteen FM pre-sets on the radio. The radio is Japanese of course, but *feelings* about a motor car are never going to be rational, are they?

There are three reasons for my happiness.

One, Clive is deeply in the cack. Joyously so. Up to his eyebrows in the stuff. Why all the fuss, you might ask, just because the bloke you booked to whip up a kleftico and mouth a few worthy platitudes turns out to be some gobby chancer, rather than a fully paid-up member of the cloth?

(Gratifyingly, it was all over the weekend papers, and now the religious authorities have entered the fray because the show counts towards the channel's quota of *obligatory religious programming*; it's cheaper *and* it gets more viewers than hymn singing.)

I won't bore you with a detailed commentary. Just think of it as a feeding frenzy of envious newspapers, craven MPs, 'concerned' bishops and powerless regulators which has created the most delightful shitstorm, at the smelly centre of which sits the dejected figure of Clive Wilson, the show's producer, traditionally the figure who *carries the can*.

Clive even slunk into my office at one point yesterday – Olivia's father is still hanging on, by the way – and cast himself down on the comfy chair.

'Fucking bad business,' he confided.

'What a nightmare,' I sympathise.

'Can I have a cigarette?'

'Course you can.' *Christ, I nearly added 'mate'.*

He smokes it gingerly. It's a very great effort to keep a big, fat grin off my face.

The second cause of my advanced state of happiness is that this morning Yasmin marched through my door, dropped her smoking book on my desk, and proposed a return Martini session tomorrow night. She stayed a few minutes for a cigarette and, as she sat there, her bony knees pointing at me, I swear to God I could feel . . . *heat* coming out of her skirt. The hairs on the back of my arm were stirring.

She's *drawn* to me. I know she is.

And third, I'm bombing down the Westway towards town in my shiny new black car. It's not *rattling*. Nothing is *juddering*. The radio's playing Farley Dines' *Song for Wendy* (I know, sad, isn't it? But hey, I'm *dealing* with it). Those are my tail-lights disappearing round the bend. Here are the tall buildings of the Marylebone Road rising up to meet me. Come on then, London, swallow me up.

To [illegible] we were [illegible] about twenty four
hold [illegible] [illegible] and [illegible] the [illegible] under the
Chinese [illegible] the [illegible] [illegible] the [illegible]
[illegible]
eyes [illegible] [illegible] delight [illegible] [illegible] on [illegible]
Bloody [illegible] looking [illegible] [illegible] the [illegible]
Shakespeare's book [illegible] [illegible]
[illegible] Henry Sedgman [illegible]

FOUR

1

Clive has been promoted and Yasmin's getting married. Otherwise, it's been a very promising day.

To begin where it began, however, twenty-four hours ago, Yasmin and I in the Pharmacy, under the Canestan tube again, *our* spot, like the clock at Grand Central Station, me barely able to take my eyes off her, she delightfully banging on about bloody smoking, puffing away all the while like Stephenson's Rocket. I'm not doing a bad impression of The Flying Scotsman myself.

'Have you looked at that book I gave you?' she

asks me as the second pair of Martinis arrive. We pause to watch the waitress setting them down gingerly on our table, a moment of solemnity as the poisonous, *sexy* fluids lap at the edges in their fragile containers. We're pausing out of *respect*. For the transparent lethality of this classic cocktail, all the more dangerous for being set in those innocent Y-shaped glasses. Y, they proclaim. Why? To which, of course, there is only one sensible reply.

Why not?

We clink and slip gently under the influence of Martini number two. As far as I know, there is no nickname for the second of the night, but in my book, it's always been The One You Shouldn't Have. The one that goes straight to the part of your brain that deals with caution and turns it off like a lamp. We've said we're only coming in for a couple, but I think we both know – I certainly do – that *that* is impossible.

'*The Easy Way to Stop Smoking*? No, I'm afraid I haven't had a chance to open it.'

But this is a lie. I did open it and the first words that my eyes fell upon made my stomach shrivel. Written in biro on the title page in a rudely confident hand: *To Yasmin, darling please read and inwardly digest. Lots of love from Nick xxx.*

'It's very good about the ridiculous efforts smokers make to convince themselves they need to smoke,' she says, parting her lips to admit a fresh Camel.

'I can tell you are a convert,' I reply deadpan,

firing her up with Hilary's big silver Ronson. The huge eyes gaze at me, unblinking, as the end of her cigarette glows orange. Her nail varnish, I notice, is a shade of blue you don't find in nature. I count off the seconds before the nicotine sandbag whacks her across the back of the head. *Five, six, seven*. And then the great horse face slowly tips back and she sends a river of smoke off to mingle with the light fittings.

'You said it yourself,' she says. 'That you smoke a lot when you're writing. That smoking helps you concentrate. I know you sincerely believe that to be true because I am the same.'

We're the same.

'But look at it this way.' She swings one long leg over another and leans towards me intently. I'm looking. 'You've got a deadline, right. You're working on some vital document that has to be ready by lunchtime. But your office door is open and the conversation outside is distracting you . . . what do you do?'

'Close the door?'

'Exactly. So now you're hammering away at the keyboard, but you realise the TV set is still on. It's Jerry Springer. Men Who Want To Be Women – and The Women Who Love Them. Kind of tacky and you'd love to watch for a bit. But you have a deadline to meet. What do you do?'

'Hmm. Difficult. OK, fuck the deadline. Turn up the volume and watch Jerry?'

A patient smile assembles itself on Yasmin's face.

'OK, I turn off the telly.'

'Now you are free to really concentrate on this brilliant thing you are writing. Except there is one more distraction. A final niggling irritant to get rid of before you can devote a hundred per cent of your talent' – *my talent* – 'to the task. Can you guess what that is?'

I drain my Martini glass.

'The strange-looking woman who sits directly in my view whom I ache with longing for. I ask her to kiss me. Or move her desk. One or the other.'

Actually I do not say this last piece of dialogue. I merely think it.

'It's the itch-itch-itch of desire for a cigarette,' she says, doing a sort of scritchy-scratchy gesture with her index fingers. 'The constant background withdrawal craving of nicotine addiction. So to silence that last remaining bit of . . . *noise*, you light a fag. And now you can concentrate. And that's why you think cigarettes have helped. When in fact they are the problem.'

I have stopped listening. I am wondering, what would it be like to *be* her cigarette? To be trapped between her long, bony fingers, to be brought up to that implausibly wide mouth, to sit there for a while, held gently but firmly, and then to be sucked so fiercely that you glowed.

That is definitely a two-Martini thought. But she is continuing.

'Or take the case of someone who can't finish a meal without a cigarette.'

‘Yes, Hilary, my girlfriend, is like that.’

The Hilary mention is revenge for Nick. The scribbled dedication in the book, the fact of him, his whole damn being. Except she doesn’t look particularly wounded.

‘You’ve had this wonderful dinner, right. Lovely food. Lovely wine. Good company. From a food-and-drink standpoint, you’re completely satisfied. Carbohydrate, protein, fats, sugar, water, alcohol, coffee. All your needs and desires ticked off nicely. Except one. The final piece of the jigsaw that stands between you and absolute contentment.’

‘Line of cocaine?’

‘Very close. Just as addictive, but not as much fun.’

Now she drains her Martini. I know, I just *know* that she’s going to suggest we have a third. And then we’re done for.

‘You see, I buy this man’s theory about smoking, like totally. I agree with everything he says about it. But I still can’t stop. What’s that all about then?’

And she looks at me with something very close to despair on the features of her extraordinary face. Now she says something truly shocking.

‘I want to do it for Nick. He’s asked me to marry him.’

In the circumstances at this point, one might normally say something like, that’s wonderful. Congratulations. Fantastic news. Except her expression does not speak of joy. She looks alarmed, hunted. Like I say, desperate. But she's asked me a question and, to answer it, I lean towards her for dramatic effect.

'Yasmin,' I tell her in a low voice, 'I think you've *got to want to*.'

What's she thinking? The eyes are as wide as I have ever seen them. But, after a few seconds, she drops her head slightly to one side and puts a peculiar, rather dopey, half-smile on her face.

Of course.

Same again, I tell the waitress.

2

Funny how a few words can affect your psychic well-being. *There's no easy way to say this* never fails to send a cold chill through me. *Ladies and gentlemen, Jim Davidson* has much the same effect. On the plus side, the best two words in the English language are known to be, *It's benign*.

So Yasmin and I are at the Zen Master Martini stage – four I'm afraid – except this time I do not feel any particular clarity or transcendence. Instead I am prodding at the little bruise that began to form in the moments after she said, *He's asked me to marry him*. I have not mentioned it again, out of consideration to my own tender feelings on the issue. And I suppose I am pleased that we've got the sort of relationship where she can tell me stuff like that. But it's pretty bloody radical, isn't it? You don't propose to a member of the opposite species unless you're well up a tree with them, do you? On the other hand, there's the curious question of her singular lack of happiness when the subject came up. In my experience, whenever a woman announces to the world that she's been asked to tie the knot, the occasion is marked with 100-kilowatt smiles and the blinking back of tears. So, as Steve says in his more laconic moments, it's a rum do and no mistake.

Actually it's a good thing that we've had a few to drink, because something else has arisen that I think would worry me if I were sober. Yasmin's been filling me in on all the excrement that's been flying off the fan blades as a result of the *Holy Delicious* scandal. Columnists have fulminated – *should we believe anything we see on our screens?* – MPs have raged, one even demanded an inquiry (OK, a newspaper asked him to), and various top TV people, Montgomery Dodd not least, have been exquisitely embarrassed by the affair. Clive has, sensibly dammit, toughed it out, sitting grimly in his bunker under a hard hat waiting for it all to go away. And now that it looks like they're not going to sack him (the luckless individual who booked the bogus priest turns out to be a media studies student at Belvedere on work experience) he's gone on the warpath, publicly declaring in the office yesterday that when – not if, *when* – he finds out who tipped off the papers, he's – and here I quote – going to cut off his head and shit down his neck.

This is not the sort of language Clive normally employs, so I assume he is particularly annoyed.

How do I feel about this? Well, largely indifferent, I suppose. There's no suggestion from Yasmin that she, or anyone else, thinks I might have spread the story. Indeed I honestly can't remember telling Dave – sorry, *David* – Cleaver anything that might interest the readers of his newspaper. Actually, in view of the lateness of the hour and the large amount of drink that had been taken, I cannot remember our conversation full stop. I guess I just phoned him up to chew the fat. Talk over old times. Must get together and have a beer, that sort of thing.

So that's all right then.

Er, except something is stirring uneasily beneath the pool of vodka in the pit of my stomach. A horrible thought that I do not wish to confront. I gaze at Yasmin.

'Can I show you a trick?' I ask. 'Bet you can't do everything I do in the next sixty seconds.'

'What's the bet?' she asks sportingly.

'Loser buys the next round.'

She pauses. She's going to say she's had enough. *We've* had enough. It's been a lovely evening, but . . .

'Go on then.'

This is a woman to gladden your heart. Game as a peanut, and can drink you under the table. Under the floorboards by the look of things.

OK, I tell her, the time starts now. I scratch my

ear. She scratches her ear. I tap my nose. She taps her nose. I pick up my cigarette. Inhale. Exhale. She does the same. I take a good slug of Martini. Yasmin likewise. I stroke my chin, she strokes her chin. I drum my fingers on the table, she drums as advertised. Neither of us has said a word. She's staring at me, intrigued. I look at my watch, run my fingers through my hair, interlace my fingers and crack my knuckles. She does all the above.

And then I pick up my glass and, bringing it up to my lips – she's doing it too – I purse my lips and *slowly, triumphantly, squirt the unswallowed slug of Martini back in*.

Your move, honey.

She's fixing me with a level gaze, but now – I cannot believe this – now, a perfect stream of vodka is flowing out of her mouth and into her glass. I am speechless.

'Learned it in the sixth form, didn't I,' she says. 'Your round, I believe.'

3

So the Bearded Lady is *radiating* disapproval this morning, plucking at her skirt, twitching around in her chair like it was infested or something.

'You woke up in her flat.'

'On her sofa. We didn't . . .'

'. . . No.'

'I mean, I'm sure nothing happened . . .'

'. . . Yes.'

'Though I barely remember the end of the night . . .'

'. . . You had had some drinks.' *Well, that's certainly one way of putting it.*

'We'd had this great evening, and I suppose I didn't want it to end. So I suggested we went back to my place.' *To smoke a joint or two.* 'And she'd said could we go back to hers because she had to feed Satan. Her cat. Funny, because I wouldn't have taken her for a cat person.'

'And what *is* a cat person?'

'Oh, you know, sad spinster type. Self-help books in the bathroom and cat hairs everywhere.'

'And did she have self-help books in the bathroom?'

'Copy of *Vogue*. Does that count?'

I am too hungover to protest at the irrelevance of these questions. So I lapse into silence, the events of last night going through my head like a movie trailer. One minute we are in the Pharmacy, and the next (jump cut) we're getting out of a taxi outside her flat in Queen's Park. And now a black cat is swirling round my ankles in the hall. And now we're in the sitting room, an intriguing hybrid of groovy and scruffy, and she's rolling a joint, and I'm trying to focus on the spines of her CD collection, and I'm amazed and delighted to find Leonard Cohen's *I'm Your Man*, but working the stereo is beyond me and, as she leans across to press the right buttons, I silently inhale a gust of her perfume.

We smoke and we talk and we listen to the great gravel-voiced poet, and she's rolling another joint and at some point I must have fallen asleep because, when I'm next awake, it is six in the morning and I am lying on the sofa and Satan is breathing in my face.

Only in the minicab home – I found a number by the phone – does a little scene come into my head. Did I dream it or did it happen? We are on the carpet. And our kiss goodnight has lasted just a bit too long for two colleagues parting at the end of a nice evening. So we try another. And that's no better. The third, if anything, is even worse.

But this, as they say in connection with black holes, is the *event horizon* of the night. No further light can escape the gravitational pull of the alcohol, the dope and the fatigue.

Except now that I am lying here thinking about it, a pair of snapshots come back to me. In my delirium, I must have book-marked them for later. Two tennis rackets – *his 'n' hers?* – leaning against one another intimately in the hall. And on a hook on the bathroom door, a man's shirt, deep blue. Nick's, beyond a doubt.

'Actually, there is something I am moderately worried about,' I tell Augusta Tuck.

'I'm afraid our time is nearly up,' she says, 'but OK, quickly.'

'I spoke to an old friend of mine on the phone last week. A newspaper reporter. He specialises in showbiz, actually. I have a feeling I may have told him something that, with the advantage of hindsight, I perhaps wish I hadn't. You see it was quite late at night and I was half asleep and . . .'

'. . . You perhaps had had a drink.'

Ouch.

I suppose even shrinks can't resist putting the boot in now and again. Yes, as Austin Powers so perfectly expressed it, *very* ouch.

4

The rather unsatisfactory fifty minutes I spent with the Bearded Lady at forty pounds a pop, or put it another way, eighty pence a minute – some premium-rate phone lines are cheaper than that – we call that therapy. But how would you describe the three minutes and forty seconds of Todd Rundgren's *I Saw the Light*? Wound up loud on the Westway. What may turn out to be the most enjoyable three minutes and forty seconds of the whole day. The week. The next five years. Well it was certainly *therapeutic*, in the sense that I feel better now than I did before. It was free. And although I guess the wholly modern combination of fast forward motion and pop music can never really solve your problems, merely mask them, I think I'd settle for the phrase *pure pleasure*.

There's a Chinese proverb:

If you want to be happy for an hour, get drunk.
If you want to be happy for a year, get married.
If you want to be happy for a lifetime, get a garden.

I'm sure Confucius would have put in something about Todd Rundgren and the Westway, if he'd known about them.

Belvedere Television seems to have a higher energy about it this morning. A buzzier buzz, the molecular motion of the boys and girls who work here, a little accelerated. The first thing I notice when I reach my floor is that Yasmin is not at her post. This is simultaneously a disappointment and a relief. And when I get into my office, the phone is already ringing.

Hilary.

'Michael, I've been worried about you. You must have got home terribly late.'

Yes, very. Only time to change, shave, and listen to five messages from Hilary featuring updated details about when she'd be going to bed and the latest time I could call her.

'Yeah, it was a bit of a late one.'

'What did you get up to then?' she asks as cheerfully as she can manage.

Never lie. It only complicates things horribly. The truth is always simpler.

'I had drinks in the Pharmacy and I think we must have forgotten to eat. I ended up spending the night on the sofa. At Steve's.'

'Really? Because I spoke to Steve. He rang last night about ten o'clock. Looking for you.'

Shitshitshit.

'Yes, he said. I was with some of the gang from the office first. Look, I'm not explaining this very well. Can we talk later? My brain feels like a dried pea in a bucket.'

And now something even more disturbing is happening. Across the open-plan floor, Clive is marching towards me with an unpleasant expression on his face. And as he gets to my glass door – no pantomimed courtesies, *Have you got a minute? Can I have a word?* that sort of thing – he strides straight in and throws himself down in the comfy chair, picks up an old copy of *Broadcast* magazine and begins to flip irritably through the pages, waiting for me to come off the phone.

'Er, Hilary, look I'm just in a meeting as it happens. Can I call you back?'

I hang up. The palms of my hands feel tropical.

'Clive.' As matter of fact as I can make it.

The horrible little cunt is all dressed up for some reason. Dressed up by television standards that is, which in his case involves smart chinos, a shirt and tie and, ridiculously, a *blazer*. Not quite shiny brass buttons with anchors on, but very nearly. And now I come to look at it, the tie could almost be regimental. I can't quite see from this angle, but I suspect we may also be talking tasselled loafers. On Clive, the overall effect is total prat. He's only the producer of a daytime cookery show for God's sake, and even then, only just.

'Michael,' he begins, needlessly fingering the

unfamiliar knot at his throat. 'There's no easy way to say this. Someone in this building tipped off the papers about our . . . little local difficulty.'

He's badly rattled. He looks pale and I notice a twitch that wasn't there before in the pouch under his left eye. I feel both better and worse at the same time. I'm enjoying my enemy's discomfort, but he could be dangerous.

'Really? Who would do a thing like that?' *Don't answer that.*

'I couldn't say at the moment but I mean to find out. I want your help, Michael.'

He's Michael-ed me again. And at this man-to-man stuff, I feel slightly sick. I mean, I don't mind having the creep as a nemesis figure, but he shouldn't try and get all pally with me. If that's what he's up to.

'What do you think I can do?' *What in the world do you imagine I would* ever *do for you, dick brain?*

'You used to be a journalist, didn't you?'

'Still am, really.' *And you came into television from where exactly? Oh yes. University.*

'Well. Would you talk to your contacts? To someone who might know this Cleaver creature. Who might be able to find out who gave him his story.'

Is he serious? He *is* serious. What a . . . chump.

'Well, I could *try*. But if this chap – who did you say he was, Cleaver? – if he's any sort of journo, he will protect his sources to his dying breath.' *I sincerely trust.*

'Oh, I don't know about that.'

I begin to have a sinking feeling.

'What makes you say that?'

'Because I've spoken to the bastard. He had the nerve to ring me up for a quote. Christ, they've got some neck these tabloid reptiles. He more or less admitted straight away he had a mole at Belvedere. Even referred to his source as a "he". I think he was a bit pissed, which doesn't surprise me from what I've heard.'

Delete *sinking* feeling. Insert *sunk*. He gets up to leave.

'I'm determined to find this . . . traitor, Michael. There's no room for people like that at Belvedere. Will you see what you can do?'

'Sure.' I can feel sweat forming on my upper lip.

'By the way, Olivia's father has regained consciousness. The stroke seems to have affected his speech. He's talking, but in a peculiar voice. They're assessing what the permanent damage is likely to be.' And with a nauseating manly nod, he exits.

So many thoughts are in my head, I scribble them on a Post-It.

1. **Since when did Clive care so much about Belvedere?**
2. **Was he indirectly accusing me? Telling me he can't prove it, but he *knows*.**
3. **Does Olivia realise that I know Dave Cleaver?**
4. **Will she realise this is the same Cleaver who is the cause of Clive's miseries?**

5. **Has she been too busy with her father to be included in the Dave Cleaver loop?**
6. **Now that he is recovering, will she put two and two together?**
7. **Where is Yasmin?**
8. **What to tell Hilary about last night?**
9. **Warn Steve.**
10. **I was right about the tasselled loafers.**

5

More bad news. Though not unexpected. Electra Fuchs has passed on *Stir Crazy*. Apparently she finds the contrast between the lovely food and the sad daily lives of the prisoners a little tasteless. In other words, exactly what she first *liked* about the show, she now dislikes. Par for the course in this business. But according to Montgomery Dodd, who's just phoned, she's 'nibbling' at *The Sweet Furry Baby Animal Show*, which at this stage is precisely those six words, and no more. So my task this morning is to dream up a programme fitting that title for her nasty little channel. Naturally I'm smoking heavily – where's Yasmin? I want to hear her tell me again how cigarettes *stop* you from concentrating – and I'm trying hard to imagine what such a programme would be like. I think the best bet would be to find a personality vet (is there such a thing as a *pediatric* vet?) and have him go round assisting at various tricky births. An organic farmer's favourite cow. A pedigree lurcher's first litter (such narrow hips). *Nature's Little Miracles*, I think we'll call it. Maybe someone like Angelica Doubleday could go along too, to emote in all the right places. Or perhaps we should reinvent an unlikely figure, like Rolf Harris with *Animal Hospital*. Nicholas Parsons maybe. Or Dave Lee Travis.

I tell you, there are days when I hate this job.

So I'm torturing this ridiculous idea into shape, getting all lyrical at the keyboard – *we'll witness the exquisite moments when new life is brought into being* – when the terrible thing happens.

Plink.

To: All Staff
From: Montgomery Dodd
Subject: Clive Wilson

I am delighted to announce that Clive Wilson has been appointed to the new post of Executive Producer, Leisure Programming. He will be in overall charge of Belvedere's cooking, gardening and DIY output, the appointment to take effect when the present series of *Holy Delicious* comes to an end. As many of you may know, Clive played a leading part in untangling the mess that led to the recent unfortunate publicity surrounding the show. In his new area of responsibility, Clive will be putting in place procedures to ensure that Belvedere Television never again suffers such a regrettable and uncharacteristic lapse in what are necessarily the very highest standards of factual accuracy.

The greasy little fucker. The tasselled loafers and the absurd regimental tie drop into place. I am so outraged, I cannot write another line. So I call Steve and ten minutes later we are having an early 'lunch' in BarBushKa.

'Russian hit man. That's the answer,' says Steve returning with another Guinness and a Bloody Mary. 'I read in *The Times* about this bloke in Leningrad who used to do people in for a bottle of vodka and his bus fare home.'

We have formed the recurring tableau. Urban gentlemen smoking, drinking, snacking and passing the time in enjoyable revenge fantasies.

'Mosquitoes. Those American mosquitoes that carry West Nile Encephalitis. You release a couple of hundred through his letter box in the middle of the night.'

'Hungry females,' adds Steve. 'In search of blood.'

'Er, speaking of which.' How to bring this up discreetly. 'Do you think I could ask you a favour?'

'Fire away.'

'Would it be all right if I stayed on your sofa?'

'Sure. When?'

'Last night. Only if anyone asks, as it were.'

'Have you been a dirty dog?' Steve inquires cheerfully.

'Not at all. Just. Well. It's a bit awkward to explain to be honest.'

'What's she like? Yasmin whatnot.'

'Lovely. How did you know?'

'It's obvious. Who else could it be? Just like it's obvious who tipped Dave Cleaver about *Holy Delicious*.'

Only by a series of heroic air exchanges, swallows and similar manoeuvres in the depths of my mouth and throat do I avoid expelling a significant portion of Bloody Mary back into BarBushKa.

'How did you find out about that?' I ask when the crisis has passed.

'Michael, think about it. You and I are the only people at Belvedere who know him. I know *I* didn't tell him . . .'

I can feel myself blushing.

'I think I did it when I was pissed.' I light another cigarette. 'Listen, if anyone finds out . . .'

'Don't worry,' says Steve. 'All your sordid secrets are safe with me.'

I feel a profound wave of affection for my old, skinny friend.

'One for the *strasse*?' I ask, using one of Dave Cleaver's battery of hail-fellow-well-met catchphrases. None of us on the *Wrexham Examiner* could ever understand why he talked like that. His father was a Rural Dean in Shropshire.

'Why not, chief.' Another Cleaver-ism.

'Do you think Chum Cleaver is the sort of feller to . . . compromise the anonymity of his confidants?' I wonder out loud.

'Cleaver is the complete professional,' says Steve. 'He absorbed the first law of journalism – never shit on your contacts, laddy – with his mother's milk. You could put the bugger to torture and he wouldn't reveal a source.' There is a horrible pause. 'Offer him a pint of lager though . . .'

Why am I laughing? This is my career we're talking about.

6

You know where Yasmin was? Only at the building society with bloody boyfriend. Talking about a joint bloody mortgage. But when she dropped into my office after lunch to smoke a fag, there was no song in her heart as she brought me this news. Instead, she wore a kind of weary, God-how-boring-and-grown-up-I-must-have-become sort of a look. She actually rolled her great eyeballs to the ceiling on the phrase 'endowment policy' and at 'six point five per cent APR', I believe she technically shuddered. Her enthusiasm for the forthcoming union appears to be that of a drowning man preparing to merge with a shark. Or maybe I'm kidding myself. And she's sparing my feelings. Letting me down gently.

We compared hangovers and agreed we'd had a hell of a night. I thanked her for the use of the sofa, but as neither of us mentioned the mysterious snog – *was* it a snog, or just a fond goodnight? – I'm none the wiser.

So now I'm standing in a foul bar near Liverpool Street waiting on the arrival of Dave Cleaver, 'hotfoot from the open prison in Docklands,' as he'd put it when I called him earlier this evening. The place is packed. I'm earwigging groups of office workers discussing which train to catch, the young men and women in their lustrous suits laughing and drinking and squirting clouds of pheromones over each other, the floor a troubled sea of pints and bottled beers, vodka and tonics, and dry white wines. Across the surface, every now and again, a face turns, tilts, and blasts a jet of cigarette smoke at the ceiling, like sperm whales breaking the waves to blow off water.

'Evening, chief.' Cleaver has materialised at my side.

How does he do it? The man does not age. Well, not in the conventional sense of running to flab or balding. Instead Cleaver somehow *hardens*. Becomes a better and better caricature of himself. Still dark. Still curiously handsome. And still – thank you, God – inescapably tiny.

'Sorry I'm a bit late. I've been de-briefing this, er, actress who's going to tell all about a certain member of the England football squad on Saturday. Had to open a few bottles of shampoo to get her going. Filthy stuff. Gasping for a pint. What are you having?'

Despite the anxiety he's put me to, it's oddly good to see him. I guess you always feel like that about people you go through some early baptism with. And although this man is a tabloid hack to his toenails, although he's certainly sold his granny twenty times over for a story, I feel a certain cynical comradeship towards him. After all, what's so very different about newspapers and television? As he'd no doubt put it himself, we're all pissing in the same pot, aren't we?

'How's the goggle box treating you?' he asks before I can reply. 'That dodgy vicar story got a lovely show, did you see it?'

What did he tell me his thesis was about? The Romantic poets? Imagery in Chaucer? A textual analysis of Shakespeare's tragedies?

With the lounge lizard's facility for snagging a barman's eye, despite his lack of feet and inches, he rapidly procures drinks and we squeeze into a tiny corner between the bar and the ladies' toilet. Cleaver gulps down half his pint alarmingly quickly, makes that exhaling noise that satisfied lager drinkers make when they want the world to know that *this is good, satisfying lager*, and lights up a B&H.

'Are you in receipt of your ill-gotten what-nots,' he asks. 'I should think in view of the splash we made, you'll get at least five hundred.'

'What?'

'Well, seven fifty maybe.'

'Dave, are you mad, or is it me?'

'Sorry, chief, it's the going rate. I can *try* and

squeeze a little more out of the bean counters if you like, but they're a bit fierce on this sort of thing. Cracked down on expenses horribly. Whole place run by accountants now. Same everywhere.' And now his eyes dart round the bar, checking for spies, an absurd gesture since all he can see are armpits. 'They sacked a bloke for carelessness last week,' he whispers gravely. 'Put in a receipt for dinner with a footy manager. The restaurant's been closed for *two years*.'

'Dave, I didn't tell you about *Holy Delicious* . . . to go on the bloody payroll.'

He looks at me perfectly levelly. The gaze expressing nothing. His reporter's 'go on, say more' look. Creating the awkward silence that the other feels obliged to fill.

'It was late at night. I . . .'

'You were arseholed, that's what you were, matey. You kept going on about "cunt-chops" and how much you were going to laugh when he went tits up over the fake bubble story.'

'Fake *bubble*?'

'Bubble and squeak. Greek.'

'I wouldn't have said "tits up". Tell me I didn't say "tits up".'

'No, that could be one of mine as well. But you definitely called him "cunt-chops". You were most insistent on that point. Indeed, as I recall, you were very much of the opinion that cunt-chops deserved to die. There was talk of drugging and the feeding of said chops to pigs. Or dangerous fishes. There was mention of incorporation of chops within the setting cement of a motorway flyover under construction. Or possibly bypass. Sir Chops must have done something very bad indeed to annoy you, Michael.' And he tips his head back and pours the rest of the pint down his throat as easily as if he were watering a plant.

Remarkable how little I remember of this phone call beyond the fact of making it. Certainly none of these colourful details.

'Let's just say he's one of the world's bigger shit-bags, Dave, and I felt it was my public duty, if at all possible, to land him right in it.'

'Oh, that's interesting,' he says, snaring the attention of the man behind the bar with impeccable timing and a cleverly flourished fiver. 'You told me he'd once nicked your bird and you'd never forgiven him. Pint of lager, chief, and a vodka and tonic. No, I'll get these, Michael. I'll put you down as a "studio insider".'

7

'So he didn't,' he says. 'Go tits up. Not even a bit?'

The bar is half empty now, the boys and girls in the suits have caught their trains, and we are perched on two of those drinker's high chairs with the long legs and nice, safe wrap-around arms so you can't fall out. Beneath his sharply cut black jeans, I notice Dave Cleaver is wearing cowboy boots. His legs swing well clear of the foot-rail. There is a pool of empty glasses in front of us. He offers me another B&H and I light us up with Hilary's Ronson. If Steve were here, we could be back in North Wales.

'No, they found someone else to blame. He had a few wobbly days but now, like I say, he's been promoted.'

Actually, give him his due, Dave Cleaver has been very reassuring. No of *course* no-one will ever discover the source of the *Holy Delicious* scandal – what do I take him for? – and no, nobody at his newspaper knows who tipped him off, and rest assured, Michael, not even in the course of medicating his stress with a few glasses of weak beer, would he *ever* breathe a word to another living soul. My secrets are safe with him. Only the grave is more silent, chief.

Weirdly, for all his rat-like cunning and slippery professional skills, I think he means it. I think he too feels that peculiar loyalty and kinship born of working together in the same dismal Welsh town. In fact, when the conversation drifted round to dopey Electra Fuchs, he told me the most amazing story of what she apparently got up to in the toilets of a certain central London hotel during an industry awards ceremony recently. Plus a cracking bit of gossip about who's about to be the new presenter of *Who Wants To Be A Millionaire?* Oh yes, and a very funny – sorry, tragic – tale of how a particular TV star is now so fat, he daren't leave the house for fear of being photographed.

He drains a third off another pint. Where does he put it all? Maybe he never eats.

'So they've made cunt-chops head of whatchamacallit.'

'Executive Producer, Leisure Programming. It means he's in charge of all the cookery, DIY and gardening.'

'He's a floater, isn't he?' declares Cleaver philosophically. 'You know, it's all shit but some sinks and some . . . floats.'

Maybe I'm pissed, maybe just flooded with relief that Cleaver is a sturdier vessel than I had supposed, but this strikes me as a rather profound thought.

'I'll tell you who's another one,' he continues. 'Electra bloody Fuchs. There's a talentless cow for you.'

'Do you know, Dave, five years ago she used to be my researcher?'

He shakes his head sadly.

'It's all so phoney, isn't it? The *real* talent doesn't get a look in.' Another third of a pint follows the former. 'Angelica Doubleday,' he says, warming to his theme, 'she's another one. All that smiling and gooing and flirting with the camera when everyone knows she's batting for the other side.'

'How do you mean?'

'Oh God, don't tell me you're the last to know. Heavy handbag, sensible shoes? She prefers *girls*, Michael.'

'Oh I knew *that*. It's just . . . it's not all that interesting.'

'No, I agree it's not that interesting in *itself*, it's the *pretence* that's so hypocritical. I mean why does she pretend to be a cute little dolly bird when *everyone* knows she's diddling that techie.'

'Dinah the vision mixer? No, they just go out for dinner together. Dinah's a sort of mother hen. There's one in every TV company. Even you would tell her your troubles.'

I can't remember the last time I heard anyone say *dolly bird* outside the safety of a nice pair of inverted commas. But irony has bypassed Dave Cleaver. Unless he's being *post-ironic*. Would he know how to do that? He drains the last of his pint.

'I'm full, chief. In the immortal words of the great Les Patterson, I'm as full as a fat girl's sock. Shall we call it a night? And Michael,' he says, commencing his descent to the floor, 'don't worry about the *Holy Delicious* thing. It'll never come back to you. Scouts honour. Dib dib dib and all that malarkey-pookey.'

Only after he leaves, do I remember that I haven't asked whether he's ever met Olivia.

8

I've been thinking in the cab what to tell Hilary about last night. And she's still up when I get round to her place. But instead of what I was expecting, her version of a boot-face and the third degree – *'What I don't understand, darling, is how Steve got in touch with you when your mobile was turned off'* – she is curiously unconcerned, never even raises the matter. Instead she asks if I've eaten, and am I interested if she rustles something up, and blow me down if she doesn't grill me a nice rare fillet steak, served with a perfect cross-section of raw red onion and a portion of microwave oven chips, English mustard and tomato ketchup on the side. In short, the ideal dish to set before the intoxicated Londoner whose last best hope up to that point had been Kentucky Fried Chicken.

'Fan-bloody-tastic,' I compliment the chef when the plate is bare. 'There aren't many people who know how to cook a rare steak, but you are one of them, Hilary.' We're sitting in her kitchen and I am grateful. Really I am. For a dinner that has hit the spot with surgical accuracy. For the fact that she hasn't given me a hard time. And for her sheer, irrepressible . . . being there for me, I suppose. When I light a cigarette, she joins me in her nightly Lambert and Butler.

'So tell me,' she asks, a knowing smile beginning to creep on to her face. 'What gives you the most satisfaction? On a sliding scale of pleasure. The steak or the cigarette?'

Satisfaction? Pleasure? Sliding? I have a funny feeling about the way this conversation is heading.

'Well, the steak was definitely a positive addition of pleasure,' I state, trying hard to muster the logic. 'Particularly taken as a whole in the light of the onion and the mustard.'

'Not a mere cancellation of hunger then?'

For a moment, I think she's got me. What is life after all, if not an endless series of needs that you go around satisfying? Hunger, thirst, sex, nicotine. The desire for stimulation. Excitement. A decent haircut. A complete set of Queen's Park Rangers programmes. Whatever lights your lamp. Satisfying the various demands of body and soul is like being one of those circus performers who spin plates on sticks. Easy to spin some of the plates, some of the time. But the trick is to get *all* your plates spinning at the same time. Only then do you hear the applause. Only then, I suppose, are you fully happy.

But there is a flaw in the foundations of this house of cards. I simplify the argument and present it to Hilary.

'Bollocks.'

She is oddly unimpressed by the force of my rhetoric. I expand.

'Eating that steak was a natural act. Every living creature eats to survive. They don't all eat so *well* of course. But I was right at one with nature there. Smoking that cigarette of yours is wholly unnatural. We are the only species who smoke. You don't see any big game lounging around the Serengeti with a Marlboro on the go, do you?'

'We are the only species who drive cars. Or watch television. Are they unnatural?'

'Actually, you're wrong about television. There are zoos in America where the monkeys watch a lot of television. They particularly like wildlife documentaries. And the news.'

'You made that up.'

'What if I did? Anyhow, I *need* to drive to get to work. Where I *need* to watch television because it's part of my job. No-one *needs* to smoke.'

'You do. You can't function without a cigarette.'

'That's because I'm *addicted*. I can't function without food, water or sex either, but they're *natural* cravings.'

Hilary gets to her feet, picks up my plate and puts it in the sink. Then, returning to the kitchen table, she suddenly sits herself upon it, in exactly the same spot where my steak and chips had been so recently. The mustard and ketchup are stationed by her right hip. Her legs are bumping into mine. And the look she's giving me is that dumb, insolent one again, the one that women know men like.

I eye up the old oak table. Seems reasonably robust.

'I really didn't think I could manage a pudding,' I tell her afterwards.

9

We're in bed, reading. Hilary's the fastest reader I've ever met. I think she may have learned a special technique at university. The way she turns the pages

– maybe four of hers to every one of mine – reminds me of Woody Allen's story about taking a speed-reading course. Afterwards, he said, he was able to read the whole of *War and Peace* in half an hour. It's about Russia.

'Who's Yasmin, darling?'

The little light bulb of pain pings on under my arm.

'Who?'

'Written in the front of this book you left here. *To Yasmin, darling please read and inwardly digest. Lots of love from Nick xxx.*'

Now I see what she's reading. *The Easy Way to Stop Smoking*. I'm a bit annoyed for some reason. When did I leave that at Hilary's?

'Oh, she's someone at work. She lent it to me. What happened to *How to Live Forever*?'

'*The Physics of Immortality*? Finished it on the tube.'

'Really? What happens in the end?'

'We are never extinguished. We live on, recycled into the material of the universe.'

'Oh, that's a relief. For a minute there, I thought this might be all there is.'

'Goodnight, Michael.'

And she snaps off her light, burrows down under the duvet, and I swear is asleep by the time you reach the end of this sentence.

My head is too full for sleep. So I pick up Hilary's *Independent*. And here I find it. A story about a man who was walking home from a pub one night, carrying a wooden table leg in a plastic bag, who was killed by a police marksman. Apparently police arrived in response to a 999 call from a member of the public who claimed that a man matching the victim's description had left the pub *carrying a sawn-off shotgun* tightly wrapped in a blue plastic bag. The man was shot in the head when he turned in response to a shouted warning: 'Armed police.'

I drop the paper over the side of the bed, turn out my light and shut my eyes. It's perfect. Why mess around with alcoholic Russian hit men or swarms of killer mosquitoes, when with one discreet phone call you can get a trained professional to do the job? But how to lure Clive on to the bait? What's a nice shotgun-shaped object that he can be induced to leave a pub with? Collapsible fishing rod? Does the bugger fish? Telescope? Has he the remotest interest in the night sky? Some specialist cooking implement? Fish kettle? Asparagus steamer?

Cricket bat. The fucker's almost certainly a cricket player. Maybe even turns out for a pub side. We can work with this. I believe I drift off with a contented smile on my face.

Three a.m. A phone is ringing. A mobile. *My* mobile. In Hilary's kitchen where I left it. I stumble downstairs. There's been some disaster. Accident, injury, the death of a relative.

It's Montgomery Dodd.

'Michael. Sorry to call you so late. I need you to go to New York tomorrow. There's a big story there that I think we've got to ourselves. I'll fill you in properly in the morning but, in a nutshell, there's an old Nazi, eighty-something, lives in Queens, who's ready to talk about what he did in the war. He hasn't been charged or indicted by anybody yet. He just wants to get it off his chest before he dies. I think it could be very big, Michael. The pictures will sell all over the world. Are you up for it?'

'Of course.'

'Good man.'

'Monty?'

'Yes.'

'I'll need an AP. A body to help out on the ground.'

'Of course. Have you got someone in mind?'

'Well, Yasmin Swan is very . . . capable.'

'I'll call her now.'

When I finally get back to sleep, it is with a smile on my face *and* a song in my heart.

2

FIVE

1

'Warm nuts, sir?'

Things have started very well. We've been bumped up to Business Class. Someone must have phoned ahead and used the magic word 'television'. The angle of the air hostess's eyebrows suggests an appreciation of irony, not usually found in Economy.

'Yes, please. And the same again.' I indicate our empty glasses.

'Certainly, sir. Two *large* vodka tonics.'

Confession: I am frightened of flying. I mean, just consider the sheer *implausibility* of getting inside a couple of hundred tons of metal, plastic and aviation fuel, rumbling down a runway for a mile or two and then *leaping into the air*. Quite aside from maintaining this idea for seven hours, all the way across the Atlantic Ocean, and then somehow putting down on land again in one piece. At speeds of over 500 miles per hour. At heights of over 30,000 feet. In air temperatures fifty degrees below zero. Sorry, but I lose my nerve during the safety demonstration. Well, it is a bit of a giveaway, isn't it? That thing about 'in the event of a sudden loss of cabin pressure, place the mask over your nose and mouth and *breathe normally*.'

So I'm afraid this is the only way I can manage it. Comfortably numbed from the existential *horror* of what is happening to you. I mean I really appreciate the lengths they go to, trying to pretend it's not really a big scary aircraft you're getting aboard. By the time you've made your way through the *sealed walkway*, you could be taking a seat in a cinema, couldn't you?

So then the thing starts rolling along the ground – OK, now it's a train – and it taxis for ages, long enough so you can just about forget it's planning to take off. But then the hideous burst of acceleration – you can see gold braid on the pilot's sleeve as he pushes the throttle forward, *this'll scare the shit out of them*, he's thinking – and I'm silently yelling: *no don't be silly. Let's keep going along the ground. We're fine like this. We'll get there . . . eventually*.

And then it's too late. The cinema is pointing

uphill. There's the horrible bit where every time I think, oh Christ he's going to scrape the tail on the runway, like doing your car exhaust on a speed bump. And the ghastly grinding and bumping of the undercarriage retracting, like when you were a child on a swing, tucking your legs under the seat to go higher.

And then, *only* then, the sweet relief of the clinking of the drinks cart – *we're alive! we're alive!* – and hopefully by the time we attempt a landing, I shall be pissed enough not to care if we end up in a blazing fireball.

You may think I exaggerate but, when the seat belt signs go off, I find I'm gripping Yasmin's hand so tightly there are nail-marks.

'Sorry about that. Nervous flyer,' I tell her. 'Cheers.'

We clink glasses. And I reach for my Silk Cut, my hand reflexively dipping into my jacket pocket, a piece of behaviour now so well ingrained, it feels hardwired. But you're not allowed to smoke anywhere on this plane – especially, they've been keen to stress, in the toilet, where there are smoke detectors. So I tip my seat back and gaze with something like wonder at my miraculous travelling companion. She has put on headphones and is experimenting solemnly with the various channels of entertainment on offer.

Clive, of course, cannot have been best pleased that Yasmin was summarily hoiked off his show. And I'm sure he enjoyed it even less when he learned who she was going with and why. But, happily, there was nothing he could do – I mean this is real journalism, not 'lifestyle television' – so I got another one of his sickening, masculine nods when we crossed in Montgomery Dodd's doorway this morning.

'Hey, sorry about hijacking Yasmin,' I tell him, just to cheer myself up even further.

'No problem,' he assures me. Is his manner a little more businesslike, more *managerial*, this morning? 'Did you manage to speak to anyone about Cleaver, by the way?' he asks.

'Not yet. Don't worry, I haven't forgotten. I'll make some calls first thing when we get back.'

When *we* get back. Love that *we*.

Monty was gratifyingly *conspiratorial* about the whole thing. Bit of a long story, but he got the tip from a contact of his in the States who'd heard it from someone who'd heard it from someone who goes to the same émigré café in New York as the Nazi. Who actually turns out to be a Ukrainian, one of those Ukrainian Fascists that the Germans got to do their killing for them behind the Eastern front. Very assiduous they were too. Much more unpleasant than their SS commanders. At the end of the war, rather than fall into the hands of the Red Army as a Nazi collaborator, our man somehow disappeared into the chaos of Europe in 1945, surfacing in New York where he posed as a refugee from Communism. He became an American citizen and worked quietly at various jobs before settling on the career that took him to retirement, that of school-bus driver. For the last twenty-five years he's been living in Queens. His name is Czeslaw Waldzneij. Monty's given me a whole pile of notes to read about him.

Yasmin has found something to look at on the back of the seat in front of her. It seems to involve Hugh Grant. And at the sight of her, smiling slightly, sipping her drink, watching the movie, my heart lifts like this big old 747 limbering into the sky. Or 757. Or whatever the hell 77 it is. Lift and thrust over weight and drag. That's the formula that keeps these bastards in the air, isn't it? The forces of *up* over the forces of *down*. Me and Yasmin over Clive and . . . who?

Olivia? Hilary? Nick?

Anyhow, we're going to be spending a lot of time together. No need to rush anything. Be cool, Michael.

I tug the nearside headphone off her ear.

'How are we going to get through this flight without a fag,' I ask.

Without taking her eyes off the screen, she lifts the bottom of her blouse a couple of inches away from the top of her jeans. And there, stuck to the skin like some horrible secret, is a nicotine patch.

2

We've both been here before. But we agree in the taxi, as it bursts out of the tunnel into early evening

Manhattan, there's something about this place that never fails to blow your socks off. I tell her I think it's the massiveness of the straight lines involved; the hilariously tall buildings that make you say *fuck* and laugh when you look up at them; the rectilinear tyranny of the avenues and streets; the amazing *straightness* of the concrete canyons whose lines, shooting away to infinity, finally converge on the brown smear of pollution you only see at a distance. And then, as if in opposition, there's the sheer exhilarating curvyness, the *loopyness* of the population who will not be trammelled by . . . well, trammels.

Actually, I do not put it quite like this. I'm still a bit woozy from the flight. So I say what I always say at my first glance of this city. In an American accent. 'Noo York . . . just like ah pictured it.' And happily – we're made for each other, I'm sure of it – Yasmin gets my quotation from Stevie Wonder's *Livin' For The City* and completes it: 'Skyscrapers and ev'thang.'

'Crazy motherfucker.' The yellow-cab driver swings us violently into the next lane. Yasmin has been thrown across the back seat and is squashing into me delightfully. There is a riot of car horns. 'Didja see that? Motherfucker nearly ran into me. Holy fuckin' mother*fuck*.'

And now, as we try to separate ourselves, though I have few options in the matter, we take a sharp right, apparently in pursuit of the driver referred to earlier, and she's pressed even closer. Her hair is in my face. I can feel her breast against my arm. Goodness, I *am* enjoying this trip. We draw level, screeching to a stop at the lights.

'Where d'you fuckin' learn to drive, mother-fuck?' our driver yells out of his window. In the car alongside, a very old man, a lizard in a base-ball cap, turns slowly in our direction, lifts a hand limply in apology. Or maybe it's an old-guy way of saying, Up yours, pal.

In any case, the fight has left our driver. He manages a *sotto voce* 'mother*fuck*', guns the cab through the green light and brakes traumatically at the next corner.

'Your hotel's right here. And that'll be thirty dollars. Welcome to New York.'

As Yasmin rearranges herself on the kerb, I tip him generously. After all, he was an *excellent* driver.

3

Of course we've got separate rooms. *Adjacent* separate rooms. Rooms you're allowed to smoke in. With ashtrays. And mine smells like someone's done an awful lot of smoking in here. We've agreed to meet in half an hour in the bar, so I fill the time by doing that hotel-room thing, wandering around lazily, opening drawers, casing the mini-bar, hanging up the hideously creased suit, seeing if the window will open – it won't – bouncing on the bed, checking out the exotic foreign TV – *Friends,*

The Simpsons, ER – inspecting the bathroom – look, a paper seal across the toilet, no-one has slashed here since it was last cleaned, the proof; look, even a *phone* in the bathroom. Look, it's ringing.

'Hello?'

'May I speak with Michael Roe, please?' A man's voice. Odd accent, half English, half American.

'This is he.' *He?* Why do I become Bertie Wooster the moment I leave United Kingdom airspace?

'Michael, this is David White. I'm an associate of Montgomery Dodd.' It's Monty's man with the Nazi.

'Good evening. Monty said you'd be getting in touch. Extraordinary story we've got here.'

'Sure is.'

'I've read all the notes. Absolutely fascinating. But, excuse me for asking, we are quite sure Waldzneij is, or was, what he *says* he is? Or was.'

'Why would he lie? It's going to make him *very* unpopular.'

'Well, I wanted to ask you about that. I mean war criminals don't tend to make a habit of coming forward. Why *is* he talking?'

'One word, Michael. Guilt. This is someone who's been carrying a terrible secret. Listen, for fifty years the guy goes to a particular café on the Lower East Side to eat Sunday lunch. With a crowd from the old country. He's known as kind of quiet, doesn't talk much. But for the last few months, each week he ends up crying into his soup. No-one knows why. A lot of old people have bad memories they don't like to talk about, so they don't push him. Finally, he tells his best friend. A woman from the same town. Tells her during the war he was a *Hiwi*, a *Hilfswilliger*, that's German for "willing helper". Says he did a lot of terrible things. Says no-one's ever going to bring him to justice, because no witnesses were left alive. Says he wants to unburden himself. As weird as it sounds, he says he wants to apologise to humanity.'

'Why not confess to a priest? And avoid the . . . bad publicity.'

'He says he doesn't believe in God. He says nobody could, who's seen what *he's* seen.'

Through the open bathroom door, *Wheel of Fortune* plays silently on the TV. I am suddenly aware of the huge energy of New York's traffic, dimmed to a faint background drone by the double-glazing. I see myself, as if from a very long way away, twelve storeys up in the air, taking part in a surreal discussion about evil, contrition and the existence of God. I feel slightly sick. I badly want Yasmin's hand in mine again. Even her hair in my face would do.

'Sorry, I think I may have missed a step. How did you come to get . . . included in the loop, if I might ask?'

'The woman from Waldzneij's town? She tells her bridge partner. And the bridge partner tells me.'

Silence falls on the line.

'Sorry, I hope I'm not being too dim. The bridge

partner is . . . a friend of yours? I'm just trying to establish the, er, evidential chain as it were.'

Did that sound as pompous as I think it sounded? There is a longer silence.

'The bridge partner is my grandmother.'

His grandmother? He got this story off his *granny*?

'Michael, I should tell you, we are beginning to experience a little heat from the opposition on this.'

'What opposition?'

'Newspapers, TV networks. They haven't found him yet, but they're sniffin'. They sure like stories about bad guys here.'

'Oh dear.' This sounds a bit pathetic, so I add, 'Can't we think of something to . . . protect him from them?'

'I'm driving out to Queens right now. Get him signed hopefully. You and me'll talk tomorrow evening. I'll get him to meet you the next day. Then I'll hire a crew for you to do the interview as soon as you like after that. How does that sound?'

This sounds marvellous. Because it means that before I need to give another thought to this *highly dubious* weeping Nazi, there's a clear twenty-four hours to frolic around in The City That Never Sleeps. With you know who.

So it is that ten minutes later, she slips on to the stool beside mine at the hotel bar. She's changed into something clingy and chic. Earrings are dangling where before none dangled. Perfume wafts. A pair of vodka Martinis stand before us magnificently.

'How's your jet lag?' she asks.

'Fine. How's yours?'

'Not bad. Apparently it's all about resetting your body clock to local time.'

'So what do you make it then?' I inquire.

'Oooh. Time for a drink I should think.'

We clink. And, at the first cold chill of cocktail, inside my head Frank Sinatra's backing orchestra kicks in with the opening bars of *New York New York*.

Dah dah, da-da-dah, dah dah, da-da-dah . . .

Easy, Michael. As Frank recommends in another of his famous ditties, let's take it nice and easy.

4

'It's got to be bollocks, hasn't it?'

Yasmin lights a Camel and considers her reply. We are both flagging, but we remain afloat thanks to the buzz of the city, plus a serious contribution from fags and drink. We've been strolling around midtown in a bit of a dream, soaking up night-time New York while trying not to be run over. Once, we look up and find the Empire State Building floating above us, its uppermost storeys floodlit purple, summit poking dramatically into the low cloud; corny, but somehow rather moving. Times Square, however, is a grotesque neon tourist-trap, so we've cabbed it down to the East Village which Yasmin says is groovier. Now we're sitting on a ruined sofa in a grungy-stroke-hippy music spot where a young man fronting a three-piece band in a bowler hat and goatee is reminding me powerfully of Bob Dylan. So much so, I have a horrible feeling that any moment he will announce he ain't gonna work on Maggie's farm no more.

'Why bollocks?' Her sleepy face is lovelier than ever.

'Because people who've committed wartime atrocities don't usually turn themselves in. In fact they do everything they can to take their secrets with them to the grave. This is a fake. Or a scam. It doesn't feel right. I tell you Carruthers . . .' – and here I assume my best Alec Guinness spymaster accent – '. . . there's something about this fishy tale that smells strongly of fish.'

Yasmin laughs. And, not for the first time this evening, I wonder how tonight will play itself out. Clearly any sort of *move* is out of the question. Whatever happens must just happen . . . organically.

'Have you phoned Nick?' Why did I ask her that? It's not like I *want to know* or anything.

'Yes, but he was out. Have you rung Hilary?'

'No. I think tonight is reading-group night. Might have to leave it till tomorrow.'

Roe, you are an absolute wanker, I think to myself. What a pointless, fruitless . . . utterly *retrogressive* piece of dialogue to initiate. We're supposed to be decently forgetting about the Nicks and Hilarys. Growing closer, bonding in the face of this exotic foreign assignment. Allowing the excitement and strangeness of the city to work its magic on *us*. Failing that, at least a touch of Stockholm Syndrome where she identifies with her captor. Viz myself.

'Do you know any good tricks?' I ask, desperate to change the subject. 'I've shown you my best ones.'

'Yes. Have you got a silk handkerchief?' she replies. 'Or an ordinary one. Actually a ratty old bit of tissue would do.'

Men do not carry ratty old bits of tissue as a rule, though women, in my experience, are never without them. From my jacket pocket, I fish out a big, blue manly job. Not too disgraceful happily.

She takes it gingerly by one corner – a bit of stage business or disgust, it's hard to tell – and drapes it over her closed left fist. With the thumb of her right hand – are you following this? – she pokes a depression, a well into it, through the gap between left index finger and thumb. Her face is a mask of inscrutability. I love this stuff. I am fascinated.

She takes the cigarette from her lips and, shooting me an enigmatic glance, she pokes it – *lit end first* – into the hole. If it was your precious silk scarf, this would be the moment you'd start to worry.

Now she takes the cigarette out and has a really big drag. And another. And now she puts the cigarette back down the hole, blows a huge cloud of smoke over it, and dramatically squeezes fist, fag and handkerchief together in the air.

'Hey, careful . . .' The words seem to have slipped out of my mouth before I can stop myself. But she receives them as a compliment to her magical arts. And now, taking a corner of the handkerchief, she shakes it out theatrically.

No burns to handkerchief or hand, and no cigarette either. Just a wisp of disappearing smoke. She actually says, 'Da daaah!'

Another confession: because I have looked in more books about magic than is good for me, I know how this trick is done. I know the cigarette never really entered her clenched fist the second time. It's still hidden inside her *right* hand, the filter tip gripped in what they call the 'crotch' of her thumb. Significantly, the palm of that hand has been turned away from me since the trick began. But she's performed it very well. And I don't want to spoil her moment of glory. I begin to clap politely.

'OK, where is it?' she asks me.

'What?'

'Where's the cigarette?'

'Er . . . you've magic'd it away.'

'Come on, I know you know. Where is it'

'Well, you did ask,' I reply sadly, and I flick my gaze on to the back of her right hand.

'In here, huh? Wanna bet?' God, I *like* this woman.

'Got to be.'

'What's the bet?'

'Next round?'

Slowly, shockingly, she turns her right hand to reveal the palm. It's empty. Both her hands are empty. I am *seriously* confused.

'Where do you think it is *now*?'

It feels like there is a stupid smile on my face. 'Fucked if I know,' I admit.

'Good, isn't it,' says Yasmin. 'My brother taught it to me.' And bringing two fingers up to her lips, she slides the *lit cigarette* out of her mouth into their safety. 'You need quite a big gob to do this properly. Your round, I believe?'

I am speechless.

5

I think we are actually going backwards. Because, when we return to the hotel, it isn't even a chaste kiss, it's a straight 'Goodnight, see you tomorrow' and she's inside her room, door closed. So I lie on the bed for a bit, flipping through the forty or fifty channels, Letterman joshing with Elton, Leno fooling with Sting – maybe the other way round – I even watch the thirty seconds of porn they allow you before it shows up on your bill. She has the TV on too, I discover when I put my ear to the wall between us. (Is that a *very* bad thing to do?) And then I hear the low buzz of her voice. The unmistakable rhythm of one half of a phone call.

But who can she be talking to at . . . at nearly midnight in New York, nearly 5 a.m. in London? Quietly, I open my door, take a step along the corridor and put my ear gently against hers. And here's what I hear.

'No honestly, I *tried* to call but you were out . . .' (pause while she listens) '. . . because we were downstairs in the bar . . . we had some drinks and a bite to eat and then we went for a walk into Manhat . . . you know, for a look *round* . . . Oh for Christ's sake, don't be such an arse' . . . (long pause. Happily no-one passes through the corridor) . . . 'No, I *haven't* had a chance to think about it. Look, can we discuss this when I get home?'

I creep back into my room, being *very* careful how I close the door. Haven't had a chance to think about *what*?

A couple of hours later, when I wake fully clothed on the bed, TV still playing, the red message light is flashing on the telephone. Damn this jet lag. Was that there before?

'Hi, darling, it's only me. Wondering how you are. Hope you had a good flight and New York is wonderful. Hugo says absolutely *the* place to go for smoked salmon and bagels is Barney Greengrass on the Upper West Side. He says it's practically an institution. It's on Amsterdam Avenue between 86th and 87th Street. And Julia was raving about the Metropolitan Museum of Art. She says you've *got* to see the Nineteenth-century European Collection. It's an absolute must, apparently. Anyhow, darling, give me a ring when you've got a moment. You're five hours behind, aren't you, so I suppose your evenings are my middle of the nights. You could try me at work when you get up if you've got time. Oh, Olivia rang. She wanted to ask you something about her father so I said you'd be back in a few days. Anyway, darling, I won't witter on. Have a good time. If you *have* got time, it would be great if you could pop into Barnes and Noble or any of those big bookshops and see if you could find that book I was telling you about, about human consciousness all being an illusion. I'm almost certain it's called *Lights On, Nobody Home*. But only if you've got time. Big kiss, darling. Bye now. Bye.'

Wrong number, I guess.

Only kidding. Hilary of course. The odd thing is, when I call her back at home – 7.30 a.m. London time – there's no answer. Early yoga session, maybe?

6

We are walking across Central Park in bright sunshine. One of those perfect New York days in that part of the year when the city has escaped the stifling humidity of summer but is not yet so bitterly cold that the birds fall like stones from the sky. I could give you the date, but this is a story, not a travel brochure, right?

'Michael, this is really . . .' She searches for the right word. 'Nice.'

Nice will do I suppose, though if she'd just slip her arm through mine, I think my happiness would be complete. A dangerously old woman, all tragic flesh and wraparound sunglasses jogs past us. If she was moving any slower, she would be overtaken by insects.

'So which was your favourite?' asks Yasmin. She is referring to the New York Metropolitan Museum's collection of Nineteenth-century European art, which we have just rattled round at my suggestion (well, it is an absolute *must*, isn't it?).

'If I could have just one, which would it be? The Pissarro, I think.'

Actually, I did find it oddly moving. A view of a Paris park. One of a series that he painted from the window of his apartment at different times of the year. Here it's late autumn, the light is falling, and the crowds seem to be moving slowly along the paths towards the gates, melancholy dots in the landscape, heading home. Overhead hangs a huge bruised sky, a particularly sad splodge of cloud floating above distant steeples, seeming to speak of nights drawing in, summer's pleasures coming to an end.

'I thought the green of the grass was wrong,' says Yasmin. 'It was too green for the time of year.'

She's right of course. Now I bring it to mind, the grass was too bright. But maybe that was the only green Pissarro had left. If he painted it on a Sunday – and it did look like a Sunday crowd – perhaps he was planning to nip round to the paint supplies shop on Monday for a tube of darker green and forgot. What was it some famous artist said? When critics get together they talk about spatial relationships. When painters get together they talk about turps.

After the uncertainties of last night, this feels like it is shaping into a much better day. We only spent an hour or two at The Met, but the sheer abundance of the place was breathtaking. Like America itself, the museum seemed to say: we can *have* everything. What a pleasure it was to stroll past the lovely oil paintings – 'Oh, let's not bother with Degas,' she'd said, 'all those boring ballet dancers' – *in the company* of someone whose features would have happily preoccupied any great artist through many a season. And right now, after the warm glow of the oils, in this park, the roar of the city turned down a few notches as if the neighbours have complained, loud sunlight is banging off her hair and face. The huge eyes drink it all in, the trees turning to gold, the wall of skyscrapers beyond.

Impressionism, post-impressionism, all those other isms . . . what are they against this *real life*? Bright, shiny and ready to eat.

'Are you hungry at all?' I ask. 'Only I think we're very near *the* place for smoked salmon and bagels. If you like that kind of stuff.'

7

Hugo was right about Barney Greengrass. And it's already become the top sight of the day as far as I am concerned, Yasmin's teeth, as if in slow motion, sinking into – in the order named – tomato, raw onion, smoked salmon, cream cheese, toasted bagel. It's one of those old-fashioned family concerns which has been dispensing smoked fish to the *cognoscenti* since 1929. A quote from Groucho Marx on their leaflet asserts: 'Barney Greengrass may not have ruled any kingdoms or written any great symphonies, but he did a monumental job with sturgeon.'

Afterwards, we saunter down Broadway, make a left back to the park and find ourselves standing with a knot of reverential gawpers outside the Dakota building, where John Lennon lived and died. Not as I'd imagined, a spare modernist classic, but a heavily ornate European mansion block. As we pause to smoke cigarettes, two youths hurry past.

'Mets *suck*,' says the first. His friend's reply sounds to me like poetry.

> 'Mets don't suck.
> Mets gonna *win* this thing.
> Mets gonna *kick* the Yankees' ass.'

I believe they are referring to baseball.

We walk. Yasmin in her oversized trainers. Me

in my slightly crippling London shoes. We walk for hours down the length of Manhattan, allowing it all to wash over us. Gaping at the junctions, each street offering a vista to infinity or New Jersey, wordlessly absorbing the varieties of humanity extruded within the soaring architecture. A finely dressed woman with a disastrous facelift. A scabby bum slumped against Trump Tower. An old white guy with a stick, walking arm in arm with a young black woman. A girl on a bench, smoking a pipe. And, everywhere, people talking to themselves. Lots more than you'd see in most big cities. Not only weirdos or obvious crazies, but quite middle-class-looking folk too. And not just lips moving, but actual words coming out. Chattering away, so very many of them (they presumably *don't* realise they're doing it) that I'm beginning to wonder if I haven't been doing it as well.

In Washington Square we pause to watch the chess hustlers, guys who make a living playing chess for money. One, a Native American in a cowboy hat, is playing a furious endgame against a scruffy old white guy in an anorak, their fingers flying between board and chess clock. At the next table, people are playing Scrabble. Good grief, are there Scrabble hustlers, too?

'Yasmin, it's Brad Pitt.' Walking towards us is an extravagantly handsome young man, unshaven and shabbily dressed, with a fabulous husky dog on a lead. Both seem utterly oblivious to the crashing chaos of the huge city around them.

'No. But he'd like to be. That's probably the only living creature he's capable of forming a meaningful relationship with. They say that about New Yorkers and their pets.' The dog's ice-blue eyes peer into mine as we pass.

Exhausted but exhilarated, we limp back to our hotel. In my room, I dial up Hilary. It's ten o'clock in London. But still no reply. She's probably gone out with her people from work. I watch a bit of TV news. Leaf through my complimentary *New York Times*. It's official, there are now six billion people on the planet. Golly. The Phillip Morris Company who make Marlboro are finally admitting that smoking is addictive. Well how about that? Who says there's no news in the papers any more? But hang on a minute, what is *this*? Scientists at Princeton have challenged the long-standing belief that the brain is the only organ in the body that doesn't grow fresh cells. *Sorry*? I have to read it twice, it's so amazing. Like, here was a universally held truth, the view that when brain cells are killed off – through excessive drinking, let's say – they're never replaced. Er, well scrub that now apparently. Because what they've discovered is that new cells appear in the brain *every day*. Thousands of them, a great stream of neurones, generated in the brain's central chambers, which migrate outwards to nest in the cerebral cortex, the brain's outer rind where 'higher intellectual functions and personality' are centred. Stuff like, who you think you are, where you see yourself in five years' time, what you want for Christmas. OK, so they did the research on macaque monkeys, but we're very alike apparently, apart from the thing about climbing trees.

I'm so excited, I have to tell Yasmin when, half an hour later, we remount barstools, prepare to swallow restorative cocktails and await the arrival of David White, Nazi-hunter.

'Did you see the *New York Times*. The best news . . . all *year*.'

'What, about cigarettes being addictive? Bit of a shock, I must admit.' She lights a Camel and eyes the drinks list.

'No, the thing about the brain regenerating itself. Fantastic news. We don't just have a fixed supply of brain cells that we're killing off slowly with drink and drugs. *We get more*. They come every day, Yasmin. Did you read it?'

She looks at me seriously. Out of respect, or because she thinks I am an idiot, it's impossible to say.

'I thought it was only in macaque monkeys. A champagne and cranberry juice, please.'

'Yes, yes. Macaques today but it'll be us tomorrow. Dry vodka Martini, please. With an olive. I mean, just think of all the times you've *forgotten* something, like a birthday, because you got a bit pissed and those particular birthday brain cells died. Well, maybe this is the way you have completely *new* thoughts. They come riding into your head on the back of the new brain cells.'

It's not respect. It's idiocy, I'm almost certain.

'I mean, why did you ask for champagne and cranberry? Where did that thought come from? Have you ever asked for one before?'

'Can't say I have. It just sounded rather nice.'

'There you are. Maybe your desire for a champagne and cranberry was a brand-new thought from a brand-new brain cell. A thought that wasn't here yesterday, because if it had been, you would have asked for one then.'

Yasmin blows a stream of smoke at the ceiling, digs her pale fingers into the bowl of nuts. Pops an almond in her mouth. Starts chewing. Now another. Now a Brazil. She's thinking. As far as I'm concerned she can eat as many nuts as she likes. I can watch these features in motion for a very long time.

'Well,' she says finally, 'what is true is that when I lit this cigarette, it wasn't *me* who wanted it, it was a small, but very insistent part of my brain. I mean, it's a puzzle, isn't it? It's like, one bit of my brain knows it doesn't want to smoke, wants to give up, even reads books about how to stop . . .'

'. . . Your cerebral cortex,' I add helpfully, 'the sensible part.'

'Right. But another bit, the nasty little cluster in charge of addiction, some horrid grey blob the size of a baked bean probably, is absolutely *insisting* on a fag. Right now.'

I try and imagine Yasmin's brain, the squidgy mass of blood and tissue cupped snug in its cavity behind the remarkable face not three feet from mine. Its tangle of intricate connections, its small electrical *glow*. Linked through nerves and fibre to her eyes, her tongue, to everywhere.

'Bloody ridiculous. Grown adults at the mercy of a sodding baked bean. Here, I couldn't steal one of your Camels, could I?'

8

I was at university with a bloke called David White. So I have a mental picture of the David White who will be joining us at the bar at 8 p.m. Absurdly, it's that of a straw-haired layabout in tight jeans and a filthy T-shirt covered in dope burns. Optional *Daily Mirror* rammed into his back pocket. *My* David White wasn't really a student – there was certainly no question of him attending any lectures – rather, I think, he was one of those characters who operated on the margins of student society. I suppose the confusion arose in my mind because of his friendship with a tramp-like Welshman called Dylan who was obsessed with philosophy. I assumed *he* must have been a student, so great was his passion for the subject in general and Nietzche in particular. When he embarked on some excitable philosophical discourse – to explain to me or Ralph or Olivia or Dave why, or how, the universe was most likely constructed in this way, or that – the fat, uproarious Celt reminded me most, I think, of a mad person. I worried for him. What real job in the real world could he ever do, this overheated intellect? Would he end up chewing the carpet like the object of his hero-worship? Or would he one day just think, oh fuck it, and go on to become a senior manager with the Severn Trent Water Authority? His pal David White meanwhile was a follower of an obscure belief system known as being a Coventry City supporter, a philosophy noted for its cruel emphasis on loss and despair. David read the football pages of the *Daily Mirror*, the first real person I had ever seen do this.

'Michael Roe?' The man suddenly at my side is the appropriate age and build, but the clothes are wrong. Posh suit, tie with a pin through it, a diamond ring affair on the hand he's thrust out for me to shake. Fit-looking, fair hair, big teeth. If memory serves, my David White had big teeth, 'I'm David White. Guessed it was you. Us Brits aren't all that hard to spot.'

'Really, why's that?' I ask, shaking, trying to unpack the accent. Either a Yank trying to be British or the other way round.

'Smoke signals. No-one smokes in this town any more. And this,' he says swivelling ominously towards Yasmin, 'must be . . .'

'This is my colleague, Yasmin Swan,' I reply, as if she was incapable of introducing herself. I hope she noticed I didn't say 'my *assistant*' as Clive would have done.

David White's mouth breaks open into a smile to reveal a truly shocking exhibition of huge white teeth. They seem indecently plentiful. More coming into view every moment, as the smile gets wider. Molars, canines, the lot. A *wall* of dentition. The last time I've seen teeth like this, they were passing the winning post at Lingfield Park.

'Hello, Yasmin Swan,' say the teeth creepily.

'Hello, David White,' she replies, partly ironically, but partly something else. Hideously, in those few seconds, I realise they have begun to flirt with each other.

'Let's move somewhere a little quieter where we can talk,' he says, leaning in to pick up her glass and no doubt giving her a good hosing down with his big-teeth pheromones.

We move towards an alcove of seats away from the bar and immediately somehow I have lost the body-language game. It's *his* body that seems to be choreographing our relocation from stools to booth. When we sit, Yasmin is manoeuvred into the middle between us. Placing a black leather attaché case on to his knees, he snaps open the locks with too much brio for my liking, and produces a mobile telephone. He sets it on the table portentously.

'I'm glad we have an extra hand, Michael. And particularly – how can I put this? – such an attractive one. I have a feeling Waldzneij may respond better to some feminine input.'

This oily prick can't possibly be the same David White I used to get stoned with on winter nights in Manchester. It's merely a coincidence of name. There have to be loads of David Whites in the world. Yet weirdly, there is a disturbing similarity. The hair looks right, though it's been expensively cut, not self-hacked with blunt scissors in a bathroom mirror. And the timbre of the voice could be his too, if not the ridiculous accent. People can change a lot in fifteen years. But what about the teeth? Surely the *real* David White never had so many?

Come to think of it, the real David White was never that interested in women, preferring in the main to spend his time on cannabis and Coventry City. I don't know what exactly, but Yasmin is definitely *doing* something in this man's presence that I've never seen before. Holding herself in a different way. Her head, shoulders, elbows, knees . . . everything seems to be at a subtly different angle from normal. She's smoking like a furnace. My God, she's even twirling a bit of hair in her fingers. I've got a horrible feeling she fancies him.

He's been explaining how Waldzneij is still on board but hasn't yet signed a contract. How he's a difficult old bugger, by turns tearful, paranoid, petulant, furious. How we need to meet him tomorrow morning to press the flesh, reassure him that we will solemnly hear his testimony blah blah blah. But I'm not listening all that hard. Since most of his remarks have been aimed at Yasmin, with the odd courtesy cut in my direction, I am studying his features. The cold way he's looking at her when he's serious. The way when he smiles, which he does needlessly frequently in my opinion, the great baboon grin overwhelms his face. And why is she lapping it up? Is it because he is radiating sexual attention and she is responding like a plant to sunlight? Surely she can't actually *like* this . . . well, oily prick I think are *les mots justes*.

Can she?

9

I've worked it out. What she liked about him. It was a gob thing. The genetic attraction of one big mouth for another. It's true what they say, people choose themselves. It's why fat people often get together. Or mad boozers. I once knew two people who got married with nothing more in common than they both had red hair. God knows what they talked about after they'd exhausted that topic. They were divorced in less than a year. Mind you, they reckon we have thirty-five per cent of the same genes as a daffodil. I think that speaks for itself, doesn't it?

So, all in all, it's a pretty ghastly evening. Fuck-face leads us off to some terrible fancy-shmancy restaurant where he continues to gibber and make ape faces at Yasmin. And she . . . well, she isn't actually gooing and gurgling but she's definitely encouraging him in a subtle, female way. Flapping her eyelashes, cocking her head this way and that, and generally not letting him know what a complete tosser he is. And while she isn't actively ignoring me, I do feel as if I have in some way been *cancelled*. Though when the time comes to pay, Slimeball says he's sure Monty will want to pick up the tab, leaving me to drop my credit card on a bill for a remarkable number of hundreds of dollars.

Over dinner, one does manage to glean a few details about Mr David bleeding White. His actual occupation is part-ownership of a Media Studies school, which accepts rich kids from around the world on surrender of 7,000 bucks a pop. And, of course, he turns out to be Monty's *godson*. His grandmother (whose bridge partner is the woman from Waldzneij's home town) and Monty's father were in military intelligence together during the war, if you can believe that. Though in which war and on whose side, he doesn't say.

'My grandmother is a very remarkable woman,' he tells us, or rather he tells Yasmin, giving her both barrels of full-on simian stare. 'She's over eighty, goes to bridge four nights a week, and can remember every card that's been played. She power-walks down Broadway from Central Park to Wall Street and back. Says it keeps her fit. And in touch.' *And, don't tell me, she's smoked sixty untipped cigarettes a day since she was twelve. And still has the lungs of a teenager.*

'God, I hate old people,' I chip in lightly.

'I'm *sorry*?' David White furrows his brow. Yasmin looks in my direction for the first time in ten minutes.

'I don't hate them because they're . . . *so active,*

putting us young people to shame in inverted commas. I hate them because they're a reminder of what we're going to be. I hate them because they're old. I think they even hate themselves for it.'

I'm in a bad mood, I'm sorry, what can I tell you? Maybe this isn't the ideal speech to make at a jolly little dinner. But then this isn't a jolly little dinner. It's torture. So when we all get back to the hotel for a nightcap, I leave the two of them sitting in the bar, mouthing things to one another through their big mouthy mouths and stomp off to bed.

Except I can't sleep. I've been watching television and dozing and listening out for the click of Yasmin's door, but up to now – it's 2 a.m. – no such click has been logged. They can't still be in the bar, surely. Have they gone back to his place?

I phone Hilary. She must be out *extremely* late, because I get the machine, unless she's unplugged the phone.

I drain the last Diet Coke from the mini-bar, scrunch the can and hurl it at the TV set. I want to be Elvis. Didn't he *shoot* a TV once?

Shitshit*shit*. It's Friday night. Where *is* everybody?

[illegible]

[illegible] Why else walk [illegible] this number. A [illegible]

[illegible]

'Good morning!' I say as [illegible]rfully as I can. '[illegible] normally prefer a slice of [illegible] toast myself. With a little Gentleman's Relish. I'm feeling particu[illegible]larly [illegible]

SIX

1

So I come down to breakfast and here she is, ploughing her way through an indecently large plate of waffles impregnated with syrup. Some in fact has dribbled on to her chin. My first thought is not a noble one. A post night-of-shagging restorative. Got to be. Why else waffles? In this number. At this speed.

'Good morning,' I say as cheerfully as I can. 'I normally prefer a slice of brown toast myself. With a little Gentleman's Relish if I'm feeling particularly zesty.'

'Oh hi.' She looks at me as though nothing has happened. 'Fuelling up to meet Mr Nazi. There's coffee here if you want some.'

'Thanks.' I sit down opposite and study her demeanour as she chews. Giving nothing away. 'Er . . . sorry for bailing out early last night. I got a bit irritated for some reason.'

'No worries.' And on she goes. Hoisting great pieces of sticky, spongy mattress into her face. Are you *supposed* to eat waffles with a knife and fork?

'What did you make of our American friend?' I ask. 'Quite a . . . character.'

She sets down her cutlery with more of a clatter than strictly necessary.

'It was completely obvious that you thought he was a total arsehole.'

'Really?'

'Not at first. But in the restaurant.'

'I think I was a bit tired by then.' *Go on, ask her*. 'What did you think then? About David White. I thought you . . . rather liked him actually.'

Yasmin sighs heavily. 'Well, he was bloody fit, wasn't he?'

'Yeah?'

'Not the clothes, they were tragic. But he's the physical type I'm a complete sucker for. And he was such a fucking flirt, I couldn't help myself . . .'

'You didn't . . .' *It just slipped out*.

'What? Shag him? Don't be daft, he's married. And I'm supposed to be *getting* married. And you're right, he *is* a bit of an arsehole.'

Oh joy. Oh thank you, God.

'What did you find to talk about till, whenever it was in the morning? Not granny, I take it.'

She laughs and picks up her knife and fork ready to on-board some more waffle.

'When a chap wants to get into your knickers that badly, there's something kind of . . . fascinating about it. It's hard to tear yourself away.'

'What was his best line then?' I ask.

'He said, "I bet you're a fantastic snogger." In that weird accent of his.'

'And . . .'

But her mouth is full of waffle and she's shaking her head firmly. No further questions.

Supposed to be getting married. She said *supposed* to be.

2

Slimeball picks us up from in front of the hotel in a grey Toyota. Gratifyingly, there seems precious little chemistry between him and Yasmin this morning. Possibly even a slight sulkiness on his part, born no doubt of expectations deliciously raised and cruelly dashed, ha ha fucking ha.

So, soon we're bowling through the iron girders of the Queensboro Bridge, Manhattan flickering away across the East River. And then into mile after mile of gas stations, factory outlets, Burger Kings and Dunkin' Donuts. Now a series of identical huge brown apartment blocks rear up. Archives of humanity, is the thought that pops into my head. Great filing cabinets of human souls. We stop outside one. David White pushes a doorbell from a choice of several hundred. Seven storeys later, plus about four minutes worth of linoleum-lined corridor, we stand outside his door. Yasmin takes an audibly deep breath. Unseen by creepo, I grab her wrist and squeeze it in a sort of *courage mon brave* sort of a way. She shoots me a grimace. Trying to smile but can't.

The door cracks open and a short old man stands before us. Unshaven, pouchy face, the whites of his eyes yellow, sick-looking. He's spilt something down his shirt recently. A cigarette burns between stubby fingers. As he looks sourly over the small group standing on his doorstep, a wave of over-cranked central heating hits me in the face. Carried upon it is old-man smell, tobacco and urine I should think, possibly a hint of cat food in there as well. He turns into the gloom behind him. Broad-backed, still stocky, he has the look of an old man who was once physically powerful. David White signals that we should follow.

We tread through a tiny hallway into the living room. A small sofa, a couple of armchairs. A TV set playing mutely. The blinds have been drawn against the brilliance of the crisp autumn day outside. The air feels like it has already been breathed too many times. I want to leave . . . *now*.

'Tea,' he barks. It's an order not a suggestion.

'That would be very kind,' says David White. 'This is Michael Roe who will be doing the interview and Yasmin Swan, our, er, colleague. Michael, Yasmin, let me introduce Czeslaw Waldzneij.'

'Hi,' we say simultaneously.

The eggy eyes of the old Ukrainian flick between us, his expression hovering somewhere between dismay and outright disapproval. Then with a kind of grim internal acceptance – *ah, what the hell* – he pads off into the kitchen. David White signals we should sit. He takes an armchair, Yasmin and I squeeze on to the sofa.

As best we can, we survey our surroundings. There's a half bottle of brandy and a glass on the coffee table. A newspaper in Russian. A pouch of rolling tobacco. A nasty souvenir ashtray full of rollie butts. By the door, a huge artillery shell-casing acts as a stand for an umbrella and a walking stick. In a cabinet under the TV, there's a collection of battered paperbacks – I recognise Tom Clancy and John Grisham – there are titles in Cyrillic and a Bible. On the TV, a church service of some kind is in progress. Poor picture quality and dodgy camera work. It's Russian Orthodox on an émigré channel, I guess. Above the TV is a framed photograph. A group of school kids, a big yellow school bus. Their smiling driver.

Yasmin screams. A yellow cat has jumped into her lap. A beautiful sleek skinny creature – the cat version of Yasmin. It turns and turns on her knees, trying to find a way to settle.

Waldzneij enters bearing a tray of steaming mugs.

'You say hello to Blondie,' he says to Yasmin. There's something approximating a smile on his face. He serves us tea, Russian style with a slice of lemon. The Ukrainian sits forward on his armchair, elbows on knees, making a fresh cigarette. We are silent while he works. When he lights it, I notice his hands are trembling.

'Now you talk,' he says to me, blowing smoke and spitting bits of tobacco. 'Tell me what you want.' His eyes seem to be angry and hurt and scared all at the same time.

I explain slowly from first principles. What we will do. Bring a camera to the apartment. Some lights. Probably film him in the chair right where he's sitting. I'll ask him to tell me his whole story. Starting with where he was born, his parents, his home, his childhood. (I don't tell him that we'll never use any of this, it's just for background and to get him warmed up.) Then we'll move into the thirties. Feelings at the time towards the non-ethnic Ukrainian population in his town. The outbreak of war, the German advance into Russia. His wartime 'career'. These . . . terrible things that happened.

The old man sighs heavily. His yellow eyes are growing watery. Careful now, Michael. Don't peak too soon here.

'All I need today, Mr Waldzneij,' I say quietly, 'is a rough idea of your story. The headlines as it were. So we can . . .'

The old man crashes his mug on to the coffee table.

'Impossible for me,' he shouts, shaking his head. He's wiping away tears with the heel of his hand. 'This is very . . . emotional subject. Very difficult to speak about. I will speak it to you . . . but I cannot speak it twice.'

Fine, fine. Whatever, whatever. That's the craven First Rule of Television, isn't it? Above all, keep the talent sweet. Even if he is a fucking Nazi.

So does he have any stills we can take a look at now? Photos, documents, records, papers, letters, *anything* to tie this man into the story he will tell us.

Nope. All destroyed naturally before he hands himself over to Allied forces in 1945.

A thought occurs to me.

'Is Czeslaw Waldzneij the name you were born with, Mr Waldzneij?'

He looks at me curiously. As if no-one's ever asked him this before. Alongside, I feel Yasmin stop scratching Blondie under the chin.

'No,' he replies eventually. 'Is the name the Americans give me. In Displaced Persons camp.' And then he actually laughs. I begin to feel slightly sick. The overheated apartment. The foul air. The horror of what this man *may* have done.

'You mean the name *you* gave to the Americans?'

'Yes, yes,' he splutters. 'Is father of Mickey Mouse. Waldzneij.'

Walt Disney. The sneaky old cunt. A made-up

name to take the piss out of the Allies. He's beaming at me. Good joke, eh?

'Very . . . clever. So what *is* your real name?' I ask with as flat a bat as possible.

'I tell you tomorrow.'

This story is getting smellier and smellier by the minute: without any supporting evidence, there's only his word that he ever worked for the Nazis. And even if he tells me his 'real' name, it's not going to make any difference. Even *if* the Nazis in their meticulous fashion had documented someone of that name having worked for them in 1942, and *if* those records had fallen into Russian hands, and *if* they are still safely in the archives in Moscow, or even back in Germany, then all it would prove is that 'Waldzneij' *knows the name* of someone who worked for the SS. It doesn't prove it was him. The whole thing is ridiculous. Worse than ridiculous, *preposterous*. A *Hiwi* butcher who changes his name to Walt Disney? Keeps his head down for fifty years and now decides he wants to 'apologise to humanity?' To admit freely to war crimes? It doesn't make sense.

'OK, we speak money.' He's unscrewing the top of the brandy bottle. Oh ho, here we are. The m-word. But now Slimeball pipes up.

'I think we have been through the issue of a fee, Mr Waldzneij. If you remember, we agreed it could be problematic for us to be seen to be paying for this interview. Which is why, if you recall, certain . . . *arrangements* have been put into place for you?'

Who did this ridiculous life-support system for a set of teeth sound like just then? Of course. Montgomery Dodd would have cooked up that weaselly bit of script. They're planning to bung him cash. Full deniability at all times. I feel a bit dizzy. The central heating seems to have kicked up to tropical.

The old man downs his brandy in one like a Cossack.

'I am sick man,' he implores, fanning his large leathery palms towards us. 'I need operation.' He makes a fist and thumps on his chest. 'Lung is . . . fucked, liver is fucked.' He shakes his head and takes an enormous drag from his roll-up. The coughing fit that follows lasts nearly a minute.

When it subsides, Yasmin says softly, 'Perhaps you should think about giving up smoking.' The first words she has spoken.

The egg eyes stare at her. He looks shocked. By the impudence of youth, or the sheer *youth* of youth? It's impossible to tell. But then, some sort of internal mechanism flicks his expression to one of amused fatalism. He waves his cigarette at her.

'Is impossible. America is only home of the brave, not land of the free. You understand?'

It doesn't come to me until we're crossing the Queensboro Bridge back into Manhattan.

Blondie.

The name of Hitler's dog.

3

So it's all fixed. David White has gone off to book a video crew to shoot the interview in Queens on Monday morning. Right now I am trying to ignore the alarm bells that are clanging horribly between my ears.

'It's a fucking scam,' I tell Yasmin. 'He's just a piss-stained old relic who's thought of a cute way to take a TV company for a few thousand dollars to pay a hospital bill. He'll grab the money, tell us a pack of lies and deny everything when he comes round from the operation.'

'Maybe he won't come round.'

'I guess that's our best hope.'

We're walking down Second Avenue through the East Village. I want to eyeball the émigré café that 'Waldzneij' frequents for myself. But when we get there, there's a film crew outside taking shots of the exterior. For wallpaper, I guess. Footage of our man's life in the New World. Clearly, Monty's bag man isn't wasting a second.

So Yasmin and I fall into the Mee Noodle Shop and Grill. From the cuttings displayed on the window, it appears New York Beat poets like Alan Ginsberg used to come to slurp here of a lunchtime. I order Chow Fun (a flat soft rice noodle) with Roast Duck (dry mix) but she's gone for Seafood with Angel Hair (in soup).

It's one of those mental Polaroids that, whatever happens between us, I just know will stay in my album for a very long time. Yasmin and Seafood with Angel Hair. Seen through a veil of steam, the amazing face floating low over the bowl, pink reflections from the exotic broth dancing across her pale skin. And rising gently into those wide, insistent lips, with only a little encouragement from her chopsticks, a twisted rope of noodles. Once, she glances up to find me watching. I am thinking, it would be the best thing that could ever happen to a noodle. To a noodle, Yasmin would be like a Goddess. And the summit of any devout noodle's ambition of course would be merging with the Deity. Becoming One with the Godhead. If it's true that there is a first time for everything in life, then this is the first time that I have ever envied a noodle.

'What do you think he meant?' I ask after a particularly long sequence of Angel Hair completes its glorious ascent. 'About America being the home of the brave, but not the land of free.'

'I think he was talking about tobacco. How addiction is more to do with bravery than freedom. The bravery of facing the awful possible consequences against the freedom of not having to smoke.'

'Oh fuck, so he's a philosopher as well as a Nazi.' I point my packet of Silk Cut at her. She takes one and I light us up. Through the plate-glass window, an ambulance screams by, its siren not just doing that skirling *wooooh-wooooh* noise, but another one, a new alarm they've obviously found effective in scattering traffic. A massive bass roar, like a metal giant farting.

Whatever he did or didn't do, I guess anyone

from that generation and from *there*, well, they would know *something* about bravery and freedom, wouldn't they?

4

I finally get through to Hilary. Having a slouchy Saturday night in. I can hear the TV in the background. Male voices, laughter. 'So no change there then,' says someone in a familiar tone. *Have I Got News For You*. For the briefest moment, I have a pang of longing for old London town.

'How was your evening?' I ask. *Where the fuck were you?*

'Oh, I went out clubbing with Julia? And some friends of hers from her salsa class? We got a bit wrecked. So I stayed over on her sofa?' *Clubbing? Wrecked? This is not any Hilary that I recognise*. 'How's New York?'

'Oh you know, mad. This alleged Nazi is a complete con. And Monty's man over here is an absoulte twat. Far too many teeth as well.'

'And Yasmin?'

'Yasmin?' *What?* 'Well, she's the only sensible person in the whole city as far as I can make out.'

Bing bong. Hilary's Terry-and-June doorbell. I look at my watch. Who's coming round to play at this time of night?

'Oh shit, let me get that, darling, hang on.'

From a hotel room in Manhattan, I listen to a TV

set playing three thousand miles away in a house in North London. 'Michael Portillo . . . Michael *Jackson* . . . Princess Michael of *Kent* (laughter) . . . and a tin of pilchards (laughter).'

'Sorry darling,' says Hilary, a bit breathless. 'It's Julia. We're having a girly session about this bloke she's met?'

'Oh yes? Who's that then?' *Julia? I thought she was doing a seven-to-life stretch with Hugo.*

'It's all very new. She's come round to work out what we think of him? Oh, by the way, Olivia rang again today. She was after your number in New York. I gave it to her. I hope that was OK.'

'Do you know what she wanted?'

'It was about her father. The oddest thing. Apparently, he's come round from his stroke speaking Yiddish.'

It takes me two, maybe three minutes to return to normal. At one point I think I might actually pull a muscle, I'm laughing so hard. When one wakes up covered in pine needles, it is reasonable to suppose one has been sleeping underneath a sodding pine tree, indeed.

'Jesus, Hilary. That is *funny*.' I manage when I have calmed down. I can tell she is not impressed at my discovery of humour within affliction. 'Did she have anything else to say. Easy now, I may have a stroke myself.'

'She mentioned Dave Cleaver. That Clive was still wondering whether or not you'd managed to find anything out about him.'

'Yes?' *Sinking feeling. Dive dive dive.*

'Well, I said that was odd, because the two of you were old friends. Or you knew him of old, at any rate. She didn't really have much to report after that.'

A metal giant is farting raucously in my head.

'Can I have a word with Julia?' I manage eventually.

'Er, she's just popped into the bathroom.'

'Really? Well, don't worry.'

'Michael, is everything all right? You're gone a bit funny.'

5

'Two dry vodka Martinis, please.'

'It'll be my pleasure, sir. Would that be with an olive? Or a lemon?'

'Olive, please.' *Just get on with it, you fawning cretin.*

'Certainly, sir. Do you have a preference for a particular vodka this evening? I can recommend a new brand we have, out of Siberia. There's a very interesting note of barley on the finish, and a faint suggestion of vanilla. I believe it's sixty per cent proof.'

'Two, please.' *And stand by for further instructions, matey. This is an emergency.*

As soon as I put the phone down on Hilary, I called Yasmin and arranged to meet here in the hotel's Crisis Management Command and Control

Centre. And in she comes, serious face on. Bless her, she's brought a notebook. I guess she presumes my 'nasty little problem' is something to do with the story. Despite her height, I love the extra little *hop* she has to achieve to plant herself on the spindly barstool next to mine.

Two Siberian Vodka Martinis appear on their little coasters, individually spotlit in the overhead halogens. We pause for a moment, as a mark of respect, then clink. At the first sip, I swear to God I can hear wolves howling.

'Yasmin,' I essay when the roof of my head has returned. 'I think I'm about to crash-land in the cack. A particularly ill-advised . . . venture of mine has, to coin a phrase, gone tits up.'

She laughs. I explain. How I was the source of the *Holy Delicious* leak. How I drunkenly blurted it out to Dave Cleaver. How Dave wrote the story. How Clive launched his mole-hunt. How my velvety black snout has been caught in the search-lights.

Yasmin thinks about what I have told her. Considers it from every angle. Sips her drink. Lights a cigarette. Reflects further. Issues her preliminary findings.

'Fuck. What a mess.'

'I suppose I *could* try and deny it, but they'll never believe me.' I conclude.

'It's my fault, isn't it?' she says gamely. 'If I hadn't told you in the first place, it would never have happened.'

'Don't be daft. I shouldn't have, you know . . . abused your trust.' Gosh, I did enjoy saying *abused your trust* to this beautiful young woman.

'Michael, to be honest, I just thought it was a funny story about a silly TV show. It didn't occur to me anyone would actually *care*.'

'No, I abused your trust. It was unforgivable.' *Not as good this time. Forget it*. 'Mind you, I was pissed,' I add in mitigation.

Fawning cretin chooses this moment to reappear at his station. His eyebrows are set at question mark.

'Would you happen to have any Ukrainian vodka by any chance?' I inquire.

'That would be Kiev, would it, sir? Happily, I think we do. Two dry Ukrainian vodka Martinis? With an olive?'

Roger on that. I look at Yasmin perched up alongside me, head tipped back, draining off the last of Siberia. I think we are managing this crisis rather well. By the time we've gone through each of the former Soviet Republics, I'm sure the situation won't seem half as shitty.

'Do you believe in telepathy?' she asks when the Ukraine takes its place under the halogen lamps.

'Is this another trick?'

She hands me her notebook and a pen.

'I've just remembered it. Write down a number between one and nine. Don't let me see.'

Call me juvenile, but I *adore* tricks. I write down 5.

'Next to it, write another number between one and nine. A different one.'

8

'Now a third number. Any number you like between one and nine.'

2

'So now you've got a three-digit number, yes?'

582. 'Yes I have.'

'OK, now reverse that number. So if you've got 123, write down 321.'

285. 'I think I should warn you, Yasmin, I only got a C in maths.'

'OK, tough part. Now you've got two three-digit numbers. The original one and the reversed one. Subtract the smaller from the larger and write down the result.'

582 minus 285. After about two minutes of pen chewing and head scratching, I'm there. 297. 'OK.'

'So now you've got another three-digit number, yes?'

'Yes . . .'

'OK, now reverse that number.'

792

'And add that to the previous three-digit number.'

'Fuck, you know this is really straining the old cerebral cortex.' 792 + 297 = 1089. 'OK, got it.'

'How many digits have you got now?'

'Four.'

'OK. We need a book. Any book.'

Lying on the bar is a house copy of a New York restaurant guide. 'Will this do?'

'Yes, fine. Take the first three digits of your final number, and turn to that page. Don't let me see it.'

Page 108. 'OK.'

'Now take the last digit. Count off that number of words, starting with the first word on the page. So if it's a five, go to the fifth word.'

The ninth word is *lobster*. 'OK.'

'Now I want you to concentrate on that word. Visualise it. Really picture it in your head.'

I recall a story I once heard about lobsters that I have never been able to forget. How somebody cooked a live pair in a microwave oven. The horrible tapping of their claws on the glass door in the few seconds before their brains fried.

'I'm getting some sort of sea creature, Michael. Would that be right?'

I don't believe this. 'You know, don't you?'

'Bigger than a prawn. Smaller than an eel. Not a crab.'

'How did you do that?'

'I see claws. Big pincer-like claws.' She's milking it. 'A lobster. Is it lobster?'

'It *is* bloody lobster. Go on, tell me.'

She sips her Ukrainian Martini in triumph. Lights a cigarette to build up the suspense. Actually, I'd like to hear her tell me that this isn't a trick, that she really *can* read minds, that there *is* such a thing as magic in this cynical old world. That in fact all along she has been a sorceress, that she has turned Clive Wilson into a catfish, and the two of us can now go off to her enchanted castle and do tricks for one another. Eventually, when we weary of sorcery, we will open a bottle of wine and fall into bed. Oh yeah, and she fixes it for Nick to start a new life as a whelk.

'Actually, the truth is rather dull,' she says. 'If you do what we did to *any* three different numbers between one and nine, you always end up with 1089. It's a mathematical certainty.'

Of course. A boring little fact at the heart of a rather brilliant illusion. 'And lobster?'

'I looked in the restaurant guide last night while we were waiting for David White. You can do it with any book. You just have to remember the ninth word on page 108.'

'And you knew I would choose this book, because it's the only book to hand.'

'Works quite well with phone directories,' she says. 'The ninth name down on page 108. If you can remember the address and the postcode as well, they think you are a genius.'

'Yasmin, you *are* a genius. You've completely taken my mind off the looming debacle. Where shall we go for dinner?'

She shoots me a Raymond Chandler smile (you know, one of those you can feel in your hip pocket). 'Well, Michael,' she says, 'tonight, the world is our lobster.'

6

Unforgivably, with all of New York at our feet, we decided we wanted hamburgers. Yasmin because, as she put it, she wanted to 'eat something's flesh', and me for reasons of comfort in the darkest hour, sort of thing. So we are in the Mercury Bar on Ninth Avenue. Dark and noisy with big screens showing the baseball. And to my joy, when I ordered a Mercury-burger – no cheese – rare, she simply said to the waitress, *Can you make that two and bring us a bottle of the Chilean Merlot*. We're chomping away, heads down. And I'm having one of those hamburger epiphanies. When the squishy beefiness of the beef, the sharpness of the raw onion, the sweetness of the ketchup and the blandness of the bun fuse momentarily with the throbbing music, the wine and the sight of the beautiful tomato-smeared visage opposite to produce a single, fragile thought: *I am happy. Take me now, Lord*.

'Actually, there's a serious scientific explanation for the popularity of burgers,' I tell her, when the moment has passed. She nods vigorously, wide-eyed. I'm sure she would say something but for the huge bolus of food products (see above) that she is currently working on with a view to swallowing.

'OK, not an explanation,' I continue, 'a theory more like. Hamburgers remind us of our primitive past. When we lived in caves. When the men came back from the hunt, they'd give the women and children a mouthful of chewed meat. The old and the sick too. And that's what burgers symbolise, the mouth-to-mouth meat thing. The bun represents the lips. The ketchup, the fresh blood. And if you think about it, the burger being *minced* feels like it's already been chewed.'

'What about the onions?'

'Bad breath. Early man, not having access to toothpaste and dental floss would have had terribly bad breath. This has all been carefully thought through, you know.'

'Why isn't Ronald McDonald a caveman then, if there's such nostalgia for the Stone Age? And what was so good about it? There were no clothes, no central heating, no foreign holidays. Life was short and nasty. You died of the first disease you caught. Oh, and there were no glasses.' Here she cocks her head playfully at my own unsuitable, unfashionable, shameful pair. 'If you were short-sighted, you were basically fucked. Even if you could tell which was the most desirable female, you'd have tumbled over a cliff edge or been carried off by a sabre-toothed tiger long before you'd ever have a crack at her. And then there's the cheese.'

'The cheese?'

'What does the cheese in a cheeseburger represent?'

Here, I admit, the theory falls down. I have no answer. I cannot imagine what the cheese could represent. Had she said gherkin, I might have come back with grasshopper, some insect, at any rate, from the ferny carpet of untamed wilderness. But cheese?

'Fat!' I cry in triumph. 'The layer of fat below the skin of the prey. It's yellow, isn't it?'

We munch onwards. But her words are floating round my head, like mobiles over a baby's cot. *Basically fucked. Desirable female. Crack at her.* You don't need to be the Bearded Lady to spot the sexual imagery. Is she reproaching me for not having a crack at her? This desirable female, who wants to be . . . no, can't be. Can it? She had a go at my glasses. A comment on my *vision* perhaps. Is there something I cannot see?

'At least people made their own entertainment in the Stone Age,' I put in after a spell.

'What sort of thing?'

'Oh, farting contests mostly. I mean there was no Channel Five in those days.' She smiles.

'And burping.'

'Burping definitely. You'd score points for volume and duration. A delicate balance to strike, actually.' Something comes back to me. A holiday in Italy. A girlfriend and I on the terrace at sunset watching the bird migration. Every evening they came over our valley, geese I suppose they were, wave after wave in V-formations. And we'd sit there, sipping Chianti and awarding marks out of ten for aerial composition. We would take account of number, the more birds there were in a flight, the harder it was for them to maintain the clean lines of their 'V'. Spectacularly, on our last evening, with the sky all pink, they didn't 'V', they *spiralled*.

Resting on a thermal she'd said, hundreds of them, slowly wheeling overhead, in a complex pattern of interlocking circles that seemed to take each bird on a path that eventually crossed the path of every other. We supposed it had arisen through evolution, to provide a refreshing change from the monotonous vista of webbed feet and arse of the migrating goose in front. We'd laughed about it and, when it was too dark to see them any more, we went inside and made love.

My companion on the *terrazzo* was Hilary, of course. Bloody Hilary who only ever wants to help. Hilary who might have just assisted my final exit from the television industry.

While Yasmin slips off to the loo, I scribble a list of contemporary brain-teasers on the napkin:

1. **Since when has Hilary been so pally with Julia?**
2. **Has Julia really met a new bloke?**
3. **If so, what's happened to Hugo? Not that I care.**
4. **Was it really Julia who rang Hilary's doorbell?**
5. **Has Olivia told Clive about me and Dave Cleaver?**
6. **What will he tell Monty?**
7. **What will Monty's view be?**

8. Is this fucking Nazi for real or what?
9. Does Yasmin want me to make a move on her?
10. Does she merely deplore tortoiseshell frames?

When Yasmin returns, our waitress bobs up and sets a rather easier problem. 'Say, would you guys care for another bottle?'

7

This time as we walk back down Broadway, she does it. She puts her arm through mine. I find it hard to speak for a minute or so, but fortunately this is Manhattan where, with so many other noises competing for our attention, it is not necessary. I love the way the length of her arm seems to fit well against mine. The way our steps have naturally fallen into synch. I bet we look good together. I bet passers-by think we are a couple. But she's only being friendly, isn't she? We're still somewhere in that confusing crossover zone between friends and colleagues. Dammit, she probably feels *sorry* for me, what with my share price currently falling through the floorboards.

In the corridor, by our hotel room doors she says, *It was a lovely evening. I'm sure everything will work out all right, Michael*, and then the chaste kiss goodnight. As I step into my room, I replay the scene on her sitting-room carpet in London in my head. The stoned kiss that went on a bit too long. The repeat effort that was longer. The third that was a full-blown snog. I've run this tape through my brain so many times that now I'm not sure it ever happened. Is it a genuine memory? Or, like the memory of something from a very long time ago, merely the *memory of a memory*, bearing little or even no relation to the original event.

I'm lying on the bed flipping between Leno with Rod Stewart and Letterman with Robbie Williams (or possibly v.v.) when the phone rings.

'Michael, it's Yasmin.' My stomach takes the speed elevator to the lobby.

'Hi,' I croak. *Michael, I'm feeling kind of lonely tonight. Would you like to come over? Maybe we could hit the mini-bar, watch a little TV together?*

'There was a voicemail message from Nick. He said there's a story on the front page of a newspaper this morning that he thinks I should see.'

'What story?'

'Didn't say. He'll have gone to bed now.'

'What do you think it could be?'

'It would have to be something to do with work. I just thought you should know.'

'Thanks.'

'Well, goodnight, then.'

'Listen, Yasmin . . .'

'Yes?'

'Er . . . are you watching Leno?'

'Letterman actually. Watched Leno last night.'

'Odd-looking bloke, Leno. He reminds me of that joke. Horse walks into a bar and asks for a pint of lager, and the barman says, "Certainly, but why the long face?"'

She is kind enough to laugh.

'How's your mini-bar?' I inquire.

'Fine thanks, why do you ask?'

'Oh, well, I was wondering . . . if I could tempt you to a late-night snifter and some crappy American television.'

'That's very sweet of you, Michael. But I think I'm only good for another five minutes.'

'OK. Night then.'

'Night.'

Oh, fuck.

Fuck squared, really.

Actually, to give it its full due, Fuckingcunting-bollockingbastardingfuck.

8

I have a terrible night. That awful state where you don't know whether you are asleep or awake. Only by waking a dozen times during the small hours, do you know you've been asleep at all. I have three dreams:

1. I'm involved in some sort of World War Two tank battle. Disturbingly, I seem to be on the German side. Worse still, the German tanks

appear to be crewed by giant rats. I try to raise Hilary on the radio transmitter. The instrumentation is very complicated and she doesn't respond. One of the rats tells me, 'It's too late, the invasion has started.' I wake in a cold sweat.
2. I am gliding in the slipstream of one of those big migrating birds. Just the two of us. When I look down, I see Hilary and I on our holiday terrace far away in the valley below. But I can't keep up, not having any actual wings to speak of (I'm up there through sheer will-power) and the white goose is flapping on ahead. Now I'm falling. My last glimpse as I look up is of the white of her wings against the blue sky, a snatch of the yellow of her beak. As I hit the ground, I wake with my heart pounding in my chest.
3. I am being chased through a bizarre landscape of Roman columns by a dwarf brandishing an axe. On an archway there is a Latin inscription which reads 'TITUS'. Weirdly, I wake from this one, laughing.

It's Sunday morning but, even so, the streets are teeming. Tourists, shoppers, people going to work, people just out there, doing stuff. I have a sudden pang of nostalgia for the Great Silence of the English Sunday morning. Between my front door in Belsize Park and the newsagents at this time of day, I'd pass no more than a dozen people. An old man paused at a lamp post with his small, nervous dog. A hungover yuppy in search of milk, fags and a *Mail on Sunday*. In Manhattan, in the short walk between hotel and the news-stand where they sell the foreign papers, I stop counting at 200.

It's not the lead. That seems to be a colourful story about Prince William and a Spice Girl. But it shares the front page. The headline in big white type on a black background reads:

SHE'S NO ANGEL!

Then in smaller type, underlined usefully:

TV Star's Night *Out* With Lesbian Lover

The author of the piece is highlighted in a tasteful little box:

By David Cleaver

The narrative commences:

Angelica Doubleday leaves an intimate Italian restaurant with new partner TV technician Dinah Phelps. The couple have become 'inseparable', according to friends.

But TV insiders say the same-sex relationship may spell the end of *Holy Delicious*, Angelica's

scandal-torn religion-meets-cookery show.

After fleeing photographers last night, Angelica and Dinah were believed to be in hiding. Curtains at the star's £1m luxury home in Highgate were drawn. The only visitor was grim-faced TV boss Montgomery Dodd.

TURN TO PAGE 2

At the bottom of the page, there are further announcements:

My Pal, Angelica – by Dale Winton P3
'Good on you, girl,' says Michael Barrymore P4
'She needs a big hug, a proper dinner and a good cry' – Read Carol Vorderman P5

Dominating the whole scene is the photograph. The famous face, so willing to take the light when evenly buttered in television make-up, is here seized by an expression no viewer has ever seen. The flash has gone off very close to them, the explosion whiting out the skin of the two women, leaving only grotesque masks of eyes and teeth. They stand frozen on the pavement, arm in arm, momentarily paralysed by the bombardment of photons. You can almost hear the ratchety whine of the camera's motor-drive. The face with the smaller eyes and mouth looks shocked. But in the bigger face – the eyes and teeth so familiar from a thousand smudgy newspaper images – there's fear and anger as well.

'Say, pal, are you gonna buy that paper? This ain't a library, you know.' The man behind the newsstand is glaring at me.

'Oh yes, sorry. It's a story about someone I know, that's all.' He surveys the tabloid's loud cover.

'Yeah, right. And I'm the fuckin' King of England. That'll be three dollars.'

9

The meaning of the three dreams has come to me.

For the last hour I've been sitting in the Union Square Café, one of the few places round here you can still smoke. Breakfast is coffee and Silk Cut and, because I've only read it fifteen times already, I read it again, a Dave Cleaver classic of innuendo, supposition and old-fashioned trouble-making. Who, for example, is the 'senior TV insider' who 'predicts the show will be cancelled within weeks'? Who are the 'religious leaders' said to be 'lining up to demand Angelica's removal'? Who indeed is the unnamed 'telly regulator' who believes it is 'inappropriate for a significant portion of the channel's religious output to be presented by a practising homosexual'? The spores of the story have spread on to other pages. There are supporting features, comment, advice, tittle-tattle; even a leader ('Angelica, the public love you for ***who*** you are, not ***what*** you are').

Now, of course, it's obvious. The dwarf with the axe? Well it wasn't an axe, was it, it was a *cleaver*. The columns were *newspaper* columns. And 'TITUS'? Very nearly an anagram of 'tits up', a nice little jokey touch there from the unconscious. The dream is a live-action pictograph of my feelings – both recognised and unrecognised – towards the small, treacherous scribbler with the heart of flint.

The tank battle is more of a mixed metaphor. But the Nazi thing is the key, I think. It's the war in the desert, if you remember your history. Rommel versus *Montgomery*. I seem to be on the side of the rats . . . or are they in fact *mice*? As in Mickey Mouse, as in Walt Disney, as in *Waldzneij*. In addition, I'm unable to get hold of Hilary and there's a fear of invasion, which is probably sexual. In short, the whole story is an expression of anxiety: that I've got on the wrong side of my boss, that the Ukrainian is going to add to my misery and that, while I'm away, someone is giving Hilary one.

You don't buy it? I'm not a hundred per cent myself, as it happens. But the Bearded Lady says the unconscious is like a shoebox. Though you can never lift the lid completely, each dream is a pinprick through the cardboard, allowing you to glimpse a tiny bit more of what's inside.

Oh, and the migrating bird who's flying away,

leaving me to fall to the ground? Probably not a goose at all. Rather, I imagine, a Swan.

I walk back slowly to the hotel. In my head, as I wander up Broadway, birds, tanks and blade-wielding dwarves give way to another kind of vision. A daydream, if you like. There's a winding creek of oozing shit. In the distance, a long, long way up that creek, you can make out the figure of a man in a canoe. Even from here, it's possible to tell that he has no paddle.

10

No sign of Yasmin. Maybe she's gone off shopping. But there's a message to call David White. To go over all the arrangements for tomorrow, no doubt.

'Michael,' he says when I get through, 'there's no easy way to say this.'

'Oh Christ, what?'

'Waldzneij has crapped out on us. He's giving the interview to CNN.'

Oddly, I have to resist the urge to laugh.

'Oh dear,' I say.

'Fucking right, oh dear.'

'Why? I mean, what made him do it?'

'I guess CNN is a bigger brand than Belvedere Television.'

'Is that what he said?'

'No. What he said was, he thought you and that skinny bitch, as he put it, were too young.'

'Too *young*? Are you serious?'

'His exact words were, "They are children. They don't understand what we went through."'

'I thought he wanted to apologise to the world, not be understood. And, anyway, how can I be too young? I'm probably the same age he was when he was out butchering civilians.'

'Let's say Mr Waldzneij is not the most logical of men. But it's a fuck-up all the same, Michael.'

'You're right there.'

A milestone. The first time, in what is undoubtedly a young person's industry, that I've ever been accused of being *too* young. The truth is that in my mid-thirties, I'm actually in danger of becoming too old. There are very few people in television over forty. If you make it to fifty it means you are the boss.

'It's absolutely hopeless, is it? No chance of getting him back on board?' Suddenly this Nazi scam-artist is beginning to feel more credible.

'None. I think they're taping the interview tonight.'

'Have you, er, mentioned it to Monty?' I ask casually.

'Left a message. His person in London says he's busy chewing the carpet about something else.'

'Oh dear.'

When I put the phone down, I remain sitting on the edge of the bed for a while, staring at the blank screen of the TV set. I feel curiously light-headed. I think it was John Osborne who said,

'After I abandoned all hope, I began to feel much better.' It's true. The little figure in the canoe has disappeared altogether.

11

I ring Hilary criminally early – 9 a.m. on a Sunday in London. The sort of slot reserved for news of the death of a close relative. There is a long time between the phone being picked up and her saying 'Hello'. Odd little scuffles on the line. As if someone else has passed it to her.

'Oh, hi,' she says breezily.

'What you up to?' I inquire as pleasantly as I can manage.

'Well, I haven't been awake very long actually.'

'Sorry. I just wanted to hear your voice.'

'That's nice, Michael.' *In the background, is that the sound of a toilet flushing?*

'How was Julia? And her new man.'

'Oh . . . not too good really. She's probably not going to see him again.'

'I thought she and Hugo were well up a tree together.'

'They've hit a bit of a rough patch, actually. She thinks Hugo may have had an affair in the States. He was over there pitching *Secrets of the Lobsters*.'

'Oh yes, *Lobster Confidential*. Did he get any bites?'

'The Seafood Channel are very interested, apparently.'

'I don't think we can get that in this hotel.'

'It's a cable thing. All Seafood, All the Time. That's their slogan. It's quite popular in Japan. And in Seattle for some reason.'

'Hilary?'

'Yes?'

'Have you got somebody there?'

'Sorry?'

'Is there somebody *there* with you? In the house. I thought I heard the loo.'

She sighs heavily. 'No, Michael. You're not going to start this again are you?'

'Well, if there *were* someone there, you would deny it, wouldn't you?'

'There's no-one here. My secret lover is away.'

'Oh yes?'

'In New York? Gone to interview a Nazi?'

'Oh. Well, it's all gone a bit pear-shaped on that front actually. The Nazi ratted on us – well, I suppose he would, wouldn't he, being a Nazi and all. And bloody Dave Cleaver has dropped me in an even bigger pile of horse manure.'

If I fail to tell Hilary that she herself has made an important contribution to my sagging stock-market valuation, it is only because of my own negligence. Clearly I should have said to her, *Anyone comes asking questions about Dave Cleaver, OK? Just say, ya don't know nuttun, ya never even hearda da guy*.

A cough. A male cough. From somewhere in the house.

'Who's that? Who's *in* there, Hilary?'

'Michael, please will you stop this?'

'I distinctly heard a man cough.'

'Honestly you didn't. No-one coughed. Maybe you heard a dog bark.'

'Don't fucking tell me I didn't hear what I plainly did hear. There was a cough. And don't give me all this bollocks about going to a club with Julia. Where did you *really* go? And who came round last night? Who *is* he, Hilary?'

'Michael, you are such a *stupid prick* . . .'

It's the first time I can remember that she has ever shouted at me, never mind sworn. I feel shocked. Her words ring in my head like tinnitus. But now, unmistakably into the silence, a male voice calls. From his words, I guess he is in the kitchen. I picture a towel wrapped round his waist.

'Where d'you keep your coffee, love?'

There is quiet on the line. There's no denying this one.

'Who the fuck was that, Hilary? Oh actually, I'm sick of this. Fuck you. Really. Fuck *you*.' I slam the phone down.

I am still standing at the window, staring out at the city without really seeing anything when the phone rings.

Hilary.

'Mr Roe, this is the front desk. There's a fax here

from London marked "Urgent". Would you like it sent up?'

'Yes, please.'

A few minutes later, a man old enough to be my father stands in the doorway breathing heavily. He's bearing a single sheet of fax paper. The badge on his waistcoat suggests his name is Tommy.

'Here you go, sir.'

I hand Tommy a dollar. He returns it. 'You keep it,' he says. 'You're gonna need it.'

12

BY FAX TO
Michael Roe
FROM
Montgomery Dodd
THIS PAGE ONLY

Dear Michael

I regret we shall not be renewing your present contract of employment with Belvedere Television Ltd when it expires at the end of next month. This is not solely due to the specific failure to secure an interview with Czeslaw Waldzneij – though that of course is a grave disappointment – but also because of certain structural changes that are to take place within the company. Development is to become the prime responsibility of the

Executive Producer, Leisure Programming, Clive Wilson, who will appoint a small team to work with him on securing commissions.

As a result of the restructuring, and in the light of certain other issues, it is felt best that you do not return to the Belvedere building. We shall honour payment of the remainder of your salary, and of course any legitimate expenses incurred in the USA, on presentation of the proper receipts. Your personal belongings will be delivered to your home by courier.

May I take this opportunity of wishing you all the best in your future career.

Yours sincerely

Montgomery T. Dodd

SEVEN

1

'Hey man, you know where Penn Station's at?'

We're standing at the corner of Thirty-fourth and Eighth. My interrogator is unshaven and bleary-eyed. A tramp, or a sweatshop worker, record producer maybe, or perhaps a Professor of Linguistics. Impossible to tell in this city. But I suppose I should be flattered. That in my own unshaven, bleary-eyed condition, dressed in thrift-store chic – scuzzy track-suit bottoms, ruined tennis shoes, Pea jacket and baseball cap – someone has mistaken me for a native New Yorker. It's not the first time it's happened in the last couple of days.

So now comes my favourite bit. In best Bertie Wooster, I announce: 'I'm *awfully* sorry, I've absolutely *no* idea. Visitor I'm afraid.'

The guy looks at me as if I may be clinically insane. Fear in his face. As if, of the two of us, *I* am the one more likely to whip out a carpet blade and stab the other through the eyeball. He breaks away and is carried off into the fast-flowing lunchtime crowd.

I am alone.

OK, a bit dramatic possibly, but nonetheless an accurate description of my state since Montgomery Dodd faxed me his thoughts (plus good wishes) on Sunday. Viz, in a nutshell, no job, no Hilary and no Yasmin. Yasmin, who after a brief, embarrassing conversation – *Michael, it's terrible, I'm so sorry, but I've got to pack, they want me back in the office tomorrow afternoon* – cabbed it to JFK and was in the sky before the sun went down.

Knowing only one other person in this town, with the sole exception of a Ukrainian Nazi, I called. A touch perverse, possibly, given my earlier hostility. But now, I supposed, we were in the same boat. The woman we both admired had escaped us. She would be riding high above the Atlantic Ocean, her great, sculptural head gripped between earphones, anywhere between the second movie and the third vodka and tonic.

'I suppose you know I've been fired,' I told him glumly.

'Yes. I heard about it. Got any plans?'

'Not really. Thought I might hang around New York for a few days.'

'Do you have anywhere to stay?'

'Nope.'

'You can camp out here if you like.'

And so it was that I appeared on a doorstep on the seventh floor of a building in the former Meat Packing District, to be greeted by the largest collection of oversized teeth in private ownership in America.

David White's place is huge and empty. Some sort of converted warehouse affair, all brickwork and massive windows looking out over the Hudson River. My bed for the last two nights has been a twenty-foot orange sofa from the 1960s which stands hopelessly lost in the middle of the vast main living space. The only other significant objects are a racing bicycle propped against a distant wall, a state-of-the-art Bang and Olufsen stereo and a TV set, roughly the size of a shipping container. In a small, unused kitchen there is coffee, a wide range of alcohol and – in the freezing compartment behind the frozen Stolly – a house brick of cannabis resin. The one book in the entire apartment appears to be the Manhattan Yellow Pages.

My host has been very generous. He's out all day running his Media Studies Academy and, on return, agreeably free with the drink and drugs referred to above. He says I can stay as long as I like. But there's something curiously disinterested about his largesse. He seems preoccupied, as if he's only putting up with me out of politeness, as though I were a relative. It has crossed my mind he might be mildly depressed. Given my present cast of mind, however, that's just fine by me.

Last night, we watched in silence as Waldzneij's sick, sweaty face got larger and larger in the creeping close-up on the massive telly. The Ukrainian wiped his brow. He told of terrible things he'd done to women and children. He wept. 'Is very emotional for me, Larry,' he'd said. Afterwards, David White rolled a joint of quite staggering power, which we smoked listening to Keith Jarrett's *Koln Concert*. The lights of the New Jersey shoreline seemed to wink in time to the sad piano.

Today I have been plodding the streets in a bit of a daze. Occasionally, someone in the streaming crowd will feel my gaze upon them and return it, a secret little animal moment; dwarfed by the buildings, hemmed between the rivers of traffic, we look into each other's eyes and instantly calculate: threat? Or not a threat? Who the *fuck* are you? Or, who *are* you?

Sorry, I'm in that sort of a mood.

Further along Eighth towards Chelsea, I come across someone selling secondhand books from an old blanket on the pavement. As I pause to look at the titles – the usual surreal mish-mash, *Coma*, *Riders*, *Don Quixote*, *The Gulag Archipelago*, *Tom Clancy's Op Center* – a shabby, bearded figure I take to be the bookseller is in conversation with a very much shabbier figure, who I take to be a bum.

'Well, since you like my money so much, you can do something for me, OK?' says the bearded salesman.

'Yeah, sure,' says the other. 'But I can't bend.'

'You can put all the paperbacks in the box. You know what paperbacks are, right?' He flexes a soft cover as a demonstration. The putative packer looks as if he might benefit from a discussion of the overarching concept of *book*, but the man of literature is undeterred. 'Put all the paperbacks in the box, right, but not the classics, OK? The Danielle Steel and the Scott Turow go in the box. But not the Dickens. Or the Nabokov. Understand?'

'I can't bend.'

'You can't?' The bookseller scratches his beard. 'Well what *are* you good for, man?'

For some reason I cannot get this line out of my head. *What* are *you good for, man?*

Near Astor Place by New York University, I pass a young punk girl slumped on the ground against a wall. She's wearing a tiny skirt with ripped tights. Studs pierce her ears and nose. Glazed eyes stare vacantly at the paving slabs. By her side is a paper cup containing a few coins and a hand-written cardboard sign that reads, like a caption, 'FUCKED'.

I drop in a quarter. I know how she feels.

2

I realise I've been revisiting the places I went to with *her*. But they're not the same. They've been stripped of their magic, like seeing a favourite bar in daylight, or an empty television studio. I walked round the Metropolitan Museum again and found the pictures *irritating*. Even the melancholy Pissarro, his view of the home-going crowds, did nothing for me. This time, the sad splodge of cloud above the church steeples just looked like . . . paint.

It's the same with the buildings. The Empire State Building seen from 34th Street. Or the extraordinary scallops of the Chrysler Building hovering over Lexington Avenue. Vistas that I had marvelled at in the bright sunshine when she was at my side, were now discharged of their meaning. As if the towers had somehow turned their tall shoulders and were looking the other way.

Guess what. The Mercury, on Ninth, once a scene of epiphany and wonder, was all the time really just a hamburger joint. And don't even get me started on the Mee Noodle Shop and Grill.

Weirdly, only Barney Greengrass retains its former potency. Maybe because it alone has the *greatness* to transcend petty human concerns. What does it matter, I guess, if X fancies Y, or A is inconsolable over B, or C has stiffed D? All of this is transient, wisp-like stuff compared to the timeless spirit of the Nova Scotia salmon, smoked, crowned with onion and tomato, and laid to rest on a bed of cream cheese, with a choice of plain, poppy-seed, pumpernickel, sesame, or onion bagel, or bialy, toasted or untoasted. First bite, and I swear to God you can feel the beast leaping up the waterway, sun glinting off its silvery back. This is one of only two places in New York where I have managed to forget Yasmin, Hilary, and the whole of my ridiculous predicament for whole minutes on end.

The other is the reading room of the New York Public Library. David White said I should 'Check it out, it's kind of cool'. And indeed I find being in the proximity of all this heavy-duty *thought* quite a novelty, after working in a business where the biggest problem of the morning can be, who should we drop? – Tony Blackburn or Bill Oddie – they've both agreed to do the show. (Correct answer: both of them; find someone else.) Here, beneath the cloud-painted ceiling, in row after row of heavy wooden tables, heads dipped into pools of light cast by homely lamps, in the vast silence of scraping chairs, scratching pens, rattling papers and whispering laptops, there are people reading about Camus and Sartre. Ancient Greek and Electronics. More Osopys and Ologys than you can shake a stick at. There are students, mad-looking old guys researching their family history. A Korean boy playing chess with himself. Maybe a dozen former TV producers considering their position – who knows? You can see people struggling with their next sentence. Reading the same passage again and again, still not getting it. Staring into space, hoping to suck down some inspiration from the book-lined walls. I watch one woman chew her pen so hard, she inhales a piece of plastic and has a coughing fit. I love this place. There's so much *effort* going on here. Such *striving*. How can human consciousness just be an illusion? – the argument in the book that Hilary wanted – with all this sheer concentration at large? And seeing these guys grappling with their problems of course helps me forget my own.

I've mainly been sitting, brooding, reading the *New York Times*. In particular, an advert for a diet product that blocks the absorption of fat. Apparently, the only possible side effects are gas with oily discharge, oily spotting, oily or fatty stools, increased bowel movements, an urgent need to have bowel movements and an inability to control them. The third time I read it, I laugh – always a bad move in a library – and the rather beautiful Chinese student opposite me looks up from her computing textbook and quickly looks down again. She probably reckons me for a crazy person.

She is sitting at place 108. Each position in this gorgeous room has a number inlaid into the edge of the table. You could pick your lottery numbers on this basis. Choose the six best-looking women in the library and make a note of where they are sitting. If the numbers are too high, add the digits together, or drop the last digit. And now it suddenly occurs to me. I should do Yasmin's trick on her. Ask her to pick a number, and another, and another, and reverse it. And take the smaller from the larger and so on. Because by the time we get to the end, the first three digits of the final, inevitable answer – 1089 – will be *where she's sitting*. The effect would be fantastic. Too good an opportunity to miss, surely. She's immersed in her manual, some crashingly dull work about coding, no doubt. The lovely almond eyes in their perfect saucer face dance over the words. I tear off a piece of *New York Times* and scribble on it: 'Excuse me, sorry to disturb you, but are you interested in magic?' I pass it across.

She gets up and leaves without even a glance in my direction.

3

I can feel it when I sit down. The crackle of the fax paper in my back pocket with its memorable collection of horrible words and phrases. '. . . *specific failure . . . a grave disappointment . . . certain structural changes . . . best that you do not return.*' Actually, it's a masterpiece of shitty prose, moving comfortably between the insulting, '*personal belongings*', the threatening, '*proper receipts*', and the chilling, '*all the best in your future career*'. I can just picture the scene, Clive gravely reporting to Monty the news that Dave Cleaver and I go way back. His serious concern. The sober regret in his voice at the discovery, the dirty little cocksucker.

The woman opposite in the subway carriage looks

up from her paper and shoots me a look. The particular Manhattan look that says, *I have registered what you did, but I make no comment. Your medication may have worn off. You may have a claw hammer in your pocket. And anyhow, hey, this is New York City, right?* I have the horrible feeling that I have said something out loud. Specifically, the phrase 'dirty little cocksucker'.

Another milestone. I have joined the ranks of the people who talk to themselves. The not-quite-crazy, the not-quite-sane. And now, spilling through the train doors with the rest of the crowd into the clattering maelstrom of Union Square Station, I have the urge to try it properly.

'Dirty little cocksucker,' I utter in a regular speaking voice. No-one flinches. My words are completely lost in the roaring soundtrack of the city. On the steps up to the street, I have another go, this time with 'motherfucker', employing the local emphasis on the second part of the construction. It's oddly satisfying. I guess there are simply too many people, in too much of a hurry to worry about one daft bloke in a baseball cap speaking to himself. As we hit the pavement, I turn up the volume and address a further comment in the direction of my tennis shoes: 'fucking arsehole'. I feel no heads turning. This is normal for New York. I am invisible.

'Arsehole!' I am shouting now. 'ARSEHOLE! You TOTAL FUCKING *ARSEHOLE*!!'

When I look up, a small boy is staring straight at me over his father's shoulder.

In the Union Square café, I ask for a dry vodka Martini, light a cigarette and consider the arguments for and against the proposition that I am cracking up.

For:

1. **I talk aloud in the street (and not on mobile phone).**
2. **I have begun to scare young women.**
3. **I hang round in *libraries* (very damning).**
4. **I've been sacked.**
5. **Hilary – who *never* loses her rag – called me a stupid prick.**
6. **She's seeing someone else.**
7. **Only drink and dope cheer me up.**
8. **And smoked salmon @ Barney G.**
9. **Obsessed with Yasmin.**
10. **Am aimless. What am I doing here? Dossing with David bloody White.**

Against:

1. **Job loss is naturally stressful. Am probably in mild shock.**
2. **Crazy people *don't know* they're talking to themselves.**
3. **Libraries are also full of very brilliant people.**
4. **Loss of girlfriend is naturally stressful.**
5. **David White is OK really. (Apart from the teeth, obviously).**

Ten for, and only five against the motion that 'This house believes Michael Roe is losing it.' I guess if there were a show of hands right now in the old internal debating chamber, the verdict might suggest a spell in a darkened room with nothing stronger than fizzy water and the odd salad by way of stimulation.

'You stupid prick' pops up in my head, does a couple of laps round my skull and vanishes. I suppose I should feel pleased about Hilary really. After all, it was part of my masterplan to . . . let her go, as they say. I imagine that if I'd actually planned a scheme where *she* thought she was dumping *me* (while all the time *I* was really dumping *her*), then I should have been delighted with an end result where she didn't have to feel like a victim. Yet now, when it appears that she has unilaterally brought about the desired conclusion, I feel no urge to celebrate. In fact, if anything, the reverse.

Go figure, as Americans put it.

4

Hilary and I crossed the border of childhood and first became lovers at the University of Manchester. It was then – and remains, I believe – a fine institution offering young people a unique opportunity to learn vital lessons and make important mistakes within the context of a low-key academic environment. I learnt a lot there.

I learnt how to smoke marijuana, the crucial first step towards getting hooked on more addictive and dangerous substances like tobacco.

I learnt that when you are invited to a party, you should *never* arrive at the stated kick-off time because, if you do, for a long while You Will Be The Only Person There. (It happened. Burton Road, West Didsbury. I don't want to talk about it.)

During a statistics course, I learnt how to yawn with your mouth shut . . . *without* your eyes watering. This has been incredibly useful over the years. I speak as someone who has worked for the BBC.

I learnt how to drink beer. And how if you have too much, when you return from the students' union to your hall of residence and lie on the floor, the room will rotate *backwards* in a vertical plane. Always backwards, never forwards. Odd that.

I learnt how to play table football. How to get better action by greasing the metal poles with the inside of a used crisp packet. I learnt how saying 'nudge nudge wink wink' from *Monty Python's Flying Circus* would induce generous laughter in almost any circumstances. I learnt to like A Flock of Seagulls.

And I learnt about sex.

It was in my second year. Her name was Jennifer Settle. And if she wasn't Love's Young Dream, well, I wasn't exactly David Soul myself. But she liked me because I could make her laugh. And because

I was interested in her. And I was interested in her . . . because she was my exit visa from the State of Virginity.

I just knew her relationship with Dull Alan was pointless and going nowhere. In the communal kitchen of our hall of residence, she seemed bored with him, and rightly. He was one of those tragic Englishmen who are doubly cursed. Not only are they dull, they *know* they are dull. Fortunately, he was rather good-looking, so he never had to go to the trouble of developing a personality. Today I believe he is an Internet millionaire.

But Jennifer Settle sparkled for me. Her eyes (not her best feature) widened and glittered. Her lips (er, ditto) became playful and pouty. She did something with the angle of her face (a cruel joke, let's be blunt) that spoke of flirtation and desire. If she wanted a pointless, going-nowhere relationship, she might as well have one with me.

And I fancied her. No question about that. She was tall and slim. Her jeans looked like they were sprayed on. Not only could you count the exact change in her back pocket, as they said, you could tell heads from tails. In the charming phrase of the time, I wished to screw the arse off her.

Weirdly, when I got my wish, it was just how I imagined it. Maybe it always is for boys. In the silence afterwards, I recalled Sylvia Plath's phrase about becoming part of a Great Tradition. Jennifer sweetly guessed it was my first time.

The next day, walking along Manchester's

Oxford Road with an abnormally jaunty gait – and the feeling that I might have grown a bit more adult around the eyes – guess who I bumped into with a bundle of books under her arm?

Hilary, who'd become a first-year English student. In a particularly man-of-the-worldly fashion that morning, I took her to the students' union coffee bar where we caught up on each other's lives since she and her family moved to another suburb of North London.

Of course, I was aware that she would be coming to be a student in the city. My mother had warned me. And indeed I was pleased to see her. For one thing, I was dying to tell her – tell *anyone* – about last night. And also, when she took off her Afghan coat, I couldn't help noticing how well she had matured in the five years since we had last met.

She in her turn was keen to hear whatever Manchester wisdom I could pass on to her. The nicest areas to live. What to do at weekends. How to get tickets for George Michael.

'Have you got a girlfriend?' I remember her asking casually, rooting in her shoulder bag.

'No,' I replied. 'Not really. Well . . . actually there is someone.'

And then she did something that truly shocked me. Probably as much as when she called me a stupid prick. She pulled out twenty Embassy, flipped open the lid and pointed them at me.

Wordlessly, I shook my head and watched as she expertly lit one up, inhaled, extinguished the match with a flick of her wrist, dropped the pack back in her bag, the match in the foil ashtray, exhaled, and fired up a huge grin. The same fat-faced dimpled smile that used to say, *Let joy be unconfined, the trick has worked, the magician is a boy genius*.

'Well,' she asked. 'What's she like then?'

A fortnight later, Dull Alan had forgiven Jennifer Settle. And Hilary and I were shagging one another with an intensity and desperation that only two children brought up in a suburb like Finchley would understand.

5

We stayed together throughout the rest of my time at university. Having known one another since childhood made things *slightly* weird – I mean how much respect can you have for someone who you can remember talking to dolls? But the familiarity also brought an excitement, at least at first. Our relationship felt oddly illicit, almost incestuous, perhaps even a little impossible. Like the square root of minus one: I was an only child doing it with my sister. She too, I remember, used to find it strange. Lying in bed together, saying it was a miracle.

Over the years, I have asked other girlfriends to show me their childhood photos. I think lovers often do this. The curiosity about a part of the loved one's life that you can never share. With Hilary, of course, I never needed to. I knew. I was there.

At Manchester University, if Hilary represented the joy of the Familiar, then Olivia was the exoticism of Other. Hilary, I always felt, was curiously unthreatened by her, considering how much I fancied the creamy Devonian, and how readily I would have jumped into bed with her, had an invitation been forthcoming. I thought at the time that she simply didn't notice how much attention I paid to Olivia. Now I suspect that Hilary understood, with the instant sense women have of other women, that Olivia was completely disinterested in me.

We broke up for the first time when I went off to North Wales to be a newspaper reporter. I think we both knew we would. Too young to settle for each other right away, we needed to try plenty of other people first. I started going out with a beautiful green-eyed Welsh girl who worked in the *Wrexham Examiner*'s sales department. Before we were introduced, I hoped very much that her name would turn out to be Myfanwy. In this, I was denied. Nevertheless, Brenda was the first fully functional economically active adult that I had ever been to bed with (not a student) and I suppose I felt a little like a grown-up.

Hilary meanwhile effortlessly took up with a series of sporty types. For a few years, all her boyfriends had one-syllable names like Nick or Dave or Pete or Bob. They all seemed to play football on Saturday afternoons. Or belong to cycling clubs. One – was it Les? – was a climber. Every weekend for about six months, game old Hilary, ever unable to say no, would find herself roped to a cliff face in a howling wind, weeing herself with fear.

One night, about five years later, when we were both back in London, I a radio reporter, she a junior researcher on breakfast television, we met in a wine bar in the West End. I'd just broken up with Tamara (beautiful, mad) and she had finished with Rick (videotape editor, golfer). We drank rather a lot and I expect you can probably guess the rest.

If anything, the second time around seemed even better. I suppose we had both matured a bit through other relationships. And the sex, to be bald about it, was joyous. For another couple of years we were Michael 'n' Hilary. We did all the couple-ly things that couples do. Went to dinner parties, took holidays together. Saw movies. Ate in restaurants. Attended the weddings of our friends.

When the end came, I'd supposed that it was all my fault. The growing sense that ultimately she wasn't for me. But by the time I came to tell her that there was someone else I was interested in – Myrna (beautiful, mad) – she told me about somebody who'd been paying *her* a lot of attention lately. Tim, a photographer. Oh, and a surfer, naturally.

I never even got to sleep with Myrna. Hilary and Tim stayed together for three years. Of all of Hilary's boyfriends, Tim was the one I came to know the best. Indecently handsome – Hilary once called him '*painfully* good-looking' – Tim was chronically pleasant to everyone he encountered, his only serious failing in my view. Actually, thinking about it, he didn't have much of a sense of humour either. But I learnt a lot about photography from him. I even liked him. I liked him mainly because he loved Hilary so much. He was utterly devoted to her, he would have married her without a second thought, and he was shattered when she finally gave him his cards.

'Why?' I'd asked her over steamed scallops and sake.

She wiped away a tear. 'Oh, I don't know. Tim's lovely but he never says anything . . . *surprising*.'

'It's surprises you want, is it? Well, tell me this. What fucks like a tiger and winks?'

'I don't know. What does fuck like a tiger and wink?'

I gazed into her face, held for a beat, and winked.

Hilary laughed like no-one had told her a joke for a very long time. When she eventually recovered, she put down her chopsticks, sighed heavily and said, 'Michael, can I stay with you tonight?'

The interlude with Olivia aside, we've been together ever since.

6

It occurs to me this might be a good time to give up smoking. Not when everything's going great and you'd really notice the introduction of some new misery in your life. No, do it when the world has turned to cack, when one more lump is not going to make any difference. Do it tomorrow.

On the way back to David White's apartment, a huge roach, the size of a walnut half, emerges from a crack between the paving slabs. It's practically under my feet and I shy like a horse. A mad drunk cackles with laughter at the sight.

'New York City, man,' he shouts. 'New York *fuckin'* City.'

The fanged one is seated up one end of the twenty-foot sofa rolling a joint when I get back. From the fug of hash hanging in the air, I can tell it's not the first of the evening. I take my place down the other end and watch him at work. He's rolling up on an old album cover, the sleeve of Pink Floyd's *Dark Side of the Moon*. Probably the only piece of vinyl in the apartment. Lights are twinkling across the Hudson.

'I love that album,' I say by way of an ice-breaker. He looks absorbed, distracted. 'Used to play it all the time when I was at university.'

'Where d'you go to college?' he asks.

'Manchester. Oddly enough, I used to know a David White there. Though he was more of a Dave White, I think.'

'Uh-huh.'

'Often wonder what happened to him.'

'Wanna put a CD on?'

'Sure.' I set off for the hi-fi. 'What are you in the mood for?' I yell as the orange sofa recedes into the distance.

'Whatever you like. I'm kind of . . . done making decisions today.' Oh, Jesus Christ. What's the matter with him? I'm supposed to be the miserable one round here. I put on a collection of operatic arias. Great passion expressed in a foreign language calms the soul, don't you find?

I begin the long walk back to my place. When I arrive, David White hands me the smouldering joint and I take a deep hit. After seven seconds – the time necessary for the oxidised drug products to travel from my lungs into my blood stream and then across the blood-brain barrier – I feel my various problems start up their engines and begin to move off my lawn. There is a quality to Maria Callas now that wasn't there seven seconds ago. She sounds richer, deeper, fuller. *Better*. And, yes, I believe I just heard my stomach making reservations for a portion of hamburger and fries the size of a football.

'Fuck, that's strong,' I utter after a couple more drags. I think it's only good manners to compliment the householder on the quality of his narcotics. 'Pakistani?' I ask, thinking of the mother-slab lying in the freezer.

'Something like that. It came from one of my Media students. In lieu of course fees.' He grins, a terrible prospect when sober, but now a truly ghastly thing to behold. Even in the mercifully low lighting, the huge teeth just keep on coming as the smile grows wider. More and more of the bastards, in a drug-induced multiple edit, like George

Orwell's jackboot stamping on a human face for all eternity – his definition of hell, as I recall. I have to look away.

When I look back, David White is quietly sobbing.

Oh fuck. *Tilt*.

You know when you play pinball and you're so into the game, rocking about, whacking those little flippers, that maybe you're just a bit too rough with the machine? And suddenly nothing will work any more. The buttons go dead, and the ball just rolls uselessly away down the hole. Well, it's what the pinball machine says, when its world is rocked. It's what I'm thinking right now.

Tilt. Men do not weep in front of other men. They weep in darkness at the movies. Or maybe at Loftus Road after a late equaliser. But not like this. He's dying of cancer. He can't come to terms with some ghastly compulsion. He's fallen in love with me. *What*?

'Er, what's wrong, David?' His shoulders are shaking now, great heaving sobs are squeezing themselves out of him. Horribly, his lips have peeled back into their corners and the full night-marish set of molars, canines and incisors is on view. You can probably see them from New Jersey.

'It's this track, man,' he splutters. 'It always does me.'

I begin the long trek to the CD player to check out the label. And also to remove myself from this embarrassing spectacle. It's from *Cavalleria Rusticana*. Santuzza, the peasant girl, is singing of her tragic love for Turiddu, a young soldier who is himself in love with Lola, who is married to Alfio. (A fuck-up, in other words.)

By the time I return, he's composed himself sufficiently to begin rolling another joint, the first one still smouldering away between his lips.

'Sorry about that, man,' he says.

'Please. No worries,' I assure him. As if grown men burst into tears in front of me four or five times a day.

'It's when she sings *io piango, io piango, io piango* at the end. Means "I weep" in Italian. Fucking gets me every time.'

'Just as well she's not singing Italian for "I shit myself",' I toss in merrily to lighten the mood.

This doesn't play as brilliantly as I had hoped. Indeed I think he shoots me a dirty look. Or maybe it's just his regular expression, it's kind of hard to tell. Anyhow, David White is clearly not a man to bear a grudge because he mashes out the original joint, lights the second, takes half-a-dozen drags and sportingly passes it over.

'How long have you known Yasmin?' he asks after a while.

'Couple of months. Why?'

'Classy chick.'

'Er, yes.' Outside of a seventies movie, it is a while since I've heard anyone use this expression. Is he being ironic? Post-ironic even?

'And a very beautiful lady.' Where's he getting this terrible dialogue?

'She spoke highly of you too.' Might as well cheer the sad fuck up a bit.

'Reminded me of my ex-wife.'

'I didn't know you'd been divorced,' I say as kindly as possible.

'She . . . we broke up last year.'

'Had you been together a long time?'

'Five years.'

'I'm sorry. That must be tough.' Hey, he's not the only one who can do corny lines round here.

'What happened?' I ask after a short pause for respect. 'Did it just fizzle . . .'

'. . . She sent me an e-mail. Said she was sorry, but we'd grown apart. That there was no-one else.' He takes a deep breath. 'Apparently the things about me that first attracted her, now repel her,' he adds bitterly.

I leave an extra long p for r. 'You didn't have any children, I take it.'

'No. Diane doesn't want any. She's in love with her work.'

'Really. What sort of work does she do?'

'She's a dentist.'

For a while, it's touch and go. I have to contrive a major coughing fit to conceal my hilarity. Even minutes later, I can still feel my mouth twisting with the appalling urge to hoot with laughter.

7

'Mike, Yasmin is the first woman who I've come anywhere near wanting since Diane left.'

For a start . . .

1. **No-one calls me Mike.**
2. **We're four joints and half a bottle of frozen Stolly to the bad.**
3. **He's been drivelling on about Y. If it weren't for the drink and drugs (see 2, above), the stunning view and the incomparable stereo system, I'd be bored shitless.**
4. **But I've worked it out. The essential tragedy of David White: he is irredeemably cheesy. He can't help himself. Everything that pops out of his mouth is a cliché. In that ridiculous half-English, half-American accent.**

'And I know, I just *know* she was attracted to me. A guy feels these things.' *See what I mean?*

'It's a bloody tragedy,' I sympathise. 'Fine girl like that marrying a great plank of wood called Nick.'

'You met him?'

'Well, no. But I can just imagine.' I picture a fit, blond male. Cufflinks and a tennis racket. No, Yasmin would go for someone cooler than that. I see combat trousers. The impression of a six-pack stomach through a tight T-shirt. Hair cut with a pair of secateurs. But what about the his 'n' hers tennis rackets propped against the wall? Cool people don't play tennis, do they? It's too undignified.

'You know how women want to be wanted, Mike? Well, I really turned it on for her. Gave her all my killer stuff. And she was buying it. Big time.'

'Really? What happened?'

'We were getting closer and closer. She's looking directly into my eyes and I'm looking directly into hers and this is the moment. So I do the exact same thing I did to Diane on our third date. I lick my finger, I touch my shoulder, I touch her shoulder and I say,' – *oh my God, he didn't* – '"How about you and I go back to my place and get out of these wet clothes?"' *She didn't even tell me his worst line.*

'Like I say,' I say, 'it's tragic.'

'You know what? Life is slipping me by, Mike.' I feel unable to protest. About the Mike thing, about the life thing. 'Oh sure, I'm making a ton of money out of the Media Studies Academy. Thank God for all the rich kids who want to come to New York and learn about TV for a thousand bucks a week. But . . . I'm going to be forty in two years.' He looks at me as if he has just been diagnosed with a fatal illness. 'Whatever it is I should be doing, I'm not doing it. Whoever she is I should be with, I'm not with her. I mean, life is not a rehearsal, right? Gotta seize the fuckin' moment.'

Oh Jesus Christ. Not again. Life is not a bleeding rehearsal.

'There are six billion people alive on the earth right now,' I explain. 'I read it in the *New York Times*. They can't all go round seizing the moment. There'd be chaos.'

I pour another pair of frozen Stollys into the tiny shot glasses and expand on my theme. (I think the fourth joint may have been particularly powerful.)

'I object to this whole seize-the-moment mentality. I think it's fucking weird enough that we are here *at all*, never mind having to snap to it and seize the moment before someone else does. I think everyone should just calm down and recognise that our lives are . . . miraculously pointless. I mean, tell me. What is the actual *point* of all these people out there? On the street, in the subway, getting in the way. What's the point of everyone? Apparently it's not to be happy, fulfilled and purposeful. Not a lot of that going on so far as I can tell.'

David White gazes at me blankly. And now I hear the words of Montgomery Dodd. It was the night of the Belvedere Christmas party a couple of years back. A small gang of us including Steve, Clive, Monty and I are shoving our way through Leicester Square. Finding it difficult to actually make progress, so thick is the crowd. I'm sliding past eight-foot Swedes in slippery parkas, pressing into red-faced office workers with lipstick on their cheeks, snagging on people's overcoat buttons; at one point I hiss tetchily, 'God, what is the *point* of all these people?'

'The *point* of all these people?' says Montgomery Dodd who is struggling alongside me. 'The point is *To Sell Things To Them*. Mobile telephones, CDs, TV shows, fried chicken. Everybody wants the same things.' At the time it felt like a nasty little revelation.

'I guess Yasmin could have turned out to be one big bitch. Just like my wife.'

Oh give it a rest. 'I guess so.'

'I guess there are no rules,' he says gloomily. 'What you think you want may not in the end be what makes you happy.'

'Actually I think there *are* a few rules,' I say just to be difficult. 'Never play poker with anyone called Doc. That's a rule I read somewhere.'

'Why not?'

'Oh, you know. Because you'll get skinned alive. Same reason you should never eat anywhere called Momas. Always leave the party when someone starts singing *American Pie*. That's another one. And *never* . . . fuck with the Mexicans.'

'That is so fucking true, Mike.' And David White's head drops forward and he is asleep.

I walk over to the B&O and flip through the CDs. And because I haven't heard it for ages, I put on The Rolling Stones' *Let It Bleed*.

A few minutes later, if someone watching from New Jersey, through a high-powered telescope let's say, were to alight on a large illuminated window on the seventh floor of a particular building in the former Meat Packing District, they would witness

– instead of the hoped-for beautiful young woman getting ready for bed – a male figure in unfashionable glasses (and in need of a proper haircut) bopping ridiculously. There are outbreaks of air guitar and the blatant miming of rock vocals. Once, twice, five times in all, after exactly the same interval, he disappears from view for a short time and returns. A seasoned observer of such male nocturnal activity might correctly guess that the figure is paying repeated visits to a sound system to re-start a favourite track. But would he guess that tonight the figure has found a wisdom and acceptance in the words, music, and above all, the title of that track – *You Can't Always Get What You Want* – that had previously gone unnoticed? That tonight, despite his various troubles, the figure is oddly at peace with the world. And that by this time tomorrow, he'll be riding back over the Atlantic Ocean to Merry Old London Town.

3

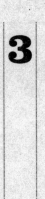

EIGHT

1

The radio alarm clock is playing as I step through my front door.

'. . . And your luxury?' There is a deep and pregnant pause. Then a male voice, the rich, deliberate sort that can belong only to an actor. 'I think, I should very much like a really splendid leather armchair.' Arm *chair*, he says. As opposed to arm sofa or arm stool. 'I should like to spend evenings on the island, sitting in my arm *chair* . . . reading, thinking . . . and remembering all the really . . . *good* times one has been lucky enough to enjoy.'

She thinks it can be arranged. What a fucking relief *that* must be. I hit the off switch. Dear old England.

My flat looks the same. As I drift from room to room – no burglary, no water leaks – all the *stuff* of my old life rears up to claim me. An unwashed mug in the kitchen sink, the last coffee before the minicab to Heathrow. The worrying towers of paperbacks and videos, their architecture as familiar and as unchanged as that of Haverstock Hill itself. My reflection in the bathroom mirror, stubbly and red-eyed, seen through a homely dapple of toothpaste spit. A *lot* of messages on the answerphone.

1. **My mother. Her loopy friend has helpfully told her there is a madman on the loose in New York bashing people over the head with bricks. 'So, be careful. Don't go to any funny places.'**
2. **Hilary. 'Michael, where are you? We need to talk.'**
3. **Steve. 'Sorry to hear about what happened. What an absolute bummer. Give us a call sometime and we'll plan revenge on you-know-who, who seems to be in charge of everything now by the way.'**
4. **Mouse. 'Sorry to hear your bit of bad luck.' *How the fuck did he find out?* 'If you fancy a few jars to drown your sorrows, give me a bell at the office.'**

5. **Claudia. 'I'm so sorry. You must come over for dinner.'**
6. **Hilary. 'Michael, the hotel say you've checked out. There's something you should know.'**
7. **Howard (old friend; never calls). 'Been a while. Just wondering how you were. Give us a ring sometime.' *He knows.***
8. **Denise (minor ex). 'How *are* you? Be great to catch up.' *She knows.***
9. **Nicole. 'Calling about the Jack Russell.' A wrong number. *Does she know?***
10. **Jane Farnsworth. Belvedere's 'Human Resources Manager'. When would I like the courier to deliver a 'bin bag' of my personal belongings?**
11. **Olivia. Do I know anyone who speaks Yiddish? And by the way, she is very sorry to hear about my 'news'. Yeah, right.**
12. **Hilary. Am I going to call. Or what?**
13. **Hilary. 'All right, *be* a stupid prick and *don't* call. Actually there's someone I want you to meet. He's called Vic.' *No, don't tell me. He's a potholer.***

Not a peep from Yasmin. I don't feel like speaking to anyone, with the possible exception of Nicole about the Jack Russell. Especially not Hilary.

I recall Steve's theory of friends rallying round in the face of adversity. They're not really phoning to commiserate, he reckons. They're phoning for the *details*.

So I sit down to open my mail. Of course, it's all window envelopes. You only see actual handwriting these days on your birthday and Christmas. So it's the usual collection. The mobile-phone bill. Offers of health insurance. The *Sunday Times* believe I should be in their Wine Club. Someone's going to *pay me* to select six free paperbacks. Oh, and here's a cheque from a tabloid newspaper for one thousand pounds.

I pick up the phone and dial.

'Dave Cleaver, entertainment.'

'Dave, this is Michael Roe.' I hope he can hear the permafrost in my voice.

'Oh hello, chief. You calling about your money? Sorry to hear they gave you the Black Spot, incidentally.'

'You've got some fucking . . . neck. Is there anyone you won't turn over for a story?' A pause on the line. As if he's considering the question.

'Michael, if you mean the piece about Angelica, that'll never come back to you, scouts honour. We're as tight as a gnat's chuff at this end. Got a lovely show, did you see it?'

'Yes I bloody did see it.'

'There'll be another little . . . consideration for that, if it'll make life easier, chief.'

'Do you actually have a grandmother, Dave? And if so, how much do you want for her?' The biting sarcasm is wasted.

'Clive Wilson has bobbed up nicely again from what I hear,' he offers cheerfully.

'Yes. So I gather.'

'Tell you what. So there's no hard feelings, let's have dinner next week. We'll go somewhere splashy.'

'What makes you think that I ever want to be seen with you again, Dave?'

'Don't be like that, I'm buying. I'll put you down as a "leading media analyst". Seeing as how you're no longer a "studio insider".'

2

Quit when it's shit.

That was the slogan doing circuits in my head during the seven hours of cold turkey better known as the flight from JFK to LHR. I did everything I could to take my mind off the gnawing desire for a single – always a single – cigarette. I drank heavily. I watched the movies (everyone smoking like a train of course). I watched the air hostesses, one in particular, very pretty in an obvious sort of way. Melanie Potts, it said on her badge. In fact I developed a full-blown fantasy about her in which, as the plane makes a terrifying emergency landing, she unaccountably finds herself in my arms. 'Melanie Potts?' I say as the great 747 pitches and yaws on its hellish descent. 'Yes?' she replies. The fuselage shudders violently and she whimpers in fear. 'Melanie Potts, if we come out of this alive . . . can I see you again?' She looks into my eyes. Her teeth are chattering. 'Yes,' she says. I squeeze her tightly to me. We feel the undercarriage rumble into place. 'Melanie. I know this is a non-smoking flight. But *please* . . . could we have just one last fucking cigarette?' She whips out a packet of Marlboro that's been tucked up the sleeve of her blouse. We both take one and she fires us up with a gold Dunhill lighter. We smoke. And that's it. That's all that happens. The plane doesn't crash, or not crash, or even land. We just hang there, on our final descent, smoking Marlboro, me with pretty Melanie Potts sitting on my lap.

But in real life, I haven't actually smoked. Not even in the minicab back to Belsize Park. Quit when it's shit. Let there be one good thing to come out of this mess. Worth a shot, surely.

So I've taken myself for a walk on Hampstead Heath – well why not? It's a beautiful morning and I haven't got a job to go to – and I'm lapping up the space and the silence after the teeming, clamorous pavements of Manhattan. The leaves are going brown, there's that first tug of autumn in the air and I guess I should feel liberated: after all I'm being paid to do nothing for six weeks before I have to even think of looking for work. But this doesn't feel like liberation to me. This feels like deprivation. Oh fuck it. This feels like I want a cigarette.

I pass a young woman walking an improbable Borzoi. If this were Central Park I'd probably have said, 'Hey, great dog. Is that a Borzoi?' But as this is North London, convention dictates that we remain silent unless I too have a dog – in which case it wouldn't be considered eccentric or dangerous to exchange information about breeds, ages, temperaments and worming tablets.

What was it Yasmin told me she had read in the book about how to stop smoking? That you should think of your withdrawal pains as the death agonies of the nicotine monster inside you. Each pang is his cry of anguish. Take a masochistic pleasure in your own suffering, because it is the monster's suffering. And in . . . three weeks, did she say? . . . it will be dead.

Three weeks? How am I going to last three *hours*?

Quit when it's shit, that's my motto. Let it be an atoll of success in an ocean of disappointment.

I'm approaching a couple on a bench. They're in their forties. Even from yards away, it's clear they're having a heart-to-heart. She has his hands in hers, and she's staring intently into his face in a way that I know would make me want to slap her.

'I was so bewildered when you started that thing again yesterday,' she says. Happily, I miss his reply.

I pass a father and son; father in elephant cords and a v-neck, son, early teens, overweight and awkward. A terrible silence hangs between them. A little further along the path, I get a lingering look from a strange young woman in odd yellow trousers.

The world is full of people and their stories. Weird David White, still weeping over a woman who only wanted him for his teeth, and then not at all. Czeslaw Waldzneij, killer of women and children, rolling cigarettes in his dark, overheated apartment. At the thought, I have a powerful, almost *physical* surge of desire for a cigarette. A roll-up. The lovely moist brown tobacco, its caramel smoke gladdening your lungs. That Nazi bastard obviously smoked all his life. How did *he* get away with it?

I am a hedonist. I love all the pleasures life has to throw at me. How could I deny myself a single one? I hear Yasmin's reply in my ear. Because it's *not* a pleasure, you just think it is. Not the addition of pleasure, merely the cancellation of pain. Pain that was caused by learning to smoke in the first place. I wish Yasmin were here now, to cancel some of my pain. The pain of not seeing her. Pain that was caused by getting to know her in the first place.

Is Yasmin like smoking then? If I hadn't met her, I wouldn't miss her, that's for sure.

By the time I make it back to the pond at the bottom of Parliament Hill, I have a new list of things to do. Shorter, as befits my new unemployed status.

1. **Call Yasmin.**
2. **Find the *real* David White. The one I used to get stoned with in Manchester. What the hell happened to him?**
3. **Don't smoke. Do anything else . . . but not that.**

3

But.

Have you noticed, there's always a 'but' hanging over everything? Call Yasmin, yes, but what if she's suddenly all distant with me? Find the real Dave White, OK, but actually, why? What if we've got nothing in common any more? Don't smoke, but . . . what will I do *instead*? And how will I ever manage a bowel movement again?

So I've gone to see the doctor. I'm sitting in his surgery watching him fumbling through my notes trying to remember who I am. My GP is very old, but that's fine. I trust old doctors. They've seen it all before. And mine is Methuselah. I once bumped into him coming out of the local undertakers, where he'd gone to write a death certificate (they can't bury you without one). When I told him that I was one of his patients, he looked a bit alarmed and replied, 'It wasn't one of mine, you know.'

'Ah yes,' he says, his nose finally emerging from the notes, 'we last prescribed some drops for a minor eye infection. All cleared up nicely, I assume. Now, what can we do for you today?'

'Well, doctor, I'm very concerned that I may die prematurely.' Actually I do not say this. You're not allowed to in doctors' surgeries, it's thought to be in bad taste. In fact I say, 'I want to give up smoking.'

'Excellent. How can I help?'

'I was rather hoping you might be able to give

me some . . . medical backup. Are there any pills to make it easier? Or maybe some horrible facts would help.'

'I'm afraid there are no pills. And I'm sure you know all the horrible facts, as you put it. You'll just have to endure some mild withdrawal symptoms for a few weeks. Motivation is the most important factor, you know. Try not to weaken. If you really want to give up, then you will. Millions have. Now, is anything else troubling you at all?' *Stop wasting my time. Get out of my surgery. Get a grip. Grow up.*

'What about nicotine chewing-gum? Or patches. Would you recommend either of those?'

He peers at me over the top of his spectacles.

'Mr . . . er . . . Roe. I'm very glad you want to stop smoking. It is the single most effective measure you can take to improve your health. But nicotine is a deadly poison. Did you know that seven drops of pure nicotine will kill a horse?'

I am ready for this one.

'I wasn't aware nicotine was a big issue with horses,' I joke winningly. 'There were none in the waiting room.'

He looks at me as if I were mucus on a microscope slide.

'Other physicians may take a different view,' he says, pressing the tips of his fingers together annoyingly, 'but I am fundamentally philosophically opposed to any treatment which *perpetuates* the addiction, albeit in a different medium. The best way to stop smoking is simply to stop. Now, is anything else troubling you at all?'

'Well, I did get this funny pain under my arm.'

'Aha.' All of a sudden the old goat is interested. He starts asking questions and scribbling in his notes. When did it start? Stabbing or throbbing? Always in the same place? Or does it move around? How often does it appear? He tells me to take my shirt off, gets me up on the ramp and has a feel about.

'Well, there's nothing there. All perfectly normal,' he says when we're all sat down again. And then he does it. He leans back in his chair, pushes his specs down to the end of his nose, looks over the top of them, pauses for timing and asks, 'Anything happening in your *life* at all?'

It comes spilling out. The work thing. The Hilary thing. The Yasmin thing.

'I'm not surprised you've been getting the odd twinge,' he says after I give him edited highlights of my recent life. 'Losing your job and this business with . . . the ladies sounds very stressful. I'd say your pains were what we call somatic. You were expressing the pain in your life by putting them in your body.'

'But that's the funny thing. Since everything's gone belly-up, they've stopped.'

'That's exactly the pattern I would expect. Still,' he says rising to his feet, 'it's better to be alive with a few worries than dead with none. Do try to enjoy your time off.'

4

If this were a movie, there'd be a music sequence now. The actor playing me – Hugh Grant, let's say – would be seen going into the optician's trying on various absurd pairs of glasses. There'd be lots of shots of him striking poses in mirrors, trying to decide. You know the sort of thing . . .

CLOSE UP on HUGH seen in mirror. He's wearing a particularly silly set of frames. HUGH does a 'well, what do you think?' expression with his eyebrows. The camera then SHIFTS FOCUS to the background where the ATTRACTIVE FEMALE OPTICIAN is sensibly shaking her head.

He finally settles for some of those narrow rectangular specs that all the young people are wearing these days. Then we cut to the hairdresser's. Hugh's in some ultra-groovy salon, full of male models and pop musicians. Lots of snippety-snip. Extreme close ups of sideburns being shaped, ear-hair being trimmed. When we're finished and Hugh has a nice Julius Caesar job, the camera pulls back to reveal his male stylist is totally bald.

And now we're in Islington. Hugh's wandering through secondhand furniture shops looking for a filing-cabinet. He's inspecting old wooden ones, trying drawers, blowing the dust off surfaces and coughing. He's looking at an architect's plan cabinet, opens a drawer, and it comes right out, spilling blueprints of long-demolished buildings all over the floor. Eventually, he decides on an old four-drawer metal jobby, stylishly stripped back to the original steel. The quaint stallholder puts a SOLD sticker on it.

And now we dissolve back to my flat. It's early evening. A high shot of the sitting room. The new filing-cabinet stands nicely in the corner, a lava lamp blobbing away on top. I am sitting on the floor, in the middle of a sea of printed material. Old photos, credit-card statements, council-tax bills, newspaper cuttings, letters, takeaway menus, electrical-appliance guarantees, piles and piles of the *stuff* of one's life. I am sorting through it, arranging it in heaps, and putting the heaps into files. I am writing things like 'MORTGAGE' and 'CAR INSURANCE' on the hanging-file tabs. I am taking control. Organising myself. As the music dies away (*Getting Better* off *Sergeant Pepper*), the camera finds me on the phone.

'Are you *supposed* to keep your Visa statements? And what about old bank statements. How long are you supposed to keep them for? I mean no-one ever tells you any of this, do they?'

'I just bin it all myself. Nothing seems to happen.' In the background there's a familiar *ping-rasp*-(pause)-*snap*.

'And how about this, a cutting about tennis holidays. I thought I might go on one. It's what, five years old? Keep or chuck?'

'I think you know what to do,' says Steve darkly. I screw up the yellowing piece of newspaper and add it to a growing pile. There is something very therapeutic about Sorting Things Out. Sad too. Cards bearing endearments from defunct girlfriends (file under 'MISCELLANEOUS PERSONAL'). Orders of Service from their marriages years later. Invitations to the Christenings of their children. In some ways the Visa statements are even more telling. Measuring out your life in credit-card impressions. Jet Service Station, Sainsburys S/Mkt, Odeon Camden Town, Oddbins, Our Price Records, Waterstone & Co. The dreadful inventory of Taj Mahals, China Gardens, Siam Cottages, Sushi Bunkers and Villa Biancas.

'I've stopped smoking, by the way,' I remark. I can practically smell Steve's cigarette down the other end of the line. 'So don't offer me any.'

'I won't. What technique are you using?'

'The do-anything-you-want, be-as-badly-behaved-as-you-want-but-just-don't-smoke technique. Combined with some philosophy of nicotine. And plain old masochism. That's helping too. The main thing is to feel like it's a liberation, not a sacrifice.'

'Sounds like a very mature approach. Still, these things aren't for everyone.' I hear the end of his fag crackle as he takes another deep drag.

'So, tell me, changing the subject. Shitbird rules the world, eh?'

'He does,' says Steve. 'They're calling him Executive *Editor* now. The most horrible detail is that he's gone out and bought a couple of expensive suits to look powerful in. And you know how some people just can't carry it off. Well, he *can*. The bastard looks groomed for it.'

'God, he must be enjoying this so much. Perhaps we don't have to kill him, maybe he'll just explode with his own self-importance.' I recount to Steve the story about the man carrying the table leg who was killed by a police sharpshooter. 'What do you think we could get him to carry on a dark night that a trained marksman might mistake for a weapon?' I ask.

'I don't know. But I know what he'd love to do.'

'What?'

'Win an award. You know, actually go up and collect one. A Golden Rose of Montreux. Or a Bafta. I can just see him, springing up the stairs, buttoning the Armani on the way. Thanking all the little people who made it possible.'

'You're right. Fuck, he'd even leap at some dopey little prize, wouldn't he? TV Show of the Year . . . as voted by the readers of *Incontinence Pants Monthly*.'

'Or the award for Best Use of an Aubergine in a Factual Programme.'

'Yes, the premier honour in the gift of the Aubergine Advisory Council.'

'The Golden Aubergine of Kidderminster. A perspex aubergine, mounted on a plinth.'

'Know what, Steve? Oddly enough, I think we may have something here.'

When I put down the phone, I sit for a moment

and survey the paper slurry that is obscuring a significant portion of the sitting-room floor. The trouble with organising your life is that, as well as being therapeutic and occasionally moving, it can also be a pain in the arse. Does it really matter that you can't *immediately* lay your hands on the trouble-shooting guide for the dishwasher, as long as you know it's *somewhere*? No, sorry. That's entirely the wrong attitude. It *does* very much matter, but maybe not just this minute. I pick up all the sub-heaps and assemble them into a master-heap. The master-heap, gratifyingly, fits perfectly into the bottom drawer of the filing cabinet.

Sorted.

Buy groovier specs ☑

Get a proper haircut ☑

Buy filing cabinet ☑

Give up smoking [?]

Don't know what to do about that last box. Bit presumptuous to tick it. But bad faith not to. Well, as I used to say last week when I was a television producer, let's not worry about that now.

I pour myself a glass of red wine, pick up the phone and – God, I'd love a cigarette to accompany this call – dial a number in Queen's Park.

5

'What's the score?' Yasmin's standing at the net, red-faced, hand on hip, panting slightly. Dead leaves are blowing round our feet, but it's one of those crisp, bright days where a game of tennis has the power to make you feel more alive than almost anything else I can think of.

'Thirty-fifteen,' I yell back. Five games all, first set. Sunday afternoon in late September. A public court in London, England. I'm having a hard time concentrating on the game. I mean tennis is kind of . . . *sexual*, isn't it. Not in the sense of tiny skirts and a flash of knicker – good grief, she's wearing a baggy T-shirt and shapeless tracksuit bottoms – no, it's more to do with the rampant physicality of the thing. A man and a woman bashing a ball back and forwards between them. And of course there's the corny old matter of the language of tennis. Your head is full of words like *Love. Advantage. Game. Match. Serve. Service. Receive. Deep penetrating cross-court return.* To say nothing of *high toss* or *new balls, please*.

She doesn't play like she did in my dream (where if you recall, there was no question of any T-shirts or tracksuitings). For a start, she's got a silly serve. It looks fine until she comes to hit the ball, and then she *squats* slightly, as if she were laying an egg. Nor does she step into the shot, or follow through so the racket head ends up over her shoulder. But she's scarily . . . not bad. As the score suggests, round about as not bad as me. She's a solid safety player, getting everything back, not hitting any winners, letting me make the mistakes. And I'm making plenty. Over-anxious to shine, I'm hitting them all over the shop. But I don't care. I'm just happy to see her. Her presence has cancelled the pain of her absence.

When I called, she'd said Nick was away for the weekend. And, yes, it would be *lovely* to get together. I'd suggested the tennis and she'd said great, let's play at her local courts, grab showers back at her place, and then find a nice spot for drinks and dinner. 'Yasmin,' I'd said. 'I can't think of anything I'd rather do.' Which wasn't strictly accurate of course.

At 5–6, 30–40, and I'm serving to stay in the set, she hits a deep one and utterly uncharacteristically runs to the net. This so unsettles me, that my certain forehand passing-shot winner clips the edge of my racket and soars into the air, disrupting the flightpath of some passing gulls. I hear nearby small children laughing. She wins 7–5.

As we walk back through the park, I ask her. 'When you rushed the net on set point. Did you do that deliberately to rattle me?'

Her eyes flash in the autumn sunlight. She raises an eyebrow. Maybe two. 'I did actually,' she says. 'You've got to seize the moment, haven't you? Shit or get off the pot, as I believe the expression goes.'

Do you think she is trying to tell me something?

6

We come back to Yasmin's flat. Satan does that cat-round-your-ankles thing where you're meant to think they're being friendly but actually they're smearing you with a territorial marker. (I've never felt the same about cats since discovering that one.) Yasmin cracks open a bottle of white wine and goes off to take a shower, leaving me to play with the CD and flip through her books and mags. There's *Vogue*, *Hello!*, *Time Out*. On the shelves I clock the copy of *The Talented Mr Ripley*. There's obvious university stuff like *The Canterbury Tales* and *Daniel Deronda*. But here, too, are copies of my three favourite novels, *Lolita*, *Tender is the Night* and *Brideshead Revisited*, all looking as though they've been well read. Never mind the squatty serve, we'll get past that. I have no doubt in my mind, this is the woman for me.

So shit or get off the pot. You heard the lady.

When she returns, it's in jeans and a jumper. Her feet are bare and her hair is still wet. I have the powerful thought, *She's been naked in the shower. Rubbing soap, God knows where.* Yasmin curls into an armchair, closely followed by Satan and lights a cigarette.

'You look different,' she says. 'Have you done something?'

'I've shaved my beard off.' I reply, slightly stung that she didn't notice my transformation instantly.

'No, come on, what is it?' I do what the doc

did, push the glasses down my nose and peer over the top of them. 'Of course,' she says. 'New specs. They suit you. Very hardcore.'

'I was looking at your books,' I say to change the subject. *Let's just forget the sixty-quid haircut, shall we?* 'Did you like *Lolita*?' I ask her. 'I adore that book.'

'I read it at school. I think I thought he was a dirty old perve.'

'Yes, a lot of women read it too young. It's a very beautiful love story really, you know.' *Calling Humbert Humbert a perve is like calling Bertie Wooster a twerp. Not at all the point.*

'What about *Brideshead*?' I inquire.

'That might be Nick's, actually.'

I go off for a shower without asking about the Scott Fitzgerald. The man's blue shirt that was hanging on the bathroom door is missing today. Nor in the jumble of toiletries on show is there anything suggestive of a regular male visitor. When I return to the sitting room, lamps have been lit, low music is playing and Yasmin is bending over my wineglass filling it very full. Much fuller than is normally considered polite.

Blimey, if that's her attitude, fuck polite. Let's drink.

7

We haven't gone out. Darkness has fallen and we've moved on from white wine to White Russians

– vodka, Kahlua and milk – the preferred beverage of the central character in the movie *The Big Lebowski*. We've agreed this is one of our favourite films of recent years, though I'm sure The Dude (Jeff Bridges) didn't mix them with *supermarket* vodka as Yasmin has. OK, not a crime against humanity, but still in pretty poor taste if you ask me. Nutritionally, White Russians are a good source of milk (contains calcium for teeth and bones), worth remembering if you don't eat breakfast cereal or prefer your coffee black. The taste is not unlike Baileys, but *unlike* Baileys, of which it's impossible to drink more than a few thimbles, an excess of White Russians can lead you to wake up the following morning in a neighbouring county with a radical new identity.

I like them enormously.

Yasmin hasn't noticed that I haven't smoked a cigarette yet. She, of course, has been going like a train since we arrived. The White Russians have dulled my craving for nicotine, though they have done nothing for my craving for her. She is rabbitting on about some play she's seen above a pub in Hammersmith, and I am wondering what it would be like to undo the buttons of her baby-blue jumper.

She's curled tightly into her chic junk-shop armchair, Satan draped across the back. She's wiggling her long thin toes and gabbling away (this play has greatly impressed her) and I'm staring at her, not hearing a word (goodness me, the author must be a sodding genius) when, for a moment, she seems not a goddess to me any more but, well, more like a madwoman. She looks bonkers. The great eyes are blazing and, I feel like she's forgotten I'm here, and . . . was that a bit of spit that just flew out of her mouth?

But now, just as suddenly, she stops. The eyes, as if after a long time away, swivel back on to me. I feel pinned to the sofa. 'Sorry, was I going on a bit?' she asks. My mind returns to the baby-blue buttons.

'Not at all. Sounds brilliant that play. Must go and see it. You don't want to see it again do you?' *Of course, I'm fucked if she tests me on the title.*

'Shall I roll a joint?' she asks. This has all the makings of a splendidly quiet night in.

'Definitely. I'll round up a couple more of those Russians if you like.' The labour divided equitably, I trot off to the kitchen with our empty glasses and open the fridge.

Slightly unpleasant, although I suppose it all depends how strong your views are about opened tins of cat food mingling with the brie. I notice a bag of tomatoes deliquescing quietly at the back. There's an onion with a bright green shoot. About fifty cans of Diet Coke. The milk however is fresh and, being organic semi-skimmed, our cocktails can be officially classified as Health Drinks. I prepare them to my preferred formula: one part Kahlua, five parts vodka, enough milk so it looks like a glass of cold cocoa.

'So where's Nick this weekend?' I ask when I return with the refreshments. I don't care about bringing his name up this time. We seem to have moved on somehow. I walk over to the window and look out at the street.

'Some sort of team-bonding, think-tanky thing in Oxfordshire,' she replies. It occurs to me that I don't know what Nick does, or what he looks like. Nor, I suppose, do I particularly wish to.

'Are you really getting married?' I ask. A lone dog is walking along the opposite pavement. It stops at a garden gate, assumes a timeless position and begins to strain. When I turn back to Yasmin, she has a hand to her forehead. 'I didn't make it too strong did I . . .?'

She's crying.

For a few seconds I am frozen to the spot with horror. *Oh fuck. What?* I step across to her armchair and put my hand gently on her shaking shoulder. 'Yasmin, what is it?' She shrugs me off with a loud inhalation of snot.

'Just leave me alone for a moment.' Without looking up, she thrusts the joint at me. 'Light this, would you?'

I retire to the sofa and ponder the dilemma. Tobacco is my enemy, and this little number is loaded with it. But it's not technically, a *cigarette*, right? Its primary purpose is not the delivery of nicotine.

Within seconds it's alight.

Ah. Now that's better.

8

Yasmin wipes beneath her eyes with a tissue, looks up from her armchair. 'What's it like?' she sniffs.

'Hitting the spot,' I reply. Actually I've begun to feel my head floating away from my shoulders. I've never been sure whether this is a good or a bad thing. I pass the joint to her and she takes several deep drags.

'Sorry about that,' she says.

'Don't worry.' I reply. I add nothing. She'll tell me if she wants to. There's further business with the tissue. Some nose-blowing. General feminine realignment. When she speaks again, it is in a flat, defeated tone.

'He's a really decent chap,' she says. 'A Good Man, if you know what I mean. A proper person. Not a flake like me. He loves me to bits. And I know he'd make a fine husband and father and be a good provider and all that. All my family love him. And his lot like me. We get on very well . . . physically, and all he wants to do is marry me and eventually, when we're ready, have a family.'

'And you've said yes.' *They get on very well physically*.

'And I've said yes.'

'But.'

'But I just can't do it, Michael.'

'You can't.' *Because you've fallen for me*. 'You can't because . . .'

'Because I don't really believe in it. He's so solid

and dependable. He hardly drinks, he never takes drugs. It's not that he's no fun – he can be – it's more that we're on different wavelengths. He doesn't see me the way I really am.' *The way I do*. 'Does that make any sense?'

'Yes, it does actually. It makes perfect sense.' Two sets of eyes stare back at mine through the bank of cannabis clouds. Hers and Satan's. 'Have you told him?'

'No, not yet. But things have been a bit shitty between us lately. He's no fool, he knows something's wrong. He isn't going to make it easy for me though.' She sighs heavily. 'Shall we have another joint then?' she asks.

'I think we'd better.'

If this isn't the moment to shit or get off the pot, it must be bloody close to it. But we need to get a bit of distance between us and the Nick confession.

'Do you know The Magician?' I inquire. She smiles. Shakes her head. *Bet Nick never does any magic for you, does he?* 'The Magician is a very great man. Would you like to speak to him?' She nods, the smile widening. 'Have you got a pack of cards? This isn't just a boring old card trick by the way.'

She goes off to find some, and I force myself to think clearly about how to do this one. Mouse and I have been pulling The Magician stunt since we were at school together and, right now, I'm praying he's at home this evening, because the only other person who can help me out is Hilary.

Yasmin drops on to the sofa and hands me a battered deck of cards. 'There might be a couple missing,' she says.

'Doesn't matter,' I reply. I spread them out, face up, on the carpet in front of us. 'Pick a card. Any card.' She gives me a *very* long look, bends down and pulls out the Nine of Clubs.

I lift her cordless telephone out of its cradle. 'May I?' I ask politely. She nods. I dial Mouse's number.

'Hello?' he answers after a suitable interval.

'Can I speak to The Magician please.' Yasmin is watching me intently. Pissed and stoned though she is, she's going with it. I press the phone tightly to my ear so she won't hear the other end of the conversation.

'Oh God, aren't we too old for this?' says Mouse. In the background I can hear the twins smashing furniture. 'OK, OK, you're trying to impress someone. I'll go through the suits first. You speak next after the suit you want. Here we go. Hearts.' (*pause*) 'Diamonds.' (*pause*) 'Clubs . . .'

'Yes, that's right,' I say, 'I'd just like a quick word with The Magician. I'll hold for him.' I wink at Yasmin. I do believe she's fascinated.

'OK,' says Mouse wearily. 'Clubs it is. Counting down now. Stop me when we get it. Ace. King. Queen. Jack. Ten. Nine . . .'

'Ah, good evening, O wise one. Let me put you straight on to the young lady.' I hand the phone to Yasmin.

‘Hello?’ she says cautiously. ‘Yes, I have selected a card.’ And now the wonderful moment, as the smile falls off the tear-smeared face. Because I know Mouse is putting on the deepest, spookiest voice he can manage and he’s saying, *Your card is the Nine of Clubs. It’s the Nine of Clubs. Is that correct?*

‘Yes. That’s right,’ she says. Mouse hangs up, and she’s looking at me in something like amazement. As if *I’m* The Magician. ‘OK, how the fuck did he know that?’

‘He’s The Magician, isn’t he? He’s The Man.’

‘Who the fuck *was* that guy?’

How very gratifying. For once, she doesn’t know how I did it.

9

We’re still sitting on the sofa. She’s still holding the Nine of Clubs and we’re looking at one another through a haze of drink and drug fumes, just like the rest of West London.

But she’s no longer a goddess. She’s only a woman. Let me number the reasons.

1. **She thought *Lolita* was about a dirty old man.**
2. **She serves like she’s taking a dump.**
3. **She hasn’t noticed that I haven’t had a normal cigarette all evening.**

4. **For a moment back there, she looked like a crazy person.**
5. **There's an open tin of Whiskas in the fridge (rabbit and pilchard if memory serves).**
6. **She fancied David White.**
7. **She's had sex with Nick.**
8. **She buys supermarket own-label vodka (very damning).**
9. **She didn't immediately clock my new hair and glasses.**
10. **She didn't suss The Magician.**
11. **The brittle note in her voice when she handed me the joint and said, 'Light this, would you?'**
12. **(The tears don't count, because every woman I have ever known – and half the men – have blubbed at some point in the proceedings.)**

'Shall we have that other joint then?' she asks. But softly. Her eyes have gone very saucer-like.

'I think we should,' I say. 'We might regret it if we didn't.' And then her lips are in mine, and mine are in hers, and she tastes of youth, health and tobacco, which in my book is a pretty unstoppable combination. I can feel her heart hammering against her ribcage, like an agitated canary. Every now and again we pause slightly to re-juxtapose our noses (can't decide, should she be on the left or the right?).

Finally, she gently pulls us apart. Her face fills my world. We're so close, I don't know which eye to look in. (You've got to go for one or the other, haven't you?) Fuck it, what does it matter if she buys Tesco vodka? Let her be as mad as a mongoose for all I care. She's a goddess again. We subside into the sofa. My hands are in her hair. Heat and perfume are rising off her like a thermal. The next minute or two are among the happiest I have known.

'Hang on a minute.' She's breathing heavily. The collar of my shirt is in her fist, her knuckles are white and she looks faintly shocked. 'Michael, we can't, you know, *do* anything. You know that, don't you?' I know no such thing but I nod anyway. She tightens her grip on my collar. I feel cotton ripping. 'You're a great snogger,' she says. 'Did anyone ever tell you that?' Yes, but I shake my head. 'What about that joint?' she asks. 'We won't forget to have it, will we?'

'No, we won't forget. I can reassure you utterly on that point.' And then we're down among the upholstery again. I've bypassed the baby-blue buttons altogether and she's got her hand in the back pocket of my trousers. Out of the corner of my vision, I notice Satan leap off the back of the armchair and stalk out of the room.

Taking the reader with him.

10

'Fuck!'

There is a horrible stabbing pain as someone impales the skin of my arm to the mattress with a bony elbow. Now a highly disagreeable thrashing and disentangling of limbs. I grab a warm, skinny waist and pull it back towards me.

'Get off,' a voice hisses. Hands prise my arms away. 'It's late. Some of us have got to go to work round here.'

I'm in bed with Hilary, back in her old flat where the bed stood up against a bookcase. We're making love and, in my enthusiasm, on the final push I bang my head against the shelf, upsetting a glass of water that's been standing there during the night. It spills over us, and we come together, convulsing with laughter.

'What's so funny?' asks Yasmin. I open my eyes. She's sitting on the end of the bed wrapped in a towel, brushing her hair. 'You laughed in your sleep.'

My head feels denuded of brain cells this morning. Not to worry though, some new ones will be along in a while.

I wake again to the all-pervading smell of toast. There's a sort of swishing noise. When I open an eye, Yasmin is wriggling into a skirt.

'Miss Swan,' I croak. 'Did we smoke that joint in the end? Or were we defeated by the Russians.'

My last memory is trying to keep in mind the edict that we shouldn't, you know, *do* anything. And indeed we didn't do anything . . . if you call tumbling around under the duvet, grappling and snogging with no clothes on not doing anything.

She doesn't reply, so maybe I only *imagined* speaking.

'There's a cup of tea there for you.' Yasmin is sitting on the bed, all shiny and dressed for work. A purple mug bearing the legend SHIT HAPPENS stands steaming on the bedside table. 'You can call yourself a cab when you're ready, can't you?' I can't read her expression. Is it affection or dismay? Or a bit of both? 'You know, we really mustn't do that again,' she says. And then, placing a warm, yet somehow tentative kiss on my lips, she's gone.

'Oh no, definitely not,' I call weakly. 'Out of the question.' The front door slams behind her. I shut my eyes.

You know the sound of an old black taxi as it stands idling at the kerb? The distinctive carburettor rattle that tells you 'taxi', even from round the corner? Well, there's one parked in the bed with me.

Sorry. No, there isn't. It's Satan. I think he likes me.

I gulp the cold tea, pull some clothes on and pad round her flat. It's Monday morning and the world has gone to work without me. I drop on to the sofa and survey the ruins of the White Russians, the ashtray full of Yasmin's cigarette butts. I replay what I recall of last night. The way she held on to me. Her greedy mouth. How at times she seemed shocked by her own beauty. I can still smell her perfume. It's in my nose, on my clothes, on my fingers.

What does she mean, we really mustn't do that again? We *must* do it again . . . *soon*.

Halfway home in the minicab, the mobile rings.

'Hello?'

'Hi, this is Nicole. Did you get my message about the Jack Russell?'

'Oh yes. Listen, I think you've got the wrong number, actually.'

'No, it's definitely you. I recognise your voice. I got the mobile number off your answer machine. I'm calling about the Jack Russell.'

'Yes, I know. I don't have a Jack Russell.'

'No, *I've* got the Jack Russell.' She laughs. A *nice* laugh. Nice laughs are hard to come by. 'You must live near the Heath. I recognise the dialling code.'

'Yes, I do. But I don't think I need a dog in my life at the moment.'

'Sorry, I'm confused. I thought I was returning your call.'

'That's what I'm saying. I think you've got a wrong number. I'm afraid I'm not looking for a dog at the moment.'

'Oh, shame. Not even a small one?' She laughs again. A *very* nice laugh.

'I live on the top floor of a block of flats. I don't think your dog would be very happy there.'

'He's not my dog, actually, but I know what you mean.' She sighs. A deep sexy sigh. 'Oh well, nice try.'

'I'm sure you'll find someone who wants him. Jack Russells are very characterful, aren't they?'

'Oh, definitely. Alfie's got more personality than a lot of the people I know.'

Now, I'm laughing. 'That's his name, is it, Alfie?'

'Yes. He's awfully funny. He's just become a bit . . . *much* for his owner. Still, you're right. He'd be utterly miserable stuck up a tower block.'

'Well, it's not quite a tower block. Anyhow, why don't *you* keep him if he's such a charmer?'

'Me?' There's a pause. 'I live in a flat too.'

A young woman. Who lives in a flat. With a nice voice. And a *lovely* laugh. Who recognised my dialling code. 'Are you in this part of the world as well?'

'Not far, by the sound of things. Anyhow, sorry to have bothered you.'

'No problem. Er, Nicole. Maybe I should actually meet Alfie.'

'Really? I thought you don't want a dog?'

'I don't, but my mum's always said my dad should have one. You know, to get him out of the house occasionally. They could be in the market for a small creature who doesn't need much exercise. Something with short legs. Or very lazy.'

'Actually, Alfie needs a *lot* of exercise. He's quite a handful, to be honest.'

'I still think we should meet. Alfie and I.'

'It doesn't sound like he'd be at all suitable . . .'

'No, really. Now I come to think about it, my dad loves Jack Russells. I'm pretty sure he used to have one as a boy.'

There's a long pause. 'Do you know the café at Kenwood?'

'Yes.'

'Would you be free to meet us there tomorrow lunchtime?'

'I think I could just about manage it.'

'One o'clock, by the tables and chairs outside?'

'Perfect. How will I know you?'

'Well, I'm about five foot ten, fair, I'll have just come from the gym so I'll be wearing trainers and stuff, and I'll be with a small dog. Shall we just leave it that you'll spot me?'

Don't worry. I'll spot you all right. With or without a small dog.

NINE

1

It takes five calls to find out what's happened to the Dave White I was at university with.

The first is to Olivia, who keeps in touch with people better than I do. She gives me the latest medical bulletin about her father. The doctors continue to be mystified but confirm that the old sod is speaking authentic Yiddish. He's even called his consultant a *shtick dreck* which is rather rude, especially for Newton Abbot.

She has a number for Ralph, her ex-lover and my personal narcotics trainer, who I probably haven't spoken to in ten years. He's still in Manchester, in Didsbury to be precise, and from his description of what he's up to at the moment – 'bringing in container loads of furniture and antiques from the Indian sub-continent' – my guess is he's still helping to keep a glazed expression on the face of the North West. He thinks Dave White might have gone to Birmingham, but the person who would know is Cath, 'Cosmic Pete's sister', who went out with Dave for several years. I'll find Cosmic Pete in a squat in the Manchester suburb of Whalley Range, quite a well-established squat by the sound of things, because it's on the telephone. Ralph is pleased to hear from me, asks what I'm doing, and characterises my latest misfortunes as a 'mega-bummer'. He says it would be cool to meet up some time, though I think we both know we won't.

Cosmic Pete takes a long time to come to the phone. It's answered by a German-sounding girl who stomps up some stairs and hammers on a door. *'Pete! . . . telephone.'* Then she stomps back down the stairs. 'He is just getting up,' she tells me, a touch indiscreetly, I feel. A door slams, hers presumably. Then more stomping on the stairs and I'm in the telephonic presence of Cosmic Pete himself. He's friendly enough, considering I've got him out of bed, and he then has to travel back upstairs to find his sister's number and, of course, return. I've been to enough dope-perfumed parties in Whalley Range to be able to picture the scene: the once-grand old house, its broad, elegant staircase, its huge draughty rooms lit by bare bulbs, bed sheets for curtains, the garden a wilderness.

Cath sounds Northern and depressed. She's rather bitter about Dave. 'Always either off his head or following his beloved Coventry bloody City,' she says. She last saw him on F.A. Cup quarter-finals Saturday some time during the early nineties. But she still exchanges Christmas cards with his parents.

'Tell him from me he's a pillock,' are her parting words. I guess he broke her heart.

Mrs White tells me her son has just changed his job – *job?* – and will be in his office now – *office?* – and when I ring the vaguely familiar London number she gives me, I'm very surprised indeed to hear a cheerful voice at the other end reply, 'Good afternoon, BBC.'

2

Back then, if someone had asked me to take a shot at which trade or profession Dave White would end up in, I might have said Civil Service. Nursery teacher possibly. I'd never have guessed television. So it is with something close to amazement that I walk into his office in the big white BBC building you pass on the left when you drive west out of London on the A40.

He's older and he's filled out a bit but he's

instantly recognisable. And when he looks up from the sports pages of the *Daily Mirror* and growls, 'Fuck me, look who it isn't', I am gratified to see that he *does* have rather large-looking teeth. The straw hair, which he once used to cut himself with kitchen scissors, now looks as if another person has been implicated in the project. And the clothes too have travelled up-market, though only as far as BBC Male (off-screen, not-*too*-important) which sartorially, is roughly on a par with long-term unemployed.

On the phone he'd told me how he got here. How he'd somehow drifted into the BBC in Birmingham about ten years ago, made himself useful and had never been asked to leave. He'd worked away quietly in factual television in the Midlands – 'It's not rocket science, is it, Michael?' – until one afternoon last month, when he'd filled in an application form to be the editor of a thoughtful new programme about football and its fans – *Team Spirit* – dealing in issues of faith, loyalty and belief. To his enormous shock, he got the job. They even told him he was far and away the best candidate. Then a fortnight ago, in best BBC goalpost-shifting tradition, someone decided they didn't actually want football and its fans in that particular slot, they wanted 'fucking attitudes to fucking death and fucking dying,' as he puts it.

Dave's been in his new office one week. He's got a desk, a calendar, a PC and a TV.

'So if you want to come and produce a death

show for me, you're more than welcome,' he says good-naturedly.

'How do you see it?' I ask.

'Oh, I don't know. Keep it simple. I think we'll be all right with a group of smart-arses sitting round talking. Doesn't matter very much. It'll be on very late. No-one will be watching.'

I flash back to a sitting room in Chorlton-cum-Hardy in the mid-eighties. Dave and his manic Welsh mate, Dylan, are rolling joints in the afternoon. Dylan skinning up, album cover jammed between knees and belly, fingers furious, crumbling, rolling, licking, the odd gleeful cackle escaping from behind the curtain of hair that hangs across his face. He rolls like he does everything, in a frenzy. And now Dave is rolling too. But there's a laziness about his movements. Not a studied or mannered laziness. This is the real thing. And then they're alight, ends glowing like torches, popping and spluttering as grass seeds explode in the heat. Dylan babbling and laughing and disappearing into his own cannabis cloud; Dave sinking deeper into the ruined armchair, legs straight out, ankle over ankle. Through the windowpane, passing traffic, pedestrians and Chorlton Library confirm that Manchester in 1984 is proceeding pretty much on schedule. Inside, time is standing still.

'What happened to that friend of yours, Dylan?' I ask Dave White.

'Dylan?' Dave smiles. 'He's a plumber. He's very

happily married. He and Frances have two lovely children, I was best man at their wedding.'

'A plumber? But he was a tortured philosopher. I pictured him, you know, struggling with the problems of existence, foaming at the mouth and stuff.'

'No, he took a plumbing qualification. He says you know where you are with water.'

In the corridor on the way to the lift, it comes to me. I retrace my steps to Dave's office and put my head round his door.

'I've thought of the name for our show.'

'What?'

'Death Warmed Up.'

'Good one.' He writes DEATH WARMED UP on a Post-It Note, and sticks it on the big blank wall near the calendar. 'You'll get a call from someone in personnel,' he says. 'I doubt if the money will prove a problem.' And he returns to the back pages of the *Daily Mirror*.

3

Yasmin is plainly not overjoyed to hear from me when I telephone. She's at her desk. In the background, I can hear the happy buzz of Belvedere Television.

'I just wanted to tell you, it was a lovely day. And evening.'

'Yes. It was nice,' she says.

Nice? Nice is the sweater your mum buys you for Christmas. Nice is a sodding biscuit. Not hours of delirious love-stuff, stopping maddeningly short of actual . . . you know.

'I mean. It was very. *You* are very . . . special.'

'That's sweet of you, Michael.' *What, I'm not special too?*

'I was wondering if you'd like to go out for dinner this week. You know, we could remember to eat something this time.' *And then go back to your place and . . .*

'Actually, this week isn't that great.'

'Oh?' *Go on then, let's hear your list of lousy excuses.*

'No, it really isn't.' *Let me guess. Seeing a friend tonight. Then another friend's coming over for dinner tomorrow. The next night it's Yoga or Pilates or Tai Kwando, and then it's bleeding* Friends *and* ER, *and you never miss those, do you, and then it's someone called Cheryl's hen night . . . oh, give me strength.*

'Well, how are you fixed at the weekend? How about another game of tennis? I need a chance to win back my title.'

'Also not good, I'm afraid.' *Don't tell me. You've decided to marry Nick after all.*

'Pity.'

'I know.'

'Well, look, when you find that you have a gap in your busy social schedule, give me a call, OK?'

'Michael, don't be like that.'

'Like what?'

'Sarcastic. It doesn't suit you.'

'Really? What suits me better then? Irony? Pathos? *Bathos*? Whatever bathos is.'

'Look, if you're going to be scratchy with me, perhaps we should talk another time.'

'I'm not being scratchy. I just want . . . to see you, that's all.'

There's a pause. I hear the sound of a cigarette lighter. 'How about next week?'

'Great. When are you free?'

'Well, I know I'm out Monday and Tuesday. And Wednesday. Oh, and Thursday.'

'Looks like Friday then.'

'I haven't actually got my diary on me. Can I call you tomorrow?'

'Yeah. Sure.'

'Michael?'

'Yes.'

'I really would like to see you, you know. It's just . . . a bit difficult.'

'Sure.' *Your move, honey*.

'I'll ring you when I've got a better idea of my plans.'

'Fine.'

'Well, bye then.'

'Bye.'

Fucking bitch.

4

'You don't fancy a few drinks tonight, do you? I'm feeling a bit sorry for myself.'

'Sorry mate.' *Ping-rasp-snap*. 'Got a previous.'

'Oh, shame. Well how's the Executive Editor? Has he been promoted since we last spoke?'

'No, but the little fucker's cock-a-hoop today. He's got his first commission. Electra Fuchs has bought *The Sweet Furry Baby Animal Show*. Says it's packed with feel-good factor. All those puppies, kittens and baby seahorses. You know, something the whole family can watch together on a Sunday afternoon. Sounds fucking ghastly.'

'It was one of mine, you know.'

'Really? Well, you wouldn't guess it. Clive's got his fingerprints all over it now. There's talk of a grand launch party.'

'God, it's intolerable. Listen, do you want to come to dinner with me and Dave Cleaver this week? He's quite amusing in his way. And I'm sure three trained journalists should be able to come up with some really horribly nasty dirty trick to pull on fuck-face.'

Steve agrees. We hang up. So tonight's to be a quiet night in then. And it's not as if I don't have the ability to entertain myself. The shelves are full of unread books, the telly stacked with unwatched videos, the fridge bulging with uneaten food. If I can't face cooking, there are at least two dozen restaurants in the locality who will be only too happy to despatch a spotty youth with my dinner on the back of his moped. There's wine, beer, whisky, vodka. There's radio, TV, the stereo, the World Wide Web, the telephone. Every form of mass communication is at my fingertips. I am not living on an Orkney Island, in a lonely crofter's cottage, miles from the nearest other human (who probably wants to see me dead). I needn't feel miserable. Yet I do.

At least I haven't smoked a cigarette. My nicotine dragon is yelling blue murder in his cave, but I'm feeling *good* about this. It means he's dying. (Actually, I'm not feeling good, I'm feeling quite shitty about this, but I'm hanging on in there.)

Reading doesn't work. Books can only cheer you up if you're in a reasonable mood to start off with. The television is complete cack this evening. There's 'another chance' to see an *Inspector Morse*. Or there's some real-life thing in a hospital (I *hate* things in hospitals, particularly real-life). In the past, I've been known to pass an evening flipping between the various news programmes, but tonight's news seems especially dull. The government is to introduce new guidelines for the clearer labelling of food. There's the usual boring little film showing a 'typical' family, in this case a repellent collection from Chester all sitting round the kitchen table as Mum dishes up the contents of several packets she's just removed from the microwave. No, she had no idea she was feeding her children pure animal fat mixed with ground glass. It's the labelling, isn't it? It's not always easy to read.

I try two of the funniest movies I know, *This is Spinal Tap* and *The Producers*, but I have to stop them after about ten minutes. It's no good. I'm three-quarters of the way through dialling Hilary's number, when I slam the phone down again. No, fuck *her*.

I pour myself a very large vodka and rifle through the CDs hoping to find something to catch the jolly atmosphere. Nothing ambient. Not opera. Rock and pop out of the question. No octogenarian Cubans (far too jolly). And then I find it, the answer. Keith Jarrett, *The Koln Concert*. A gorgeous piece of melancholy virtuoso piano. Old big teeth had a copy in New York.

The CD slides into its slot, I press play, and I wake on the sofa at four in the morning with a very peculiar dream in my head.

5

The Bearded Lady has got her disapproval under control this morning. I know she doesn't like my stories of late-night frolics and alcohol abuse; out of the corner of my eye, I see her shuffling and squirming, straightening her skirt, generally embodying the concept of *uncomfortable*. But being away in New York, I have missed a few sessions. So, who knows? Maybe she missed me. Maybe while deploring the *content* of my colourful reports from the front line of metropolitan life, she's nonetheless fascinated by what *young people get up to nowadays* (so different to how things were in turn-of-the-century Vienna, or wherever she grew up). Listening to the growing pains of a handful of anxious thirty-somethings would be more entertaining on the subject of modern man's woes than your average copy of the *Guardian*, wouldn't it?

I've rattled through recent events – Nazis in New York, getting sacked, Hilary's treachery, the tantalising night with Yasmin – and she's made all the usual noises. *Mmmm. I see. Really! Go on*. And now I tell her my dream.

I'd been invited to a black-tie ball at the United States Congress. And I am dancing away – don't know who with – when I collide with Bob Hope and his wife. I apologise. Mrs Hope, indicating her husband the legendary comedian, asks me, 'Have you met the President?' And that's it.

The Bearded Lady chuckles. So here's a nice little brain-teaser we've set ourselves. What the fuck is all that about then?

She likes to start at the beginning again. 'So, you're at a black-tie ball in the United States Congress building.'

'And I'm dancing with someone, a woman, I don't know who, and we sort of bash into Bob Hope. The younger Bob Hope, not as young as in *Road to Morocco*, but not as old as when he was on *Parkinson*. About sixtyish.'

'And his wife says, "Have you met the President?"'

'Yes.'

'And it ends there.'

'Yes.'

'Hmmm.'

You might well hmmm. Hmmm indeed. Very fucking hmmm. Either you believe all dreams mean something, or you believe they're meaningless brain-chaff, in which case you wouldn't be forking out forty quid a pop to investigate them. The halfway position, where some dreams are meaningful and others are just plain rubbish is simply too horrible to contemplate. The Bearded Lady and I share a belief that dreams are crackable.

'So, what are your associations to the elements in the dream?' she asks. 'The Congress?'

'Well, it's on Capitol Hill. And *congress* is kind of suggestive, isn't it? As in sexual congress.'

'Hmmm.' A *getting warmer* sort of hmmm. 'And Bob Hope?'

'The *Road* movies of course. *Road to Singapore. Road to Utopia.* Bing Crosby, Dorothy Lamour. *L'amour*!'

'Congress, *l'amour*, utopia. This dream seems to have a particular theme.'

'Yes, but "Have you met the President?" Bob Hope was never the President. What's that all about then?'

'Well, do you have any further associations?'

'To Bob Hope? Hope . . . and glory. Hope and

pray. When I abandoned all hope, I began to feel much better.'

'In your dream, Hope is the President.'

'No! I've got it! It's not Hope is the President. It's *hope is the precedent*. You know, when you have hope in your heart, that's the precedent for . . . congress.'

'Congress with . . .'

'Well, with Yasmin, I'd imagine.'

'Is she Dorothy Lamour?'

Is Yasmin Dorothy Lamour? I suppose I've been asked stranger questions in my life, but not many. Anyhow, this was almost certainly a dream about hope being the precedent for congress. Congress, that well-known *united state*.

It's only hours later that it occurs to me. The Congress is on Capitol Hill. You know, a *hill*.

6

Nicole was lying about her height. She looks closer to six foot than five ten and she's wearing a pair of those clingy black athletic leggings with white stripes up the sides that more or less scream at you, *See, these are my legs. Long, aren't they? And look where they go all the way up to*. She's got short, boyish blonde hair, blue eyes and a fresh healthy complexion from pounding away at the Stairmaster. A third-finger-left-hand-scan has come up negative. I find I have suddenly become very interested in dogs.

'I'll fetch us a couple of cappuccinos,' says Nicole. 'You can say hello to Alfie.' And passing me the creature's lead, she sashays indoors in a way that I immediately want to rewind and play back in slow-motion.

Alfie looks up at me – clearly Alfie looks up at *everything* mostly – and wags his tail tentatively. I've heard that Jack Russells can be nasty bits of work, but this one seems benign enough. Slowly, I lower my hand and scratch him under the chin. This is one of the few places, so I've been led to believe, that dogs cannot reach for themselves; they are therefore especially grateful if you put in a bit of scratching time in that area. And sure enough, Alfie's features have spread into a dog smile. One of his back legs is spasming with pleasure, and we are getting on like the proverbial kennel on fire. I'm just beginning to think that maybe I have a *way* with animals – 'marvellous the way the dogs all gather round him and go quiet' – when he springs up to his full height (my knee), an appalling little pink penis pops out of his fur, and he's dry humping my leg.

I pull him off. Sorry, let me re-state that. I push him away. He jumps back up. I push him away again and he's back up in a flash. We repeat this performance three or four more times. Same leg. Doesn't fancy my other leg, though I should have said there was nothing to choose between them. He's a determined little beggar (though, let's face it, half of seduction *is* determination) and I'm just beginning to panic slightly, when Nicole emerges with a tray of coffee.

'Alfie! Down!' Alfie complies instantly, and shoots me a rueful look. 'Sorry about that,' she says. 'I think he likes you.'

'Yes. He does seem quite affectionate.'

She drops into a chair and crosses her legs, which seems to take about twenty minutes. Even Alfie looks impressed.

We get chatting. Nicole says she works in the music business – chorus girl was my first ignoble thought – and spends a lot of time at home on the web. She seems perfectly comfortable with the news that I work in television and didn't say, as many people do, 'Oh, that must be interesting.' She didn't even ask what I do in television – you know, cameraman or Director General, that sort of thing – so, to make it clear, I tell her I produce programmes.

'I guessed as much,' she says. 'I think it's the glasses. Do you do comedy?'

'Well, actually I'm about to make a show all about death. So not far off.'

'Really. The man I work for is very interested in death.'

'Oh? Who's that then?'

She mentions the name of one of the biggest musical acts of the last twenty-five years. 'I'm his London PA. He's got another for his home in LA.'

I'm genuinely impressed, damn it. 'Wow. That must be interesting. You must meet some fascinating people.' She releases a wintry smile. 'Didn't I see him in *Hello!* the other week? Friends converge on his lovely home to celebrate his ninety years in show business.'

She laughs. 'Third marriage, actually.' I picture the photo spread. The star and his fragile young bride. The terrible pop-legend house – its obligatory collection of gold discs up the staircase – the red-faced celebrities with their fags and flutes of champagne, household names from music, showbiz and the arts; even a cabinet minister or two.

'So why is he so interested in death?' I inquire.

'Oh, you know. One week it's death. The next it's Japanese tea ceremonies. He's famously eclectic.' Famously flaky more like. But famously famous, that's for sure.

'If he'd like to come on our little show, he'd be more than welcome.'

'Thank you. I'll let him know.'

Alfie barks to remind us of the purpose of this encounter. And I suddenly get it. Of course. Alfie is the star's once-loved dog, now being discreetly dumped. Maybe the new wife is allergic to him. Or he clashes with her new colour scheme. Or he crapped in the sofa once too often.

'Alfie is . . . *his*, isn't he?'

Nicole gives me a long hard look. No, Alfie isn't *his*. Alfie belongs to an elderly neighbour who can't look after him any more. And in fact there is still the problem of another Jack Russell called Sheena who Alfie has made pregnant, who is about to give birth any day. Alfie, clearly, will attempt to shag anything that moves, human or animal, and good on him, in fact. But I don't believe a word of this.

He's *his*. I know he is.

I tell her that I greatly admire the fun-sized Lothario and I have a feeling that my mum and dad might just take to him too (lies, all lies; my father dislikes small dogs, and my mother hates anything that is liable to poo on the Axminster). I'll get back to her in a couple of days. And then we have an odd moment, a curious little silence where neither of us seems entirely ready to leave, even though the business at hand is exhausted. As though we had enjoyed one another's company which, in a brittle sort of way, maybe we have.

'I hope I can come up with something for you,' I tell her. And as we stand up to shake hands, and I notice the way the curve of her belly presses against her Lycra leggings, a thought pops into my head that even Alfie might blush at.

7

Seven pieces of mail from the outside world reach my fifth-floor breakfast table in North London.

1. **Another cheque for one thousand pounds from Dave Cleaver's newspaper.**
2. **A contract from the BBC to produce *Death Warmed Up*.**

3. A postcard from Yasmin. 'Dear Michael, It *was* good to see you the other night. Sorry to be so complicated. Y.' *Not 'love Y' or 'Y xxxx'. Just plain old 'Y'. (Bitch.)*
4. The *Sunday Times* cannot believe that I am not in their wine club. They are not taking my disinterest lying down. Their next move, almost certainly, will be to send round enforcers.
5. I have won twelve million pounds in a prize draw. Sorry, scrub that. I read it wrong. I *might* have already won twelve million pounds. It's not the same, is it?
6. I have been summoned to appear before Dorset Magistrates for non-payment of a fine relating to a breach of the Road Traffic Regulation Act (1984) as amended. They must be a gutless bunch down there in Alum Chine, because if I merely forward the sum of twenty pounds within twenty-eight days, they are prepared to overlook the matter entirely and will send a box of chocolates or a nice scarf, by way of a thank you.
7. The Jiffy bag I open last contains a copy of *The Easy Way to Stop Smoking*. It's Yasmin's, the one bearing Nick's sickening dedication, which I

left round at Hilary's house. Hilary has returned it to me with no note, nothing. Her way of saying, fuck you too.

And at the thought of a cigarette . . . what?

I probe the wound. It's still there, the constant background ache . . . sorry, the *triumphal feeling*, but it doesn't seem quite so inextricably intertwined with the heart-starting dose of Gold Blend this morning. Perhaps this is progress. Do I feel I am making a sacrifice, or am I liberated?

It occurs to me, I might ask exactly the same question about Hilary.

I guess the answer in each case is: a bit of both.

I am introduced to the *Death Warmed Up* team, if four people – including self – can be considered a team. In the way of these things, since last Monday when I met Dave White, the project has changed status from a series to a pilot, which means if no-one upstairs approves, the programme will never be shown and the idea ditched. Dave is curiously un-moved at the news, being more concerned I think about a midweek injury to a member of Coventry City's back four.

We've gathered in our production office to 'kick a few thoughts around'. My 'team' are Anita (the PA), a BBC 'lifer' who clearly knows the place backwards and, by the look of her, will get us out of the shit five times a day. There's a dull-looking boy called Simon who's at the BBC on work experience.

(Shortly, we shall ask him very nicely if he would mind going for the teas, and we won't see him again for the rest of the day. He'll be discovered eventually, trapped in a technical area, close to tears, having wandered the corridors for hours.) And there's Louise. An Assistant Producer, tiny and exquisite like a ballet dancer, but keen as mustard evidently, perched on the end of her chair, scribbling furiously into her mint BBC notebook. She's wearing narrow black-framed glasses, so I suppose we are to take it that she is *serious* – though in my experience, people who scribble down *everything* usually haven't the first clue about what to actually *do*.

'Could we, like, interview people who are about to die?' This is Simon's opening contribution to the debate. Louise looks up from her notebook, waiting for a reaction to this suggestion.

'Not very tasteful,' drawls Anita. 'Though we would save on repeat fees.' Strictly speaking, television PAs deal with logistical matters like tapes, timings, studio facilities and rights clearances. They are not generally asked for their input on editorial matters and, indeed, many are quite content to live in a world of spool numbers and paperwork. Others, however, may at times represent the lone voice of reason.

'What about someone who's had a near-death experience?' pipes up Louise. 'One of those people who've been drowning, or dying on the operating table, and they've seen the white light, or Jesus, and have been saved at the last minute.'

This isn't a *terrible* idea. In fact I've read a few stories along those lines, how when you get to the point, death isn't really all that scary. Nevertheless, I have an urge to remove her glasses and stamp on them.

'I don't think we quite want to go down that route,' says Dave pleasantly. 'In any case, we're operating in a low-cost environment which isn't really up to drama reconstruction. I see this more as . . . sophisticated late-night philosophical meanderings. Our contributors should *review* death, as it were. From their particular cultural and religious standpoints.'

Christ. Where did that come from? Even Dave looks a bit surprised at the fully formed bit of Beebspeak that just plopped out of his mouth. I guess ten years in any institution is bound to rub off on you.

It's decided. We need to round up a sparkling panel – a godless scientist, a hardcore cleric of some hue, a doctor with philosophical leanings, an existential psychoanalyst; you know the sort of thing, a plausible collection of loud-mouthed eggheads. Together with a presenter, they'll sit in the cheapest set possible and argue the toss about the Grim R. until we tell them to stop, pour them a drink and kick them out.

'Any initial thoughts about who should front the show?' I ask the assembled company.

'What about Chris Evans? Someone a bit different, to get young people watching,' suggests Simon.

Gosh. I *am* getting thirsty. I feel a tea run coming on.

'A woman might be good,' says Louise.

Yes, it's hard to argue with that. 'Any *particular* woman?'

'Michael Buerk's very good on *The Moral Maze*,' offers Anita.

'I'll leave you to it,' says Dave, rising to his feet and sauntering off in the direction – I am certain – of the Coventry City news page on Ceefax in his office.

'Right then,' I say, eye-contacting each member of my crack team with what I hope is a down-to-business expression. 'We'd better make a plan.'

8

Steve and I meet Dave Cleaver in Mr Kong in Lisle Street. I order for all of us because, left to themselves, these guys would go for Chicken and Cashew Nuts, and Sweet and Sour Pork and miss out on the really top stuff.

I request:

Six steamed scallops (two each)
Satay eel (suspend your disgust; this is to die for)
Coriander prawn rolls

Half Peking duck with pancakes

Salted spicy squid
Half Emperor chicken (on the bone)
Deep-fried crispy beancurd with vegetables
Guy Choi vegetables in ginger
Pea-shoot vegetables with garlic
Boiled rice
Chinese tea
1 x 700 ml bottle sake (with more to follow as directed)

We do a little reminiscing about the old days in North Wales, savouring the delicious warm feeling of *escape*.

'The destinations on the front of the buses always used to get me,' says Steve. 'Coedpoeth . . . Minera.' He intones the names of the dismal settlements like Peter Cushing narrating a horror movie. 'It was like working in Middle Earth.'

'Rhosllanerchrugog,' recalls Dave heroically. 'Which means literally Place with the Unpronounceable Name.'

'Bwlchgwyn,' I chip in. 'Place Which Sounds Like Man Bringing Up Ten Pints of Guinness and Pie and Chips.'

As Parts One and Two of the food arrives, there is a serious downturn in the conversation. Chopsticks blur, sauces are applied, things are dipped in other things, sake is poured into tiny cups, and re-poured. And poured once more. Further dishes appear. We segue seamlessly into

Part Three. The last comment anyone made was five minutes ago (Cleaver: 'Fuck me, top scoff, chief'). But now, as the initial food frenzy subsides, I sense the time may be right for the conspirators to apply their brilliant brains to the matter at hand.

'Dave,' I say to the devilish little mannequin opposite, 'didn't you do your dissertation on Revenge in Elizabethan Drama?'

'Can't say I remember, chief. We've all passed a lot of water since then. Well, I know I have.' His chopsticks expertly fall upon a particularly handsome piece of squid. 'You still worried about that floater?'

I explain how the situation relating to Clive has become unspeakable. 'We must surely be able to come up with a wheeze to punish him for being such an arsehole. Can't you suggest anything, Dave? Being a master of the black arts.'

The Rural Dean's son is clearly delighted at the suggestion. His chopsticks dive-dive-dive into the banquet, three times returning to base with a significant morsel. He snares a passing waiter with an eyebrow and signals for another bottle with the tiniest gesture of his head.

'Stopping short of actual physical violence, I take it?'

'I suppose so,' I admit grudgingly.

'Hmmm,' says Dave. The first time I have known him to hmmm. 'Well, you could hire someone to chat him up in a bar, lure him back to her place, they do loads of coke and . . . I dare say the photos wouldn't go down all that well with his missus. Or his boss.'

'Too sordid,' says Steve. 'With all due respect, naturally. No, what we need here is a revenge that for years afterwards will make us piss ourselves every time we think of it. Probably based on an appeal to his vanity.'

'Ah,' says Cleaver knowingly. 'One of those. Hmmm.' The chopsticks carry away a helpless piece of chicken. 'OK, you invite him to a fancy dress party. But when he turns up, he's the *only one* in fancy dress!'

'Doesn't sound all that devastating,' says Steve.

'You're wrong there, chief. Some nasty little git did it to me once. Fucking awful, it was.'

'Why, what did you go as?' I ask.

'Hitler.'

We all laugh at the thought of it. Even Dave. 'It was very painful at the time,' he assures us. 'Imagine it. Walking into a flat in Maida bloody Vale where you hardly know anyone. They're all wearing their fancy turtlenecks and posh frocks, and you're dressed up as Adolf bleeding Hitler. I felt like a right cunt, I can tell you.'

'How long did you stay?' asks Steve, wiping away a tear.

'Well, rather a long time as it happens. There was a bird there who was really shit-faced. And she must have had a thing about Nazis. She dragged me into the coat-room and . . .'

'. . . Begged you to violate her territorial integrity?' suggests Steve.

'Yes, as a matter of fact.'

'And?' A cube of bean curd is there one moment, gone the next. Where does he put it all?

'Well, it would have been rude not to, wouldn't it?' He drains his sake cup. 'Christ, she was ugly. Still, as they say in Lancashire, you needn't look at the mantelpiece while you're poking the fire.'

More sake is ordered to refuel the mission. We continue enjoyably to spin revenge scenarios, though the image of our tiny *Führer* wriggling around on a pile of coats with his trousers round his ankles is hard to shake from one's head. I *quite* like the idea of printing up some cards with Clive's telephone number and the legend *CLIVE. LIKES TO BE SPANKED. TEACH ME A LESSON I WON'T FORGET* and plastering them in select telephone boxes round the West End – one of Dave's, naturally – but it lacks the beautiful simplicity of, say, a bullet in the brain.

'I am aware of a Jack Russell bitch who's about to have puppies,' I inform the plotters wearily. We are on our fresh orange segments now (no toffee-banana nonsense at Mr K). 'Could we do anything with that?'

'Ah,' says Steve gnomically.

'Oh-*ho*,' says Dave.

'A Jack Russell, you say.' Steve again.

'Actually, you'll never believe this. It belongs to Farley Dines. His new wife is making him dump it because it clashes with the curtains.'

A flicker crosses Cleaver's face. It's the barest

twitch, but I've clocked it. I reach across, grab him by the lapel and menace one of his eyeballs with a chopstick. 'If one word of this appears in your fucking scuzzy rag,' I say as seriously as I can (without laughing), 'I promise you, I shall make you very sorry indeed. Do you follow?'

'Easy, chief. No worries. Er, listen, are you going to eat that last bit of squid?'

9

'The Chief Rabbi won't do it,' Louise announces gravely, as though there's just been a catastrophic fall in the London Stock Market. My 'team' in the *Death Warmed Up* office this morning are working their way through a long wish-list of names for the show. Louise stares at me earnestly, waiting for some sort of official reaction to the hammer blow just received. Behind the grisly specs and horrible combat trousers, she's actually very pretty, a tiny, perfect, painted porcelain doll. So pretty, that for a moment, I cannot think of anything to say except 'Oh good' which I don't think would send out the appropriate signal of inspiration to the troops. So I manage a wordless gesture, *Oh well, still I'm sure you did your best*, and she throws herself back on to the telephone. Actually, I find myself staring at Louise rather often, the almost impossibly cute face brutalised by the shocking black plastic glasses. That thing about men not wanting to make passes at girls who wear glasses is just plain wrong in my book.

A set designer has come to see me with three sketches of what the *Death Warmed Up* studio could look like for the money we have to spend on it: a miserly sum in TV terms, but around half the average industrial wage. The first sketch is terrible, with stylised skeletons, gravestones and coffins all over the place. Designers, however, will often show you their worst stuff first, to soften you up for what is to come. And indeed, the second idea is an improvement, in the sense that there are *no* skeletons, gravestones and coffins. This time we have a Maxfield Parrish cloudscape shot through with moving pink rays of light ('If we could stretch to some dry ice, it could look amazing'). So my money's on sketch three and, sure enough, it's a classy meditation on the theme of *black*. We'd shoot the whole thing against a black background and spend the money hiring in some 'really amazing' dark furniture for the panel to sit in. He's going to get hold of catalogues and run a few groovy Italian chairs past me.

The graphics designer who will make the show's opening titles also works to the rule of three: crappest, still crap, plausible. Shamelessly she pitches them to me:

1. **A Steadycam tracking shot through a misty graveyard, ending up on a stone which reads DEATH WARMED UP. *Oh please.***

2. Slow motion footage of a big black crow. There's something funny about it. Oh yes, it's because it's being played backwards. Now the bird 'lands' on the handle of a spade. A wide shot reveals the spade stands by a pile of freshly dug earth in a churchyard.

3. A slow horizontal pan along a naked human leg lying on a steel table in a morgue. Arriving at the big toe, we see there's a cardboard label tied to it reading DEATH WARMED UP.

Number three's my man but with a twist. Just as we've absorbed the title of the show, the toe should wiggle. The designer has gone away to do some 'costings'. You know, legs, tables, labels . . . these things cost money.

At six o'clock Louise and I are the only people left in the office. Anita had to leave early for 'a doctor's appointment', the look of tragedy in her face foreclosing any further discussion; Simon was last seen two hours ago when he set off to find some stationery. Louise has been working the phones so hard, her fingers should be bleeding.

'So what are you up to this evening?' I ask her, making a bit of a pantomime of turning off my PC, tidying away papers. *Come on, you can stop now, enough for one day.*

'Nothing really. My flatmate and I might go to the pub.'

Half an hour later the two of us are seated beneath the giant Canestan tube in the Pharmacy. I have ordered a D.V.M for old time's sake but elfin Louise, who looks as if a Martini would put her in hospital, has sensibly asked for a white wine spritzer. She really is enchantingly . . . well, *pretty* is the word, I'm afraid. Somehow not quite beautiful, not *obviously* sexy, but about as pretty as you can get without verging into bad taste. Naturally, she's done everything she can to hide it.

She mainly wants to talk about *Death Warmed Up*, which is rather annoying. It's clear this is the most 'serious' programme she's ever worked on, having started life as a junior researcher on *Jim Davidson's Generation Game*. After school, she did Media Studies at the University of Central Lancashire; deplorably, all she has ever wanted to do with her life is work in television. She is so thrilled to be at the BBC, and so concerned to do well, it's sickening.

But like I say, she is very pretty.

And she doesn't smoke. Not that I'd be tempted. Not with this twisting feeling of . . . *liberation* in my belly. Oh, good God, no.

My mobile rings. An unfamiliar number on the little screen.

'Michael. This is Nicole. With Alfie, the other day?'

'Yes, yes, I remember. *Hello*.' A bit of a Leslie Phillips *hello*, but hey, this *is* a charm business.

'I hope you don't mind but I mentioned the television programme you are making to Farley and he says he'd like to hear more. Would you like to come up to the house and meet him?'

'Sure. That would be great.' *Great? That would be fucking fantastic.*

'Farley's in the States at the moment, but he's back at the weekend. How about first thing Monday morning? Midday?'

'Fantastic.' *Great or fantastic. In this line of work, it's either one or the other.*

'I'll fax you the directions.'

'Great. Fantastic to hear from you.'

I press END and gaze stupidly at the mobile for a few moments. Those long, long legs with the stripes up the side. That odd little moment when we seemed to search each other's eyes for Any Other Business.

Louise is staring at me eagerly through the cruel arrangement of plastic on her face. 'Good news?'

'Yes, sorry. Very good news. This little programme of ours may be in serious danger of becoming not at all bad. Shall we have another drink?'

10

What was it Oscar Wilde said about absinthe? After one glass you see things as you wish they were. After a second, you see things as they are not.

Finally, you see things as they really are, and that is the most horrible thing in the world.

Is the same true of D.V.M.? I expect so. In which case, here is how things really are. Louise, despite or because of the black-legged sea-creature eating into her face, has become *less* pretty but *more* attractive. She's been telling me her story. How her younger sister is in a girl band that's about to become very big. How her older brother earns £100,000 a year in the city before bonuses. How Daddy is a partner in the biggest estate agency in the North West. She tells me she's got another brother who doesn't do anything. How, actually, he's 'a bit disturbed' and lives in a sheltered community. How proud he was to see her name on the credits at the end of a programme. I tell her, surely the point of living in a sheltered community is that you are sheltered? Especially from things like *Jim Davidson's Generation Game*. Hadn't they suffered enough? She laughs, one of those swivel-eyed helpless laughs, halfway between amused and frightened. She tells me she did have a boyfriend but they broke up. 'He turned out to be a bit of a pig really.'

In the last couple of hours, Louise has turned into a real person; bright, rather sweet, and obviously terrifically needy. One of those co-dependent characters who will ultimately do anything for you. The sort who stay sober to drive you home from parties, give you money for drugs and clean up your sick.

I find I am very drawn to her.

When I do the cigarette-ash trick – with an

ashtray *from the next table*, before you say anything – the palms of her hands, when I take them in mine, are damp. Afterwards, if she has any clue how the black smear got there, she isn't saying.

At moments her face becomes rather plain. As if, to keep it pretty she must make a deliberate effort of will; occasionally, when there's a brief power failure, she can look almost ordinary. For some reason, this only makes her more attractive to me. The vulnerability, I guess. If we weren't working together, I suppose I might ask her out. Mind you, we won't be working together *forever*, will we?

'Have you worn specs for long, Louise?'

'Since the sixth form. I found I couldn't read the overhead projector.'

'Yes, me too. Would you mind if I tried them on for a moment?'

'Sure.'

Absurdly, with nothing to coalesce round, her fine features seem somehow adrift, a little helpless. I guess the word is . . . *naked*. I try on her specs and she leans in towards me to peer at the effect, maybe a touch too close. The sort of distance at which one might gaze on the face of a lover in bed. In every possible way, I realise she is quite short-sighted.

'What do you think?' I ask softly. Twelve inches from mine, I watch her eyes dancing about, considering the question. Without thinking, I close the gap to zero and place a gentle kiss on her lips.

Louise now puts on my glasses. They're not as severe, though by no means an improvement. She stares at me oddly, her lips slightly apart.

'Sorry,' I say. 'It's all this talk of death.'

'No, it's fine. You can do it again if you like.'

TEN

1

It has to be a mistake. They can't have meant to send it to me. The big white cardboard invitation – gold-edged, if you please – requesting the 'pleasure' of my company and that of a partner at a party to celebrate Belvedere Television's Tenth Anniversary and their newest programme commission: *The Sweet Furry Baby Animal Show*. They've hired a posh venue and are promising cocktails, champagne, dinner, and disco until the early hours. Someone has taken the trouble to handwrite my name in the space above the dotted line, but I can't believe they really want me to come. It has to be a mistake.

Farley Dines lives in a heartbreakingly lovely old house at the end of a private lane overlooking Hampstead Heath. Motion detectors, video cameras and, no doubt, a satellite-tracking system follow my progress past the Addams Family iron gates, along the gravel drive and up to the Great Door. The whole picture speaks of Deep Quiet Wealth. Outrage stirs in my breast. I want the capitalist pigs who live here strung up from the nearest lamp post; I want their children put to work in the fields; I want to move in myself.

Nicole stands in the entrance, wearing a pair of life-threateningly tight black jeans. She leads me through the ridiculous Baronial Lite hallway into a bright sitting room that gives on to a deliciously mature walled garden. Beyond it is the Heath. Beyond that, London.

'Farley will be down in a few minutes,' she says, friendly enough but rather more crisply efficient than when we last met. 'Do make yourself comfortable.' I watch her turn and exit, marvelling at her health, vitality, and the way she fills her trousers with such anatomical correctness.

I remember the room from *Hello!* The rather stuffy chintzy furniture and Chinese vases. The ottomans heaped with new editions and auction catalogues. Definitely not the home of a Rock Legend. More like the Chairman of the John Lewis

Partnership. Or Esther Rantzen. The picture over the fireplace in particular seems wrong. It's a reproduction Constable, a view over Hampstead Heath familiar from a thousand biscuit tins and placemats. Except when I look more closely, I get a funny feeling in the pit of my stomach when I realise it is the real thing.

'Nice, innit?'

The shock of the famous face. No, the *icon*. Much smaller than you imagined. And old, something almost frail about him as he crosses the carpet to shake hands, his face cross-hatched with the wrinkles that never show on TV. But the eyes are still bright, mischievous even, and the hair, magnificent, indecently thick, shiny and lustrous like a seal. Farley Dines, right up there in the first circle of fame, along with movie stars and world leaders. It's cover of *Time Magazine* fame. People in Russia, in China, in Iraq know your name. Even my granny's heard of you. You probably tried to shag her.

'Hi, I'm Farley.' The endearing false modesty. The voice, that unmistakable combination of honey and nails, kissed with Estuary.

'Good to meet you. I was just admiring your Constable.'

'Yeah, it's the view from the bottom of this garden. Tash wants me to move it. She says the Feng Shui's all wrong.' *Tash. Natasha. The new wife*. 'But that's all bollocks, innit?'

'Well *I* would have thought so . . .' As if I am the sort of person rock stars consult about these matters all the time. 'I think it's just . . . *wonderful* where it is.' Whoops. A wrong note. Too gushing or familiar. Driving a wedge between the happy couple. Great, would have done fine. Fantastic, at a pinch. Farley Dines drops on to a sofa and indicates I should do the same.

'So, *Death Warmed Up*. Tell me all about it.'

I give him the spiel. How death is one of those subjects rarely discussed on television. How we're going to do it *intelligently* and at *length*; how those with interesting things to say on the subject will have the time to develop their case, probe the others' arguments; maybe even change their minds. No soundbites, no gimmicks, a very old-fashioned approach in a way. He seems interested. Nicole sways in with a pot of Japanese tea and two tiny cups on a tray. How she manages to set them down on the low coffee table without internal injury is a mystery to me.

'Thanks, doll,' says Farley Dines. As Nicole straightens up to leave, I have to force myself not to watch, though I am sure I can hear fabric screaming all the way across the carpet and out of the door. The star pours for both of us with a reassuring lack of ceremony. His old man hands. Hands that have groped a thousand chicks.

'I'll level with you, Michael,' he says. 'I'm famous for my eclectic interests. And right now it's . . . extinction. It's the most grotesque thing we can imagine. Or rather cannot imagine. The idea of not being here, while everything carries on without us.

I'm philosophically . . . *offended* by the idea.' And indeed Farley Dines does look somewhat peeved, the ageing star – what is he now, fifty-five? – in his collarless white silk shirt, midnight-blue velvet waistcoat, and pale velvet trousers, sipping Japanese tea in his perfect English home.

'It's the theme of my new album. Life being no sort of preparation for the cessation of life. Do you smoke?'

He's flips open a silver box on the coffee table and lights a cigarette, a Marlboro, I should say by the smell of it.

'No, no thanks. I'm giving up.'

He looks at me a little oddly. As if the idea had never occurred to him. 'Hi darling.' Natasha, an astonishingly beautiful waif-like creature, pale as a ghost with huge lost-looking grey eyes glides across the floor towards us. 'Darling, this is the chap from the BBC who's doing the programme about death.' She lays a tiny dry hand in mine. I give it the tenderest squeeze, for fear of fracturing small bones. She slips on to the sofa alongside her new husband, lights a cigarette and considers me with the unblinking regard you might afford a visitor from outer space.

As Farley Dines rattles on about his conception of death – its gross *insult* – and I watch the two frail beings under their canopy of smoke, I can see perfectly clearly why he would find the idea of *all this going on without him* highly annoying: it's the loss of loveliness. The house, the garden, the woman, the money. For all its facets and wrinkles, his view of death can be characterised in a single phrase: what a bummer, man.

'Farley, if you would be at all interested in appearing on our programme, then we would love to have you. I think your viewpoint could be really . . . refreshing.'

'Understood.' He rises. The audience is over. 'Let Nicole know who else is appearing, and I'll give you my answer.'

Nicole is standing in the doorway. Has she been watching? Listening? She's wearing a patient air-hostess smile, the one they put on while they wait for you to stagger off the 747. But now, from the hall, comes scuffling. A male voice cries, 'Oi! Come back here.' Nicole attempts to close the door, but too late. Exploding into the sitting room, skidding across the sections of polished wooden floor, banking through the chicanes formed by sofas, tables and standing lamps, is a Jack Russell terrier closely followed by another dog of the same breed. The latter, unmistakably Alfie.

Natasha screams and jumps on to the sofa. 'For fuck's sake, Farley, will you get those fucking creatures out of my house before I fucking have them put down.'

The legend shakes my hand. 'Be seeing you, man. Love to Auntie Beeb.'

Nicole walks me to the big iron gates. I find I very much want to loosen the top button of her jeans.

'Thanks, Michael. I think Farley liked you.'

'I think he'd be fantastic on *Death Warmed Up*. Tell him if he agrees to come on, I'll definitely find a home for Alfie.'

Her smile lingers upon me for a few seconds longer than strictly necessary.

'Nicole, I've been invited to a big television thing next month, to celebrate a programme I invented. Should be rather a good party, as a matter of fact. I was just wondering whether you might like to come at all.'

The smile falls away. Behind her bright blue eyes, I can feel her coolly crunching the data: Who is this bloke? Is he worthy? Do I want to go on a date with him? (Me? Mentally I'm still struggling to get a purchase on that top button.)

Finally, she blinks. Her eyes soften.

'I'd love to,' she says.

2

'So what was he like then?'

'Farley Dines? Well, put it this way, he looked absolutely fantastic for a man of seventy-five.'

Hilary laughs. And as we've just finished dinner, she lights the first of her two nightly Lambert and Butlers. We're meeting on neutral territory, an annoying Italian restaurant off the Marylebone Road, mutually inconvenient for us both to get to. We're here to Talk About Us.

'You're not smoking much,' she observes.

'Actually, I've given up.'

She looks genuinely shocked. '*You've* given up. I don't believe it.'

'It's not a sacrifice, it's a liberation.' For the first time, I almost believe it.

Hilary has said her piece. She's been telling me how it really *was* Julia who called round late at night, that time I phoned from New York. Julia hadn't turned up to talk about her new man – there never was a new man – but to discuss Hilary's relationship with *me*, if you please. Hilary had sensed – 'It's a female thing, Michael' – that my mind was elsewhere. 'Another stupid infatuation,' was the phrase she employed. Anyhow, Julia had just read a book called *The Rules* whose revolutionary central premise is that if women play hard to get, men will be inspired to desire them more. In particular, Julia recommended a slogan from the book that had apparently worked well on Hugo: 'Be a creature unlike any other,' a modern re-tread of the old adage, *have a little self-respect, honey*.

So Hilary had taken her advice. She'd become a creature unlike any other. She had not sat moping by the phone all evening, waiting for a call from 'Mr Man' (viz, self). She had 'gone out and done things.' She *had* been to a club with Julia and some pals. She *had* stayed over. Oh, and the bloke in her house that Sunday morning? Who'd asked where she kept her coffee? That was Vic. The plumber. Who'd *finally* turned up to see to her central-heating boiler. *Yes*, at nine o'clock on a Sunday. And no, she can't help it if it sounds far-fetched, because it is what happened. And in any case, I am the one who started all the trouble with my ridiculous obsession with Yasmin. And no, I should not bother trying to deny it, because my expression said it all when she'd asked me in bed, 'Who's Yasmin, darling?' And yes, she had been angry and hurt when I didn't return any of her messages. And yes, she had finally thought, oh sod you, Michael, life is too short. And yes, there is someone who is interested in her – though she does not state whether the feeling is mutual – and yes, he does have a one-syllable name and an interest in outdoor pursuits (Lee; hang-gliding; a cameraman). Oh and yes, I can pour her another glass of red wine.

I comply, though I suspect creatures unlike any other do not generally need to ask.

Hilary is a little red in the face from her speech, on the verge of anger. She has smoked her L&B and is starting on the second almost straight away. I think she is at her most attractive in this state, though I believe it would be a mistake to tell her right now. An elderly waiter wheels a trolley loaded with cakes and puddings up to our table.

'Fuck me, the sweet trolley,' I say to Hilary in an attempt to lighten the mood. 'You don't see many of them these days.'

'You care for dessert, *signor, signorina*? Some cheesecake? Profiteroles? I have lovely *tiramisu* this evening. Very light and refreshing. Means pick-me-up.'

'Yes, that's pick-me-up as in, help-me-off-the-floor,' I quip. Hilary smiles thinly. She's heard it before too often. We both go for the double espresso option.

'So what do you want to do, Michael?'

'What, with my life? Just . . . make a contribution really. And go to more art galleries. Eat three portions of oily fish a week. Get these shoes reheeled. Oh, and finish *Crime and Punishment*.' And sleep with Nicole. Maybe Louise.

'About us.' *Usssssss*. Don't like the hiss she puts on that one.

I take a deep breath. 'I think we need . . . I think *I* need a little space. A little time to think stuff through a bit. Like you say, it's probably my fault. Things do seem to have got a little . . . buggered up between us.'

Hilary starts fiddling in her handbag for a mirror and her lipstick. She's on the edge of tears.

'Listen, Hilary, bizarrely I've been invited to Belvedere's tenth anniversary party. They're having a big splashy do. Cocktails, dinner, dancing, the whole nine yards.'

She does that pouty thing women do when they put on lipstick, but it looks odd tonight, more of a grimace. A fat teardrop falls from the side of her eye and lands noisily on the tablecloth.

'I'd love it if you came with me.'

Hilary snaps the compact shut. Sniffs loudly. 'Sorry. I might find I'm busy that evening.' She flings her make-up back in her handbag, drops a twenty-pound note on the table and walks out of the restaurant without a second glance.

I'm so amazed I order a grappa. But typical Hilary. Not, go and fuck yourself, Michael, in twelve different places. She said, *sorry*.

3

So here's the prospective line-up for *Death Warmed Up*.

There's a nasty bald scientist who firmly disbelieves in life after death and is not too impressed with what goes on before it frankly. Broadly, he agrees with Stephen Hawking that the human race is 'just a chemical scum on a moderate-sized planet orbiting around an average star in the outer suburbs of one among a hundred million galaxies. We are so insignificant, I can't believe the whole universe exists for our benefit.' He's our right-but-repulsive panellist.

Next, we've booked a lovely old bishop, camp as a row of pink tents, who'll go in to bat for The Afterlife, with a full-colour Disneyland Heaven that includes The Almighty, Jesus Christ, Pearly Gates, St Peter, Angels, the lot. (Wrong, but romantic.)

Then there's our surgeon, a distinguished member of the Royal College, no less, who has seen more dead people than you can shake a stick at. He told me in all seriousness that he's 'persuaded that there is such a thing as a "soul" which leaves the body at death and travels on somewhere else.' (I resisted the temptation to say the High Barnet branch of the Northern Line.)

There's our existential psychoanalyst who believes many of modern man's neuroses stem from a deep-seated inability to accept the fact of mortality. She's a marvellous old thing with a curious accent and specs on a chain (these matters are important in television).

Our presenter is Maeve Middleton, one of the BBC's all-purpose women-of-a-certain-age who get wheeled out to front half-intelligent arts-stroke-religion progs. Dull but enthusiastic. And cheap. (This last, *very* important.)

And there's Farley. More famous than all the others put together and raised to the power of ten. Farley, who no matter what he says, will get the show *noticed*.

Now the bad news. Our director is a frightful old stager called Miles Kilbride who seems to have dragged himself out of retirement specially for the occasion. His c.v. reads like a History of Television, he's worked with everyone from Richard Dimbleby to Dale Winton and he probably went to nursery school with Logie Baird. Every day around 12.30, he claps his hands, declaims to no-one in particular, 'Well, all work and no play makes Jack a dull boy,' and buggers off for a two-hour lunch. The period up to that time, it should be said, he has usually passed on the phone to his divorce lawyer. On the few occasions that I have raised any technical questions about the studio recording, he has fixed me with a fiery glare and growled, 'Don't worry about that, lad. It'll all be fine on the night.' Or, another favourite, 'Dear God, I remember when we just used to wing it.' And once, the impenetrable, 'Believe me, if it was easy, they'd all be doing it.' Anita, the PA, loves him of course. Simon and Louise are terrified. Actually, I think Miles will be fine for *Death Warmed Up* being so close, as he is, to the subject matter.

Louise has very decently never referred to our oddly intimate little moment the other evening. But she has grown steadily more attractive, abandoning the radical tops and unflattering combat trousers in favour of a softer, feminine look. Her outfits have become more figure-hugging. Pink and baby blue have made appearances. The phrase that runs round my head every time I look at her is *just like a woman, only smaller*. And the effect of the hard-core glasses against the girly background is devastating. Even Simon is smitten. When he's not hopelessly trapped somewhere in a parallel universe, I overhear his appalling attempts at chatting her up ('I got really shedded at the weekend') and smile darkly to myself.

This evening, Louise and I have taken ourselves for a quiet little close-of-play drink to the Pharmacy. I've spoken the mantra, 'just one', but I've got a funny feeling it's not going to work. Louise is chattering on about the show, which egghead is likely to say what and who's most liable to have a bust-up with who (*bore-ring*). I would much rather begin a conversation about the erotic aspects of eyewear. She's so dazzlingly *pretty*, dammit, even the waiters have noticed.

'Would you guys like another drink?' says an extravagantly handsome young man, directing his remarks exclusively at my companion. Now, I don't know about you, but if someone asks me if I would like something, unless there is a powerful reason to refuse I think it's only good manners to reply, Oh, yes please.

'Oh, yes please.'

'I thought we were just staying for one,' says Louise, placing a black mark against an otherwise blameless character.

'Oh come on,' I plead. 'I've had a hard life.'

This, as they go, is hardly a *bon mot* of Wildean brilliance. But she laughs, shoulders shaking, eyes swivelling like a horse, ever-so-slightly alarmingly out of control. I worry about people who do this. In the psychiatric trade, I believe they call it 'inappropriate affect'. It crosses my mind that she may be bonkers.

Drinks are delivered. 'How many cameras will we be using in the studio next week?' she asks. *Oh fuck. Quick, change the subject.*

'Five, I should think. Louise, can I ask you something? Do you like magic tricks?'

'No, I hate them actually.' *Hello*. A contrary opinion. A pile of sick she won't clear up.

'Really?'

'Yeah, I find them quite disturbing actually. They're a lie, aren't they? You believe – you're *made* to believe – that one thing is happening, when really all along, something *completely different* is going on. Like that trick you did with cigarette ash.'

'Have you sussed it?'

'No, but there must be a lie at the heart of it. And I hate being lied to. That's why I never watch magic on telly, I find it really irritating. Actually, I think the people who do it are a bit creepy.'

She's looking at me in a mildly challenging way. Her hands are on her knees and behind the brutalist apparatus on her face, she's blinking rather a lot. But ignoring the insult – she can't have meant *me*, surely? – she's right about magic, isn't she? And professional magicians.

She drains her spritzer.

'Would you like another?' I ask apprehensively. She would.

'Michael? You know that thing you did last time we were here?'

Christ, she *is* bonkers. 'Er, yes.'

'*Would* you like to do it again?'

4

The second time was much nicer.

We've been for a bite of supper to Kensington Place. (Now, I know what you're thinking. Doesn't this fool know any other decent places to eat and drink in West London? Sorry. What can I tell you? Creature of habit.) Anyhow, this was an occasion which involved squid (when doesn't it?), Chilean Merlot (see squid) and a long conversation about magic. I've asked her to explain her thesis in more detail, mainly so I can gaze in silence upon her marvellous features and not be required to say anything, stupid or otherwise. I've been imagining the moment when – 'May I?' – I gently lift the vile black plastic frames from the bridge of her nose.

I seem to recall a similar occasion not that long ago. Yasmin chattering about the illusions at the heart of smoking. The way you believe that one thing's happening (you're smoking to feel better), when all along it's actually something else (you're smoking to feel less worse). The illusion that cigarettes add pleasure to your life, when really they only cancel their own pain. I wasn't listening to that speech very closely either.

A man at the next table blows a plume of cigarette smoke at the ceiling. And yes, it's almost happening. I *do* almost feel sorry for him, rather than envy.

Afterwards, when we're standing on Notting Hill Gate by the Underground, waiting to snare her a taxi (several have gone past, but we've both pretended not to notice them), she says, 'Well, for one drink, it's been a lovely evening, Michael.'

We kiss. Don't ask me how it began. Maybe women can sense when men want to kiss them. Maybe they sense it before men know it themselves.

I think we just moved together at the same time. There's something wonderfully *answering* about the way her lovely mouth is chewing at mine, full of need and desire and pieces of trapped squid (this last, especially exciting to a lover of seafood). I feel her small firm body pressing into my own and it crosses my mind, it would be like going to bed with a ballerina.

I pull us apart, to check whether the face in my hands is the one I remember from over dinner. It is. We carry on where we left off. Young males in a passing car jeer vulgarly. Untrue that all the world loves a lover.

'Louise, would you come to a party with me?' I whisper after a particularly rigorous exchange. 'It's a big fancy-pants telly do. With cocktails and dancing and everything. I'd love it if you could come.' *And by then we'll have finished* Death Warmed Up. *And no longer be work colleagues. With all the associated . . . complications.*

She smiles. 'That would be great. Will there be anyone important there, do you think?' Before I can answer, she's grabbed me by the ears and is doing something very questing with her tongue (actually, thinking about it, maybe it would be more like going to bed with a dental hygienist). Out of the corner of my eye, I see the friendly yellow light of a London taxi approaching from the west. Without wishing to spoil a beautiful moment, I flap an arm and hope for the best. In time-honoured tradition, the cab sails to a halt, ten yards past us.

'The taxi,' I gasp.

If we can make it to the vehicle without falling over or being sick, if we don't betray any other sign of the stream of vodka and Merlot we've just hurtled down – and if she doesn't live south of the river – he *might* be prepared to take Louise home.

5

I read something inspiring that an American industrialist once said after losing a massive corporate-takeover battle with a bitter rival. Millions if not billions of dollars had been at stake. When asked for a comment, his reply was simple and to the point. 'They won. We lost. Next.'

In the absence of any practical revenge scenarios, this has clearly got to become my attitude to Clive. I mean, none of the runners really do it, do they?

1. **Clive is shot dead by police marksmen who mistake his cricket bat for a sawn-off shotgun (v. tricky to organise and probably illegal).**
2. **Alfie's family are born on his cream sofas (ridiculous, and no actual evidence that his sofas are that colour).**
3. **He turns up somewhere to collect a bogus award, and is exposed to ridicule in the trade press (pathetic).**
4. **The Dave Cleaver honey-trap with compromising photographs (sordid).**

5. Cards bearing his telephone number advertising sexual services appear in selected phone boxes outside gay pubs (oh for God's sake).

He won. I lost. Next. (Though honestly, it doesn't half stick in one's craw.)

Let it go. Rise above it. Get past it. Move on.

'Life will see to it that he is punished,' says Steve when I phone him at Belvedere. 'If you accumulate too many bad deeds, the great wheel of Karma rolls round and flattens you like a beetle.'

'I've never believed that.'

'No, neither have I.'

Gloom has settled upon me like a bank of fog. 'I suppose I just have to accept it.'

'Regrettable but mature.'

'Though they do say revenge is a dish best tasted cold.'

'Yes,' says Steve. 'You could wait forty years, then cut the brake cables on his wheelchair in the old people's home.'

'Rub cyanide on his dentures.'

'Introduce ground glass into his Complan.'

'Throw dog shit into his garden at night. Old people find that incredibly aggravating.'

'Or voracious snails. To decimate their precious bleeding begonias.'

Maybe old age does offer better payback opportunities. The trick, I suppose, is to harbour the grudge long enough.

'Changing the subject, how's Yasmin Swan?' I ask as casually as possible.

'Well, funnily enough, I saw her and some bloke together in BarBushKa last night. They looked . . . how can I put this? . . . quite close.'

Nick. Instantly I see what's happened. She's reared up in fright at the idea of marriage, had an unsuitable drunken fling with me, and then gone galloping back to the farm, nostrils flaring, for a handful of Polo Mints and a pat on the muzzle.

'What did he look like?'

'Rather fit, actually. Macho type. But huge great choppers. Quite the biggest set of teeth I've seen in a long time.'

6

'You've reached Yasmin Swan on Holy Delicious *at Belevedere Television. Leave a message after the tone and I'll get back to you as soon as I can.'*

'Yasmin. It's Michael. Did no-one ever tell you it's rude to sleep with a chap and then never call? I haven't seen you, haven't heard from you, I could be dead here. Ring me, please. I'd like a word.'

'You've reached Yasmin Swan on Holy Delicious *at Belevedere Television. Leave a message after the tone and I'll get back to you as soon as I can.'*

'Me again. Look, sorry if I sounded a bit sharp in that last message. I guess things are getting a bit urgent here, what with the show coming up on

Friday. I'd just really like to talk to you. OK, well, give us a call when you've got a minute.'

'You've reached Yasmin Swan on Holy Delicious *at Belevedere Television. Leave a message after the tone and I'll get back to you as soon as I can.'*

'Er . . . look, I'm going to be away from the office now for a couple of hours. I'm taking Maeve Middleton and our director out for a team-bonding lunch. I'll have the mobile with me, so do call if you get the chance, honestly I'll be glad for the interruption. Right then, see you. Bye.'

'You've reached Yasmin Swan on Holy Delicious *at Belevedere Television. Leave a message after the tone and I'll get back to you as soon as I can.'*

'. . . Yeah, see you tomorrow, Miles. Home safely. Cheers. Bye. (*Pause*) Fucking arsehole . . . Oh, hi. Listen, I suppose as it's bloody gone dark outside, you've probably left for the day. I've only just got back from lunch, would you believe, with the world's thirstiest man. Christ, can he put it away. We went to that jolly brasserie on Shepherds Bush Green where they do those nice matchstick chips. And I made the mistake of saying to Miles – Miles Kilbride, he's the director, Jesus what a piss artist – I said, you choose the wine, Miles. *Big* mistake. Well, young lady, he says to the waitress, peering over the top of his fucking spectacles at the menu, we'll *start* with two bottles of the South African red and two of the white. I mean, fuck me, there were only three of us, him and me and Maeve bloody Middleton. Actually, I always used to think she was a boring old trout but it turns out she's really quite a party animal. Miles was chatting her up like mad – which was a pretty nauseating spectacle to be honest – but by the time we left she was—'

'You've reached Yasmin Swan on Holy Delicious *at Belevedere Television. Leave a message after the tone and I'll get back to you as soon as I can.'*

'Yeah, your machine cut me off. Look, I won't drivel on. If you don't want to speak to me, don't. It's Michael by the way.'

'Hi, it's Yasmin. I'm not in right now, so leave a message after the beep.'

'Yasmin. It's Michael. Thought I'd give you a try at home. I've been out tonight, so I hope it's not too late but . . .'

'Hello?' *A male voice. Shit. Who's this?*

'Oh hello. Hi. Is, er, Yasmin there, please?'

'No, I'm afraid not. Who's calling?' *A deep, dark tone. Sounds like a grown-up.*

'Oh, just a friend of hers. Michael, Michael Roe.' *Silence* 'Any idea when she might be back at all?'

'I don't think I know you, do I, Michael? This is Nick. Yasmin's fiancé.' *Oh fuck. Dive dive dive.*

'Oh, hi, Nick. No, I don't believe we have . . . actually met.' (*Horrible pause. Rewind and delete that 'actually'.*) 'If we had, I'm sure I would have remembered. Look, I'm sorry for calling so late . . .' *Another pause. The guy's a cunt at these incriminatory silences.* 'Could you possibly give her a message?'

'Of course.'

'Er, just to say that, Michael rang. Michael *Roe*. And that I'll give her a bell at work tomorrow.'

'Is that it?'

'Yes, that's fine, thanks.'

'Michael, may I ask you something?'

Oh fuck. What? 'Yes, do.'

'Have *you* any idea where Yaz might have got to this evening?'

'Me? No. Why would I?' *Yaz. Its sickening intimacy.*

'Well, I know you used to work together. She often mentioned you.'

'Did she?' *Did she?*

'She enjoyed your chats about . . . addiction, I believe it was.'

'Yes, we were both trying to give up smoking.'

'And magic. She said you knew some good illusions.'

'Oh just a few silly tricks really.'

'But no idea where she might be tonight?' His voice is heavy with defeat. I have the ridiculous urge to say, look Nick, hop into a cab, come round to my flat, I'll open a bottle of whisky. I seem to have won her and lost her. You've probably lost her and found her a number of times. If we can't have her, we could at least *talk* about her.

'Sorry, no. No idea.'

'Well, goodnight. I'll give her the message.'

'Nick?'

'Yes?'

'Can I ask *you* something?'

'Sure.'

'Yasmin never told me. What do you do? For a living, I mean.'

'Well, I'm not surprised she never mentioned it. I'm with the Metropolitan Police.'

'Really? Any particular . . . branch?'

'Fraud Squad. Goodnight then.'

7

In the guttering of a house at the end of the Bearded Lady's garden, two pigeons are courting. If courting isn't too overblown a term for puffing one's neck up, and turning round in circles while nodding up and down. I've got a fine view of the proceedings from the couch and I know that, in a few seconds, he's going to jump on her back and do whatever pigeons do to each other. (What *do* they do, by the way? Do you know *anyone* who knows?) It *looks* like he stands on top of her for a moment, shakes about a bit and flies off, but there must be more too it than that, surely? Mind you, everything may be a lot simpler with pigeons. Perhaps your average boy pigeon isn't too fussy about girl pigeons. Maybe you'd never hear him say, 'Well, she's got to have a nice big beak on her, good claws – always been a bit of a claw-man myself – and a lovely pair of wings, obviously.' For him up there in the gutter, it might be anything in feathers.

'So, these young women. Hilary, Yasmin, Nicola and Lesley . . .'

'*Nicole* and *Louise* . . .'

'Nicole and Louise. You are attracted to all of them.'

'I know, it's ridiculous. They're all so different. Nicole is probably a foot taller than Louise. And Yasmin is terribly pale and dark, whereas Hilary is more sort of mousy. Louise and Yasmin are skinny. Hilary and Nicole are . . . fuller figured. I feel like that bloody pigeon. Anything in feathers.'

'Sorry?'

'Doesn't matter.' At eighty pence a minute, we probably don't need to speculate on the sex lives of the birds. 'It just seems a bit perverse to be equally drawn to such diverse creatures.'

'You wish to have sex with all of them, Hilary aside.'

'Like a shot. Including Hilary, as a matter of fact.'

Was that a twitch? Did she go to pluck at her skirt and restrain herself at the last moment, a micro-expression of disapproval?

'What's stopping you?'

'Well . . . the logistics for one thing.' But that's a good question. What *is* stopping me? Apart from the logistics and the necessary permissions.

'Do you have any dreams?' *What? Is she fed up with the sexual fantasies?* I hit her with a couple of dreams from last night.

1. I'm watching television. I can't identify the

programme, but somehow I know it's a repeat. And I'm with someone. Hilary maybe. We're watching it together and I'm sitting on the sofa, mocking this tired old show, when I suddenly realise . . . I have a burning cigarette in my hand. I've been *smoking*. I taste a crushing sense of disappointment which turns to fantastic relief when I wake up and realise it was only a dream.

2. I'm in the gallery of a TV show. We're on the air but, every time we cut to a guest, instead of a person sitting there it's a live turkey. I press the button and shout into Maeve's earpiece, 'Ask them about fucking Christmas.' But it's no good, they don't speak English. We need better guests. I quickly scramble together a replacement panel. And when we start again, it's with my mother and father, Mouse and Claudia. But they're hopeless and I'm thinking, Oh fuck, maybe we should get the turkeys back.

'Hmmm,' says the Bearded Lady. Little fear of contradiction there. 'What do you make of the first one?'

'Well, I've heard it's fairly common, when you've given up some addiction, to dream of relapse.'

'I believe so.'

'In the dream I'm mocking a *repeat*, which does kind of suggest the endless repetition of smoking. But then I'm horrified when I realise I'm actually smoking . . .'

'. . . Your unconscious is warning you, don't get too cocky. You've got to be on your guard.'

'Yes, and the fact that I'm disappointed in the dream and relieved in real life, suggests that my conscious and unconscious are in line on this one.'

'What about the turkeys?'

'It's a classic work-anxiety dream, isn't it? Fear that my show will be a turkey. The death theme echoed in the "ask them about Christmas" joke.'

'And your mother and father? And this mouse?'

'He's a person actually. I don't know what they're doing there. Feelings from childhood maybe. Not being in control.'

But now, a third dream comes back to me.

3. I am a contestant on *Who Wants To Be A Millionaire?* We've reached a big moment. And Chris Tarrant is saying to me, 'OK, this for £64,000.' The lights and the music do their thing. And here is the question. He asks me, 'Which one of the following is the right answer?' 'Is it, A: The Eiffel Tower, B: A baby with chicken pox, C: A signet ring, or D: A field of Edelweiss?'

As I've already asked the audience, phoned a friend and gone 50 50, I am entirely on my own. The clock is ticking. I have to plump for one.

'Edelweiss,' I say.

'Final answer?'

'Yes.'

'You're quite sure.'

'Yes.'

The music begins its sadistic build toward the moment of revelation . . . and I wake up. Fuck, am I right or wrong?

So what's that all about then?

'Well, there were four possible answers, weren't there?' says the Beaded Lady. 'And a little while ago we were talking about . . .'

'. . . Four possible *women*.'

'But, alas, we have run out of time. Maybe you should think about it in the meanwhile and we'll discuss it next time.'

Damn. And I didn't even get round to sacking her.

8

'OK, boys and girls. I'm hoping we can knock this bugger on the head in an hour and be in the bar by nine. So, no mistakes, please. Here we go. Good luck, everybody. Break a leg, Maeve. And . . . *run titles*.' With an arm and an index finder, Miles Kilbride makes a sort of 'charge' gesture in the direction of the wall of TV screens in front of him.

The director is looking especially natty this evening. Atop the pink shirt, swelling defiantly over the cavalry twill trousers, flutters a festive cravat. The white hair seems particularly thick and generous. And, to the usual scent of wine and cigar smoke, a new note has been added, a splash of eau de Cologne, I'd say, on a seafaring theme. Even in the dimmed lighting of the studio gallery, I can see a vein throbbing on his temple that wasn't throbbing this morning. One leg is jigging uncontrollably, freeing a canary-yellow heel from its slip-on loafer. Blow me down, he's actually excited. It's only a boring little late-night talk-fest we're making – it's not even live – but he can still hear the hunting horns and smell the fox.

'Twenty seconds on VT, twenty seconds,' trills Anita. She's sitting to Miles' left, with a pile of scripts, three stopwatches and a roll of extra-strong mints. (In common with every PA in television, Anita is trained to never be without extra-strong mints, to offer in times of crisis, when people crave alcohol, tobacco, food, or extra-strong mints.)

The titles play. The camera pans along the cadaver's leg on the morgue trolley, down to the label tied to its big toe. We read the words DEATH WARMED UP. The toe wiggles. Even though we've all seen it at least twenty times, everybody laughs. It's nerves.

'And *mix* through to camera one,' calls Miles. 'And start your move, one . . . and *lights*!'

The studio slowly brightens, the dark shapes resolving into six figures seated on black furniture. The floor is black. The background is black. The overall effect is one of brilliant pools of light in an otherwise edgeless void.

'It's a bit fuckin' black, isn't it?' growls Dave White from the chair behind me.

'Black is the new black,' I whisper to him gnomically. Bit bloody late to do anything about it now in any case.

Next to Dave sits A Very Senior BBC Person, a haunted woman who quite obviously does not get enough fresh air. These creatures do not generally come to studio recordings, so her presence here can only mean one of two things. She is taking a close personal interest in the show. Or she needs something to do for an hour before a dinner engagement.

Miles again, in director sing-song: 'Very nice, one. Thank you, Nigel. Coming to two next. And *two*. And *go*, two. And fade the music. And *cue Maeve*.'

'Good evening.' She pauses, doing something hesitant with her face, to make it seem like she's actually thinking this stuff up and not reading it off a glass screen. 'It's been called The Last Great Adventure . . .'

For a show about death, it's actually quite a good laugh. The bald scientist is a great pantomime baddy, alleging that the end is The End, and using chilling phrases like 'not one scintilla of evidence to the contrary.' The bishop quotes Nabokov: 'Life is a great surprise. I do not see why death should not be an even greater one.' He goes on about the Bible a bit too long, but I think we can easily get the scissors in there, as we TV producers like to say. The psychoanalyst explains why death plays a much bigger part in our lives than we realise. She quotes the last words of Somerset Maugham, of all people: 'Dying is a very dull, dreary affair and my advice to you is to have nothing whatever to do with it.' The doctor talks movingly about Deathbeds He Has Attended, locks horns nicely with the sceptical scientist and even manages a joke. 'I don't mind dying,' he says, 'the trouble is you feel so bloody stiff the next day.' But Farley is the star. Even though he does very little for most of the programme, by continually cutting back to his beautifully lit, iconic features, his face somehow serves to pull the whole thing together. Also, in best don't-give-a-fuck rock-legend fashion, he's lit a cigarette, actually a chain of them, and the image of the famous face, with the curling smoke picked out against the black is irresistible. He's the only thing you want to look at and Miles instinctively knows it.

'. . . So in a real, empirical sense, you *cannot* warm death up,' says the scientist. 'If you want to be poetic about it, you can say that human life, *all* life, is a candle flame burning briefly between two eternities of nothingness. Any other view is unsustainable.'

The Man of Reason looks well pleased with himself, having pissed so copiously on the bonfire. The bishop's big pink face on the monitor appears to have lost the will to live. The doctor is cranking himself up to say something boringly equivocal. The psychoanalyst is unhelpfully nodding in agreement.

'Funnily enough,' says Farley, '*Death Warmed Up* is the title of my forthcoming album.' Dave White and I glance at one another. 'Most artists get round to the subject eventually. Usually at the point where the end seems nearer than the beginning.' A respectful hush has fallen on the other panellists. 'With me, it's happened rather sooner than I had planned. It may be a year. Two at the most. Oncology is actually rather fascinating when you go into it. The word I've been given, on the best medical advice, is *inoperable*.' Farley lights another cigarette.

In the studio, in the gallery, the shock is palpable. The Very Senior Woman from the BBC, I notice, has stopped fiddling with her Psion Organiser. A lone voice cuts through the silence.

'Two, give me the shrink. Three, stay on the bald cunt. Four on the Bish. OK, Nigel, creep in nice and slowly on Farley. Fuck *me*.'

Oddly, no-one has to ask any questions. Farley simply tells his story, how thirty years of rock 'n' roll excess ended up one morning with a curious little pain that wouldn't go away. We watch what television does best. A human head in close up, growing larger in the frame. And now, as he explains how he is philosophically *offended* at the prospect of life carrying on without him (nothing to do with the money, or the lovely new wife or anything like that) tears are standing in the famous eyes. Oh my God . . . paydirt. He's going to cry. The TV equivalent of five lemons on the fruit machine.

Maeve Middleton looks like she's been slapped. I press the button and murmur into her earpiece, 'Does he believe in *any* sort of afterlife?'

'Do you believe in any sort of afterlife?'

Farley takes a deep breath. The much-imitated delivery tonight may be a bit more razor blades than treacle. 'I honestly wish I could say I did. I'm afraid I go with the candle-in-the-nothingness idea.'

It's the perfect moment to end it. As the lights fade and the set returns to the edgeless void, the Very Senior BBC Woman turns to Dave White. 'Congratulations,' she says. 'Seriously compelling stuff. But – sorry, this might sound like a silly question – wasn't it supposed to be a programme about football fans?'

In the tiny green room, cast and crew gather to glug Latvian Chardonnay. Simon has made a beeline for pretty little Louise and is no doubt regaling her with exciting tales of substance abuse. Nicole, white-faced, is being heavily chatted up by Nigel (camera one). Miles is paying all sorts of compliments to Maeve Middleton ('You have great constancy; directors love that in a performer').

Dave White materialises at my side. 'Well, I think we got away with that,' he growls. 'I guess the only danger now is they'll want us to make a whole series.'

The room, which is otherwise crowded, has left a gap around Farley, whether out of respect for his legendary or health status, it's unclear. He is in deep discussion with the existential shrink. But as he clocks me watching him, he does a funny thing. He turns away slightly from the elderly woman in order to take another drag on his cigarette. And in doing so, he is in the best possible position to send me a huge, comical, unmistakable *wink*.

'Did you see that?' I ask Dave.

Could it be that it was all bollocks about the illness? A cynical ploy to shift more product?

The awful thing is this. We know we've got a great show. We don't care.

9

So now I am famous. The news made the front page of all the papers, the clip of Farley choking up has been shown round the world and the programme itself has rapidly found a slot; it's being shown on Monday night, as a nice meaty double bill with the snooker. In fact the BBC have got very excited about the whole *Warmed Up* concept. They think *Warmed Up* could be a 'brand', like *Neighbours/Builders/Philosophers From Hell* or *Hollywood Wives/Dogs/Loss Adjusters*. They want Dave White and I to think up a dozen more 'difficult' issues we could apply the *Warmed Up* treatment to. In the unfamiliar position of being flavour of the month, we went to a bar to celebrate our triumph, got terrifically pissed and produced the following list of ideas for future shows:

1. ***Senility Warmed Up***
2. ***Incontinence Warmed Up***
3. ***Third World Debt Warmed Up***
4. ***Bestiality Warmed Up***
5. ***Folk Dancing Warmed Up*** **(third Martini really beginning to kick in here)**
6. ***Masturbation Warmed Up***
7. ***Suicide Warmed Up***
8. ***Incest Warmed Up***
9. ***European Monetary Union Warmed Up*** **(getting desperate now)**
10. ***Misery Warmed Up***

I think we may need to have another stab at this sometime.

Anyhow, I have been quoted widely. *'It came as a complete shock. We had no idea he was unwell. All our thoughts are with Farley and his family'* – and not with the surrounding publicity, oh no. The *Independent* called me Michael Rose, which was a bit annoying. And in the TV trade magazine, *Broadcast*, all the comments came from the pale Very Senior BBC Woman who managed to create the impression that the whole thing was her idea. Nevertheless, today – and maybe only today – I am hot. It is as something of a media celebrity that I hand over my big cardboard invitation and enter the function suite of the corporate hotel near Lancaster Gate chosen to be the scene of Belvedere Television's Tenth Anniversary Bash.

The bad news: I may be famous, I may be hot,

but I cannot get a date. I have been multiply stood up. Karmic retribution no doubt for inviting too many women in the first place.

1. **Hilary rang to tell me that yes, she would be coming to the party . . . but with someone else. Namely Lee, the hang-gliding cameraman who's been invited because it turns out he shot most of *Tax-Men*. Or was it *Sweet Factory*? One of Belvedere's big hits, anyway. She called him 'an admirer' so I don't suppose they are technically going out together. Well, at least not yet.**
2. **Ditto Louise. There was a nasty little moment when she collared me on her last day in the office. She wanted to thank me 'for everything' including the invite to the party, but she's started seeing something of a young man who has somehow invited her in his own right, bloody cheek.**
3. **And to complete my happiness, Nicole called to say 'thank you so much for your help, Michael' – *uh?* – that she'll see me at the party, but she'll be with Gary. Gary kind of insisted. She hopes I'll 'understand'.**

Taken together with the fact that . . .

4. Olivia will no doubt be surgically grafted to Clive's arm all evening, and

5. Yasmin will also be here (but who with?)

. . . my current plan is to hit the bar early, and often.

By the look of the place – tables all set with loads of cutlery, decorations and wine cooling in buckets – we're in for the full sit-down knife-and-forker, as these things are known to the TV fraternity. On the stage above the dance floor, they've erected a video wall: a pile of TV screens which can all either play the same picture, or a different picture, or they can all carry a separate element of what becomes a socking great big picture. At the moment, it's a shifting mosaic of Belvedere logos and snatches of the company's greatest hits, to the backing of Stevie Wonder's *Happy Birthday To Ya*, a truly gruesome touch, if you want my opinion. The guests, at the Preliminary Milling Around With Drinks stage of the evening, are already making that excited low rumbling noise that people make when they know that six hours of alcoholic disgrace has just retracted its undercarriage and the seat belt signs have been turned off.

I procure a bracing vodka and tonic and I'm eddying about, in that way you do at parties when you arrive on your own and you're not quite sure who you want to talk to, and I'm just beginning to panic slightly when Steve appears.

How we love to sneer at events like this. At the horrible hotel, with its sullen underclass of barmen and waiters; at the vulgarity and pretentiousness of Belvedere Television for picking this joint (and not a groovy bar in Soho, or even Notting Hill, for Christ's sake); at the nasty little matchbooks they've had printed up and scattered around bearing the legend, *Belvedere Television, The First Ten Years*. Of course, in reality, we're deeply envious of the company's success, in particular of the wealth that Monty and his business partners have brought upon themselves through, for the most part, old-fashioned hard work. Through simply *being bothered enough*. This is a quality that has always eluded me. Talent helps, of course. But without the *application* behind it, one achieves nothing in TV. The same is probably true of dentistry. Or tax accountancy. Or deep-sea fishing. Depressing, isn't it?

But we're not here to realise bitter truths about life. We're here to sneer. At Clive Wilson, who is mucking around with a laptop by the video wall (no doubt later on he'll be playing a key role in some terrible visual presentation); at all these young people who *believe*; who believe in Belvedere, in television, and who will be doing our jobs in five or ten years. We're here to sneer at Monty, glad-handing his way through the throng, spraying charm, bullshit and firm handshakes in every direction; Monty, who's spotted me and is heading this way. Steve does something cynical with his eyebrow and moves off in the direction of a startlingly attractive woman with wild red hair.

'Michael!' Monty is presidential, his left hand gripping my upper right arm as he pumps my right hand. 'Great to see you. And fantastic stuff with Farley Dines, by the way. A fabulous piece of TV. The Beeb must be thrilled.'

'They do seem rather pleased. But you know what it's like. There *is* no "they" at the BBC. Just a lot of separate medieval baronies warring amongst themselves. Our particular Baron – Baroness as it happens – is quite chuffed, yeah.'

Have I gone in too deep, with this critique of the Corporation? Monty doesn't seem to know quite what to say.

'Look, Michael. Are you free for lunch next week? I'm well aware this whole furry animals thing was your baby. And Clive's got far too much on his plate at the moment. And . . . well . . .' he sighs, 'maybe we acted a bit hastily over that business with the Nazi.' Monty skewers me with his full-bore sincerity look. 'I'd like to see if there's a way of bringing you back into the Belvedere family.'

I don't know whether to laugh or puke. They're shameless, these TV creatures. When they think they want something from you, they'll flatter and cajole, buy you lunch and offer you money (and yes, the greatest of these is money). But when you're no longer useful to them, you'll be off the payroll faster than you can fall through a trap door. Oh yes, they'll continue to smile and say hello to you, but only so they can feel better about themselves. I know. It's happened to me. And it'll happen to me again. And I've probably even done it to a few people myself.

'All families have their . . . misunderstandings, Michael. The important thing is to mend fences and move on, don't you think?'

The calculation is probably this: Clive is slowly being found out as the talentless tosser he always was. The bad publicity about *Holy Delicious* didn't really do any permanent harm. In fact, if anything, I gather the ratings have actually *improved*. And the debacle with the sweaty Ukrainian? A two-day wonder, which everyone has now forgotten.

Against that . . . Michael Roe is the person who got one of the most famous faces in the world to cry on television.

I should tell this salt-and-pepper-haired weasel to go and fuck himself. If I wasn't such a craven, gutless telly-type myself, I would.

'Sure. That would be great, Monty.'

'*Fantastic*. I'll get Sita to call you tomorrow. Enjoy the party.' His gaze refocuses ten yards over my shoulder. '*Angelica! Darling!* Sorry Michael. Got to schmooze the reigning Queen of religion-meets-cookery.'

I admire the way he covers the ground towards Angelica Doubleday, arms spread wide, holding her gaze throughout. The way he embraces her without crushing her gown, the two kisses that disturb neither hair nor make-up. The man's a class act, you got to hand it to him.

Angelica, of course, is beaming. Far from being

cancelled, her programme is getting a 'fresh new look', a new title – *Heavenly Bites* – and Angelica herself will be piloting a new Oprah-style talk-show in the autumn called . . . can you guess? . . . *Angelica*. Steve says the first episode is to be called People Who've Been Stitched Up By The Press (And The Journalists Who Turned Them Over).

My stomach lurches. Through the sea of heads and shoulders, Hilary pops into view. By her standards she's wearing a rather short, low-cut dress and, horribly, she's with a pointlessly good-looking young man who, from the ruffian-in-a-smart-suit look, can only be Lee the cameraman.

'Michael, this is Lee.' No 'Hello, Michael.' No kiss. No anything.

'Hello, Lee. I'm Michael,' I add pointlessly. (Well, she started it.)

'Hi.'

And now no-one can think of anything else to say. After all, what is there? From Hilary's expression and Lee's uncertain smile, it's blindingly clear that Lee (who I would guess has not yet navigated his way into Hilary's knickers) is painfully aware that standing before him is one who has made that particular trip many hundreds of times. At the same time, I am equally uncomfortable with the knowledge that here is yet another young pretender with a monosyllabic name and a passion for fresh air and danger. What's the protocol here? Come on, Hilary, *you* say something.

'So congratulations about *Death Warmed Up*,' she

says finally. 'Yours is the first name I've ever read in a newspaper who I actually know.'

'I feel a bit guilty about it all, to be honest,' I lie. 'Getting attention from what is, after all, a personal tragedy.'

As I recount the circumstances of that rare TV event – the genuine *surprise*, in a medium where everything is usually rehearsed to death – I realise Hilary and I are doing something over Lee's head. We're flirting with each other. (You can't tell from the words. We're doing it sub-textually.) I'm telling my story and she is nodding *ironically*. There's something about the set of her eyes that is taking the piss. As Hilary is not by nature a piss-taker, I interpret this as flirting. And I'm flirting back. Elaborating the tale with an extra *knowingness* that Hilary will recognise has been put in specially for her. Lee is left to play the role of good-natured innocent in a long-standing squabble. He seems a pleasant enough young man, but honestly . . .

'Anyhow,' I say, 'isn't everyone sick of bloody telly? I understand you hang-glide, Lee. That must be interesting. You must meet some interesting people.'

'Oh look,' says Hilary, to the rescue. 'People are sitting down for dinner. What table are you on?'

'Fuck, is there a seating plan? I *hate* seating plans. The terrible tyranny of who you could get stuck with.'

'See you later,' trills Hilary and, taking Lee's arm, off she wobbles on her high heels. I watch them move away together, and I'm wondering exactly how I feel about all this, when suddenly she looks back and pokes a long pink tongue out at me.

Ahh. See, she *does* care.

They've put me on a sort of middle-ranking table with a sample of middle-ranking Belvedere types and their other halves. Happily, Steve's here and he's somehow contrived to be sitting next to the startlingly attractive woman with wild red hair. He looks rather pleased with himself. My own heart skips with something close to joy when I discover the name on the place card next to me is Nicole's.

Sorry, I never really notice the *detail* of what women are wearing. If I was better at it, I'd bring you a full report. I can say however that the overall effect, when she pulls up alongside me and drops into her seat, is dazzling. The long, *long* legs that come shooting out of the flimsy black number seem to take forever to angle, bend and fold themselves politely under the table. There's a fond brush of lips against cheek. Her eyes sparkle and I think she means it when she says, 'I'm very glad to see you, Michael.'

A glance at the card at the place next to her tells me she's here with someone called Gary Saltmarsh.

'Gary Saltmarsh?' I inquire.

'Oh, thank God for Gary Saltmarsh. Such a sad story. And such a brilliant ending.' I give her one of my *do go on* looks. 'Well, you know how his widowed mother used to keep Jack Russells, don't you? How they all died in that terrible fire in the barn last month. How Gary's mother was inconsolable. So when you told him about Alfie . . . well, it's just too perfect. She's adopting Alfie *and* Sheena, *and* Basil! They're going to be able to stay together, and they're going to live in the country! In Shropshire! They'll be so happy, I just know they will.'

'Nicole. Did you say, when *I* told him about Alfie?'

'Yes. I'm really grateful to you, honestly.'

'What does this Gary Saltmarsh look like?'

'What do you mean?'

'Well, I don't think I actually know anyone called Gary Saltmarsh.'

'You do. You gave him my number. Anyway, here he is now.'

A familiar figure hovers into view.

'Ah, good evening chief. Frightful fucking crush up at the bar. Had to line the stomach with a couple of honest pints before we're forced to start drinking this cheap vino collapso.'

'Oh, *that* Gary Saltmarsh.'

'I want to thank you, squire. For making it possible for me to bring happiness into the lives of two women in the winter of their years. My old mother . . .'

'. . . Your *widowed* old mother . . .' I add helpfully.

'. . . Indeed, whose farmstead will once again ring to the yelping of healthy hounds going about their doggy business . . .' *Where does he get this shit?* 'And the lovely Nicole's elderly neighbour, whose only concern was to find a good home for her canine brood before they proved too much for her. Michael, I salute you, chief. OK, speech over, let's party.'

Later, when Nicole slips away to powder her nose, 'Gary Saltmarsh' tells me the whole story. How, through his work in the entertainment world, the diminutive scribbler became aware of Nicole; how, though they have never met, he has admired her for years from afar – 'fucking hell, the legs on that bird. Have you ever seen anything like it?' – how he never imagined an opportunity would arise to ask her out.

'So when you brought up the topic of Farley Dines' mutt at that Chinky, I knew you had to have been talking to the lovely Nicole. So I gave her a bell . . . and the rest is history, as they say, chief.'

'The tragic fire in the barn . . . the grief-stricken widowed mother . . .'

'The power of good storytelling, matey. Even fucking Aristotle knew about that.'

'And what about Gary Saltmarsh. Who's he, when he's at home?'

'Just a professional *nom de whatnot*. When, for operational reasons, I must hide my real identity under a bushel.'

'What reasons would they be?'

'The lovely Nicole must never discover the role of the Fourth Estate in this happy affair.'

'You mean you're doing it for *love*? And not a story?'

'I'm smitten, matey.'

'You don't seriously imagine . . .'

'I know, I know, my eyeballs barely come up to her tits. But you'd be surprised what you can achieve with a bit of effort. Birds respect persistence. They reward it, I'm told. In any case, they're all the same size when they're on their backs.'

'What are you really going to do with Alfie and Sheena and Basil?'

'Who cares? Drown the fuckers probably. Whoops. Say nothing. Here she comes.'

'Who do Belvedere think Gary Saltmarsh is, Dave?'

'Just another TV correspondent, come to celebrate their string of hit shows.'

'And Nicole?'

'Dunno. She hasn't asked me yet. I'll think of something.'

We munch our way through the avocado prawn starters, the warm poached salmon and the new potatoes. But honestly, fuck it . . . Dave Cleaver must know some awfully good stories because, every time I turn round to look at them, Nicole's shaking with laughter and touching her hair, or touching *his* arm in that *stop, stop, you're killing me* gesture. It's scary. Maybe he's right. Maybe women really *do* reward persistence; they want to be wanted and, if you want one enough, there's no reason why you can't have her as long as you're prepared to make a really big effort, and you don't run out of funny things to say.

'He's terribly amusing, your friend,' Nicole confides when Dave scurries off for a sneaky peek in his joke book.

'Really? I'd no idea he could be such a charmer. I think he's taken a bit of a shine to you.'

'He's quite . . .' *Quite what? Quite short? Quite ridiculous? What?* 'He's quite forward, isn't he? What does he do?'

'Who, Gary?' And now I do something that I really can't explain. I tap-tap the side of my nose confidentially. 'Don't tell anyone,' I say to her, 'but Gary is about to share in an Internet floatation which should net him – personally – to the nearest ten million, let's say . . . around a hundred million pounds. Only on paper, of course.'

'Of course.'

'He'll probably only be worth half that in real money.'

'I see.'

'Gary is a small but genuinely weird . . . genius.'

Nicole has gone rather serious. Actually, make that awe-struck. I'm beginning to wonder why I didn't tell her he was an unemployed sex-offender. 'What does his Internet company do?'

'I'm afraid you'll have to ask him that.'

When 'Saltmarsh' returns to his seat, I have to break into conversation with Steve to stop myself from laughing.

'I've told Nicole that Cleaver is an Internet millionaire,' I whisper.

'You mean Saltmarsh, don't you?'

'Yeah, Saltmarsh. Horribly, I think she believes it.' Steve introduces me to his striking companion who, it turns out, he met in BarBushKa. She's a film editor from Sarajevo. When she offers me a

cigarette, I tell her that I have given up. Her eyes flash.

'In my country we have a saying,' she says. 'If you stop smoking, you will smoke again. If you stop drinking, you will drink again. If you stop gambling, you will gamble again. But if you stop fucking . . . you won't fuck again.'

Steve looks *very* pleased with his new friend.

'Ladies and gentlemen . . . if I might just say a few words.' Monty is on his feet at the video wall. The hubbub in the great room falls to a respectful murmur. 'The last ten years have been a remarkable ride . . .'

He's good at this sort of thing. Mixing up the self-congratulatory with the you-should-all-feel-very-proud stuff, chucking in some bits about the fast-changing TV environment and how *we must all* respond to it or die (code for lower budgets and job cuts); plus the anecdotes and gags whose positive reception have been assured by several hundred bottles of Bulgarian Chardonnay.

'And now with the help of Mr Wilson and his computer . . . let me show you our vision of this company's future.'

A few feet away from Monty at the side of the stage, Clive *rat-tats* a couple of keystrokes into the laptop. Up comes a graphic on the video wall, *Belvedere Television: The Next Ten Years*. The greasy little fucker has a horribly capable expression on his face.

'Oh God, I don't think I can bear to watch this,' I murmur to Steve.

Monty continues. 'It's propitious of course that we mark our birthday year with a major new commission in the field of family entertainment – thank you, Electra – *The Sweet Furry Baby Animal Show*.'

Clive rat-tats. The graphic vanishes and is replaced by . . . what *looks* like a man fucking a horse. Laughter. A bit crude maybe, but a nice touch nonetheless, a company sufficiently at ease with itself to be able to laugh at the absurdities of television. Monty, too close to the video-wall to see what's on it properly, ploughs on. Clive rat-tats.

Another horse. With a young woman this time. Clive taps again. Here's a donkey doing something that was never intended by Mother Nature. The girls in the photos, I notice, look Slavic. Monty is wondering why his remarks about reinventing 'aah factor television' are yielding such a big reaction. Now there's a bear. Followed by a goat. Laughter is giving way to unease. Clive is beginning to panic. There doesn't seem to be anything he can do. Every key he presses unleashes yet another appalling image, each worse than the one before: dogs, monkeys, chickens – *chickens?* – snakes, cattle – a pornographic collection of quite mind-numbing depravity. The guests watch dumbstruck. Waiters, dishes in hand, stand rooted to the spot. There are cries of 'Stop it!' 'Turn it off!' Somewhere a girl has started to sob rhythmically. Monty at last has realised what's happened. Clive is very pale. His fingers peck furiously at the keyboard, but he can do nothing to halt the stream of sickening visions. Something monstrous is occurring with a huge male turkey. Now . . . Christ, is that a *wolf*? Finally, he yanks a cable out of the back of the machine and the video-wall becomes a snowstorm of static. A wave of astonished chatter sweeps the room. Someone cheers.

I realise I am on my feet. Dave Cleaver is at my side.

'Russian hardcore porn,' he says out of the side of his mouth. 'Very nasty stuff. Someone must have switched the disc on him. Sort of thing that could happen to anyone, chief.'

And he winks at me.

Monty does his best to make a joke out of it. 'I hope no-one was too offended by that exclusive preview of Clive Wilson's holiday snaps.' The laughter that follows is more from relief than anything else. Shortly afterwards the disco strikes up and, half an hour later, the incident is all but forgotten. Except that on my way back from the toilet, I pass Monty and Clive pressed into an alcove.

Monty, crimson-faced, is hissing with rage. 'This

business is all about people having confidence in you. What are they going to think if we can't even organise a glorified fucking slide show?'

'I'm terribly sorry, Monty, I've no idea how it happened.' Clive's voice is shaking.

'Well, you'd better fucking find out then.'

I believe a light smile is playing about my features as I saunter back into the party. Would you believe it, I even feel a bit sorry for the cunt? Perhaps that is a mark of anger finally softening into something like forgiveness. I procure a drink and stand at the edge of the dance floor, feeling not that far off happy. Before me is a choppy sea of lounge suits, bare shoulders and shiny hair flicking about the place. As Edwin Collins asserts that he's *Never Met A Girl Like You Before*, a spinning glitter-ball sends bomblets of light crashing into the throng below. The place is throbbing – everyone *so* much wants to forget those haunting, disgusting images – and I have one of those little party epiphanies. When every scene your eyes come to rest upon seems to bear a weight, like a music sequence in a movie. There's Steve with his new wild-woman; she doing a wild-woman dance, arms above her head, hair whipping about dangerously; he, cigarette burning out of the side of his mouth, jerking spasmodically in an acceptable male way, and clearly deeply into *her*. There's Nicole and Dave Cleaver. Waves of simple harmonic motion (if you remember your physics) seem to shudder up and down her long slender body. He meanwhile is wiggling his silly hips, he's playing imaginary maracas, clicking his fingers, pointing theatrically at the ceiling, tumbling his fists round one another; even doing that one where you wag your index finger in a 120-degree arc; in short, performing in a manner that can be best summarised by the phrase *complete pillock*. But his companion is oblivious. Tonight it doesn't matter how preposterous he is. Tonight he is not Dave Cleaver, tabloid pond-life, he is Gary Saltmarsh, Internet millionaire. I feel strangely happy for him.

Over by the bar, my first sight this evening of Yasmin, tilting her horsy face upwards and firing a plume of smoke at the rafters. She's flirting with David White, who in turn is baring his remarkable set of teeth and laughing and . . . I was about to say joking (maybe just laughing will cover it). Electra Fuchs and Angelica Doubleday have formed an intriguing little dyad, their respective fame-stroke-influence weightings being just about equivalent. Hilary and Lee are loitering near the opposite shore of the dance floor. He's kind of jigging about annoyingly, as if any moment the music might just . . . *take* him, for fuck's sake. Hilary looks a little lost, and I have a momentary urge to go and rescue her.

But here, just a few paces away from me in a gaggle of his acolytes, Clive Wilson, his face twitching uncontrollably, dips his hand into his jacket pocket and produces – the unmistakable red-and-white markings – a pack of Marlboro. Clive, who doesn't smoke. Who *didn't* smoke, until I gave him one of mine. I watch in wonderment at the practised way he offers round the box (the perfect angle at the elbow; the correct rotation on the wrist). His gang are accepting, dip-dip-dipping into the Marlies like baby birds at their mother's throat. And now he feeds himself a cigarette. Lights, winces, inhales. I watch Clive smoking. Inhaling. Exhaling. His face flinching with each hot little packet of smoke. I imagine his lungs flooding with toxic fumes, the 4,000 separate poisons invading his system, addicting his loathsome being. He looks older. There's a new, crushed set to his eyes. I realise I have not forgiven him. I am not sorry for him. I zoom in on the simple white cigarette trapped between his fingers and my heart fills with pleasure.

Oh joy. Clive has become a smoker.

Think of really good – untraceable – revenge on Clive ☑

The disco is a seething sex-pit of young women and men who've had far too much to drink. Cooking very nicely, in other words. Oasis have filled the dance floor, although, why *have* you got to 'roll with it?' What exactly are the benefits of being prepared to 'take it slow?' I mean, where is the *reasoning*? (Sorry, a bit pissed myself now.)

Someone jabs me in the back and, when I turn around, it's Louise. She's wearing some tight, spangly party number and I feel the familiar small shock of attraction to her. Two black lacquered chopsticks hold her hair up at the back. They are a perfect match for the long-limbed crustacean that has her face in a vice-like grip.

'You've got chopsticks in your head,' I point out by way of an opener (well, it's that time of evening).

'I know,' she replies. 'I've got some sweet-and-sour pork in my handbag.' This strikes me as easily the funniest thing she has ever said, and I warm hugely to the curious little creature.

'Doesn't that florescent orange sauce make the lining all sticky?' I bellow against the noise.

She looks at me oddly. 'It was a joke. I haven't really.' I can't tell if she's being ironic, post-ironic or merely feeble-minded. She tells me how happy she was working on *Death WarmedUp* and how, now that the show is a hit, she has walked straight into another job. Apparently, it's a 'new vehicle' for Dale Winton.

'So where's this new young man of yours?' I ask, trying hard to keep it cheery. *Have you had a row? Has he perhaps been tragically killed in a gas explosion?*

'He's getting more drinks.'

And sure enough, lumbering into this scene bearing two glasses of white wine, steps the hopeless figure of Simon, our hotshot on work experience.

'You found the bar, then,' I say unnecessarily.

'Kickin' party.' He grins sheepishly. 'I'm getting really trolleyed.'

Louise glows, as if her paramour has said something exquisitely romantic. 'Do you know Simon's dad then?' My heart sinks as she names one of the richest and most powerful men in television, a TV titan who Monty has been known to play golf with. There's a photo of the two of them on his office wall. 'Monty invited him tonight but he hates dos like this. So we've got his ticket.'

Now that I look at his face again, I do see something of the famous father. In the son however, the legendary pugnacity has been translated into a kind of determined gormlessness. A Will to Failure. Why had I never troubled to discover this boy's *surname*?

I leave Tristan and Isolde staring into one another's eyes. At the bar, I discover a very chipper Dave Cleaver.

'Mr Saltmarsh,' I hail the wicked little scribe. 'I trust your stock is performing well with the lovely Nicole.'

'Oh yes, chief. I'd say I was well in there. There's a *lot* of interest in these new media launches.'

'I forgot to ask you. What exactly is the nature of your Internet business?'

He taps the side of his nose confidentially. 'That's commercially sensitive information just at the moment, chief. But I can reveal our newest idea. Very hot, this one. It's a website that brings bored millionaires together with the people who want their money. There'll be loads of begging e-mails of course. Very poignant, no doubt. Indecent proposals, I expect there'll be a ton of those,' he says, his eyes lighting up at the thought, 'plus many genuine and fascinating proposals. We're calling it Just Give Me The Fucking Money Dot Com.'

'*We*? Who's *we?*'

'Nicole and I. It's her idea actually. Well, we kind of developed it together. Now let me buy you a bottle of champagne, chief. By way of a thank you for making such a beautiful gesture in the cause of Romance.'

As I wander through the tables and chairs clutching Dave's bottle of Moet, I realise I have no idea whether or not he is joking.

I find Hilary nursing a spritzer and a Lambert and Butler. Her lipstick is smudged and her eyes aren't all that well focused either. When I kiss the side of her neck, she pulls away irritably.

'What's the matter? Don't you like me any more?' I ask.

She stares at me as if I am stupid or something. 'Michael, I am so thoroughly pissed off. I am pissed off with you. I am pissed off with . . . everything just now.' (Hilary is in a bad mood, I can tell.)

'Come home with me. Let's talk.'

'Aren't you listening? I'm not in the mood.'

'You're not going home with that great . . . lunk, are you?'

'Lee? He's very *into* me, Michael.'

'So what? What do you like about him?'

She stops to think about this one. 'I like him. He's very . . . he wants me, and I like that. It makes me feel like a woman.'

Jesus. Maybe Dave Cleaver is right. Maybe all that women want is to be wanted. Want one enough and you're three-quarters of the way there.

'And I don't make you feel like a woman?'

'Well, you did.'

'Hilary, you can't just like someone because they like you. There has to be a better reason than that.'

'He goes hang-gliding. I like that about him.'

'Sorry, was that one of your great passions? I had no idea.'

'Just leave it, will you?'

'You and I have something *mutual*, Hilary. You don't just like me because I like you . . .'

'I don't like you at all, at the moment . . .'

'. . . We understand one another.'

'No, Michael. We don't understand one another. We *stand* one another.'

'Well, that counts for *something*, doesn't it?'

'Look, here's Lee. You'd better go now.'

'Hilary come home with me . . .'

'Just go, will you.'

I bump into Yasmin and David White, half-dancing and half-canoodling together. There's a blinding explosion of tooth enamel as he spots me and smiles.

'Hey, Michael. Good to see you man. This is one . . . foxy lady.'

She's embarrassed. For him. For her. For me. For all of us. She packs him off to fetch more drinks.

'Does the Fraud Squad know about him?' I ask sweetly.

'Don't be like that,' she replies. 'I think this is something I'm just going to have to work through.'

She's wearing her clingy Chinese number tonight, tigers and orchids are rampant all the way up her lithe skinny body. The music's got a whole lot louder – *Just Can't Get Enough,* Depeche Mode – so I put my mouth close to her ear. A wave of perfume wafts off her hair. 'You know, Yasmin, for a while I wondered if *we* might have been quite good together.'

'Us!' Her eyes have gone very wide. She grabs my arm and yells into my ear: 'Michael, you're very sweet but I am fatally flawed. All my life, *all my life*, I have had *terrible* taste in men. No honestly, really appalling. I'm attracted to arseholes. Not bastards . . . arseholes. There is a difference.'

'Yes, I can see that. But what about those Martinis in the Pharmacy? And those evenings in your flat. And . . . and when we ended up in bed.' Easier somehow to bellow this stuff against a wall of noise, than speak it quietly in a silent room.

She cocks her head to one side. Smiles. Grabs my earlobe and pulls it gently towards her. 'Well, I guess at times you must have been a bit of an arsehole yourself.'

David White, reappearing with two bottles of

Becks, comes swizzling round her like John Travolta in *Saturday Night Fever*. He pirouettes to a halt. Lights up a grin that's bounced by the mirror-ball to every corner of the festivities.

I think it may have been the nicest thing she ever said to me.

Sitting all by herself, smoking a cigarette and studying the wreckage of dinner with a distracted air, is Olivia. Her beautiful bare shoulders have been dusted with something to make them sparkle. From the de-focused look in her eyes when I drop into the seat next to hers, I'd say she was three-parts pissed.

'Enjoying the party?' I inquire.

'Dreadful,' she shudders. The lenses of her glasses look smeared.

'Not having a good time?'

She blasts a jet of smoke straight at me. 'Clive thinks he may be about to lose his job. Over that business with the animal pictures. He's horribly drunk and, I'm sorry to say, I'm heading the same way.'

I have a hard time fighting a dirty great grin off my face. 'I'm sorry to hear that, Olivia.'

She takes a deep glug. 'Who have you come with?'

'On my own actually.'

'Lucky you.'

'Oh?' *Doooo go on*.

'Clive is one of those people who shouldn't be

allowed to drink. He'll throw up tonight. In the taxi, if we're lucky. In bed, if we're not.'

'I've always wanted to be sick on a small dog,' I tell her. 'Just to be able to say, *Fuck me, I don't remember eating that*.'

She snorts at my effort to cheer her up. I stand and squeeze her shoulder. 'I'm sure everything will be fine,' I say, my heart singing at Olivia's misery. 'After all, it's only television.'

Her perfume is on my fingers when I sniff them a few moments later.

In the end, Clive does not throw up in the taxi or in bed. At least, I assume he doesn't because I discover him throwing up in the hotel toilet. He has assumed the classic position, on his hands and knees, head over the bowl, groaning horribly. I watch for a few moments, the sweat-soaked shirt straining across his back with each violent heave. I have a strong urge to kick him. But they say you shouldn't when a man is down, so since there is no-one else in the room, I take a certain grim pleasure in turning out all the lights when I leave. I am rewarded with a wonderfully satisfying howl of anguish as I close the door behind me, leaving Clive on the floor, cuddling the white china and retching in the darkness. (Childish, I know. But a chap can get sick of being a grown-up all the time.)

EPILOGUE

Have dinner party ☑

Be nicer to parents ☑

It took a couple of weeks, but I finally came up with a solution to my dream. The one about the £64,000 question from *Who Wants To Be a Millionaire?* Why I gave Edelweiss as the correct answer. (I won't bore you with the details; for those who are interested in these things, here's a clue: the baby with chicken pox was really a *babe* with *specs*.)

So in the end, it turns out my list was a little like Michael Heseltine's. Neither of us achieved everything we'd set out to. He didn't become Prime Minister. There are still clothes in my wardrobe I haven't worn in ten years.

It's a curious little gathering we've got here this evening.

1. **Mouse and Claudia, of course.**
2. **Steve and his new wild woman (going v. well).**
3. **Dave Cleaver *without* Nicole. She was predictably dismayed at the inevitable discovery that he was not who she supposed he was and, in fact, the author of the recent account: '*TV STAR IN PORN HORROR. Angelica Doubleday wept as graphic pornographic images were shown at a top TV bash . . .*' He is sanguine ('She was class totty, chief.').**
4. **Mum and Dad.**

I've made *roast lamb à la frenzied knife attack*. Instructions: get a whacking great piece of lamb, perform a frenzied k.a. upon it, jam garlic cloves and rosemary into the stab wounds, and roast according to the formula on the label. My companion has prepared ratatouille. She seems to think everyone likes it. (I don't know anyone who does. Do you?)

Cleaver and my father are making most of the noise. And now – horror – my father is telling a joke.

'Three old men are sitting around talking about how they'd like to be remembered. The first old man says, "When I die and people come to stand over my coffin and say a few words, I want them to say, 'He was a good father.'" The second old man says, "When I die and people come to pay their respects at my coffin, I want them to say, 'He was a fine husband.'" The third old man says, "When I'm dead and I'm lying in my coffin, I want someone to come along and say, 'Oh look. He *moved*!'"'

Thank God. A short one. And laughter too. Dave Cleaver joins the fray.

'A Frenchman, an Italian and a Yorkshireman are discussing how they make love to their wives.' My mother flicks her eyes nervously round the table. 'The Frenchman says' – and here Dave ludicrously assumes the accent – '"When I make love to my beautiful wife, Pascale, I anoint her body with Cognac, I lick it off *very thoroughly*, and she go five feet into the air with ecstasy."' A titter from Claudia. 'The Italian says' – the accent again – '"I can do better. While I am making love to my beautiful wife Lucia, I sing an aria from one of Verdi's operas, and she goes ten feet into the air with ecstasy."' Dave pauses. Glugs a mouthful of Merlot. 'The Yorkshireman says, "Well, I can do better than either of you two Johnnies. After I've given the wife one, I wipe me knob on the curtains, and she hits the roof."'

A *bit* risqué, what with parents being here and all. But he gets away with it.

'I know one,' says Claudia quietly. 'A man opens his front door one morning and finds a snail on the lawn. So he picks it up and throws it across the road. A year later . . . there's a knock on the door. And when he opens it, down on the doorstep, there's the snail again. And the snail says, "Well, what was all *that* about then?"'

Mouse: 'Egg and bacon in a pan. The egg says, "Hot in here, isn't it?" And the bacon replies, "Fuck me, a talking *egg*!"'

The dinner party has been a bit of a success. The grotesques (Cleaver, father) have been amusing. Everyone is feeling better than when they arrived. My mother has even seen fit to announce that when I was a boy I used to do magic tricks, which is how I come to be standing outside the room, waiting to be called back in. They're picking an object on the very cluttered dining table and I am going to divine which it is.

The door opens. 'Ready for you, Mr David bleeding Copperfield,' says Mouse.

I re-take my seat. 'Magda,' I ask Steve's new friend, 'may I take your hand?' I hold it gently at the wrist, asking her to point her index finger at the table below. 'I shall be picking up vibrations from your wrist,' I tell her. 'Believe it or not, you will lead me to the object in question.'

And then off we go. I move her hand this way and that across the table. It floats over the plates, glasses and bottles, across the cups, saucers, chocolates, the ashtray, the candlestick, the spill of candle wax, the screwed-up serviette, the corkscrew, Steve's cigarette packet, the empty tub of Häagen-Dazs. Over and over it all – and all again – stopping here and there to investigate a red herring or two, until finally – dramatically – I swoop her hand across the table and land her finger triumphantly on the saltcellar.

There is general acclamation. Even a little wonderment.

'It was *you*, Magda,' I tell her. 'I couldn't have done it without you. Your vibrations were really powerful.'

'Go on. How did you do it?' asks my companion. A nice touch this. Because had a movie camera been following the scene, had it craned down slowly from the hands above the table to the feet below, it would have seen a foot resting on top of my foot; pressing gently when I'm getting warmer, pressing more firmly when I'm hot, and positively *stabbing* when I'm there.

Hilary's foot.

Girlfriend 44

Mark Barrowcliffe

Since he was ten years old, Harry has had one ambition – to find the girl for him. Forty-three women and twenty years later he is no nearer his goal. He doesn't ask for much; just a beautiful intellectual who doesn't mind his constant infidelity.

Harry's flatmate Gerrard did once find true love – but he didn't realise it until the day she left him. Only two women have met his exacting criteria, and he's not hopeful that he'll find another. Even if he does, he isn't sure he can trust her not to grow old eventually. Then they meet Alice.

Alice is the perfect girl. She's the only woman in the world Harry and Gerrard can agree on. Unfortunately, she seems to like both of them.

Gerrard wants Alice for himself, but Harry will stop at nothing to win her. Friendship is forgotten and even a little light poisoning is on the cards.

'A natural chronicler of the love-lorn male' *The Times*

'Sharp and funny' *Loaded*

'I howled with laughter . . . lively, witty and upbeat' *Mirror*

0 7472 6814 2

headline

Icebox

Mark Bastable

Here's the deal.

Give Gabriel Todd your brain, and you'll live forever. Gabe'll freeze your head in a flask – and three hundred years from now, you'll be reborn in a new, perfect body. You will be immortal.

Unity Siddorn wants in. She has her own plans to save the world – with genetically pumped tomatoes, as you ask – but she's already thirty-bloody-one years old. In actuarial terms, her life is 41.3% over. She'll do anything – ANYTHING – for more time.

Don, her squeeze, is less keen. A pack of smokes and a gambler's shot at seventy years – he can live with that.

Suddenly, Gabe's theories are about to be put to the test – though circumstances are admittedly less than ideal. The police tend to take a professional interest in a freshly severed head. It's not something you can easily hide . . .

0 7472 6839 8

headline